Brighde Redefined

THE AMULET SERIES 2

Brighde Redefined

LESLIE SOMMERS & JANICE SOMMERS

4 Horsemen
Publications, Inc.

4 Horsemen Publications, Inc.
1497 Main St. Suite 169
Dunedin, FL 34698
4horsemenpublications.com
info@4horsemenpublications.com

Cover & Typesetting by Autumn Skye
Edited by Gayle Staggemeyer
Linebreak Image Pendant drawn by Niki Tantillo

Library of Congress Control Number: 2023935701

Paperback ISBN-13: 978-1-64450-962-3
Hardcover ISBN-13: 978-1-64450-963-0
Audiobook ISBN-13: 978-1-64450-964-7
Ebook ISBN-13: 978-1-64450-965-4

Dedication

Leslie—For Uncle Stephen

Janice—For my loving brother, who spent his nights reading our book.

Acknowledgments

It really takes a team to write and publish a book. First and foremost, we want to thank Alexa Bitsko, our editor. You've been our voice of reason and guidance when we were lost. We are so happy we found you and look forward to working with you on all of our books. 4 Horsemen Publications—Thank you for taking a chance on us and making our dream a reality. Nancy and Katie—Thank you to you both! Your photos of Switzerland made it so much easier to remember the landscape around the Academy. Eden, Zachary, and Anabel—Thank you for inspiring the characters and allowing us to borrow your names! Jake—Don't worry, you'll be up next! Valerie—Thank you for being you and telling us your true feelings! (Seriously, though, it's greatly appreciated.) Rita and Lauren—Without your input and help, we would have been stuck many, many times. Kristen—Thank you for your knowledge about pigs and your advice. As always, thank you to our readers—We hope you love Bridget and come back for more!

Table of Contents

CHAPTER
1

"**O**h, my goodness! He's so cute!" Annabelle gushed over Bri's new, tiny, black kitten.

"Look at those paws," I commented. "He's practically a mountain lion!" I took a swig of my iced tea.

"Lyle! Lyle! Come here, cutie," Annabelle said in a baby voice. What was it about animals and babies that turned us into high-pitched mush machines?

"Annabelle, he's a man, not a mouse," Cole said, deepening his voice.

She stuck her tongue out at him. "He's just a little kitten. It's biologically impossible for us not to gush over him!"

I cooed. Lyle jumped at the feather toy Bri dragged across the floor.

Annabelle, Bri, Cole, and I were sitting in a circle around Bri's room, entertained by her new pet. We were enjoying the last night of our high school careers drinking soda, eating junk, and chatting about the summer. Tomorrow morning, we'd be walking across the football field as they called out our names with over two hundred and fifty of our classmates at graduation.

"I can't believe I'll be heading off to Cooper Union in the fall," Cole said, changing the subject.

"It's weird to think that after tomorrow, we won't be in high school anymore," I agreed.

Bri nodded her head soberly. "This is my last summer as a counselor-in-training. As of next year, if I go back, I'll be a full-fledged counselor."

"Well, I'm excited," I cut in. "I can't wait to be done with OCHS and start my last summer as a kid. By the end of August, I'll be an adult."

"Yeah, I can't say I'm too nervous. I mean, we knew this was going to happen at some point," Annabelle pointed out.

"But after this summer, we won't hang out anymore," Bri said sadly.

"What do you mean?" I exclaimed. "We'll hang out all the time, over breaks and the occasional weekend. Plus, we can FaceTime."

"It's not the same," she replied.

"I've never known you to be nostalgic, Bri," Annabelle smiled. It was true; I would've pegged Annabelle as the sappy one.

"What about you?" Cole asked me. "Switzerland. That's the trip of a lifetime."

Two days after graduation, I'd be flying halfway across the world with my parents to visit the good old town of Adelboden, Switzerland. To everyone else, it was a graduation gift from my family, but in truth, I'd be spending my summer training to control my powers and learning the history of the Amulet so I could fulfill my destiny as a Cuardaitheoir, a Seeker. Just one secret on a mountain of information I had to keep from my friends. It sucked, honestly. It would be easier if I could tell them, but I knew how dangerous that could be.

"It should be pretty rad. I mean, every other country is practically an hour away by train. I'm going to take a tour of all the villages I can and get wood carvings of all of you. I'm going to miss you all like crazy," I responded.

Bri *tsked* and leaned in for a hug. Annabelle joined in, and I pulled back to look at Cole.

"Hug?" I asked, half-kidding.

"I guess I'll miss you too," Cole said, hugging me back.

"And you know I'll email you like crazy, so it won't even feel like you're gone," he said as he pulled back.

"Thanks." I scooped up the tiny, fuzzy creature. "I'm going to miss you most of all," I said in a high-pitched baby voice. He purred loudly, brushed his face against mine, then hopped from my hands.

"As much as I would love to stay, I have to head home," Cole said, standing. "See you all tomorrow."

"Wait, I'll come with you," I said. "Bye, you two!"

Cole held the front door open for me as I hit the bottom step.

"So, have you talked to her?" I asked Cole as we left Bri's house.

"I've sent emails, but no responses yet," he replied. There was a note of pain in his voice, the same one I heard in my own whenever I spoke about my ex-boyfriend. It'd been months since I'd heard from Trip, let alone seen him. After the Findlays up and left Corbin City last December, a hole had existed in our social circle. I was the one who had ended things with Trip, but I still wished things had been different. I wanted a second chance to fix what had broken. It got minutely easier every day, but there were days when all I could do was keep from walking in front of his house. It'd been dark since they left.

"I'm sorry," I told Cole.

"I'm guessing you haven't heard from him either?" He stopped in front of his car door. "Because if you have, you could ask him about her for me..." Cole's eyebrows drew up, and his eyes widened as he gave me puppy eyes.

I gave him a hug. "I know. I haven't spoken to him, but I miss him too."

As much as I missed my ex, Cole missed his doubly. He'd expected Deidra and her family to return at the end of winter break, but they never showed. Instead, he got a quick email saying something along the lines of *Love you, miss you, and I don't know when I'll be back. Grandma's too sick to be alone right now.* I knew that to be a load of crap. Trip had turned eighteen just days after they left, which would have engaged his powers. I bet he was off somewhere with Tomas searching for the Amulet half while I was stuck finishing high school.

Cole and I had promised that if we ever heard from them, we'd tell each other.

"I'm sorry. I wish I had something for you," I offered.

He shrugged. "I know. I wish the same for you."

"But hey, tomorrow is graduation, and we have that party on the beach to celebrate. You still going?"

"Yeah, are you?"

"That's my plan," I smiled.

He half-smiled back. "Good. See you in the morning." Cole got into his car and left. Drenched with sweat from the humidity, I walked half a block down to my car. It was only a few weeks into May, and it was already sweltering at night.

A figure was resting against the hood.

"Took you long enough to say goodbye," Cay said.

"After graduation, I don't know when I'll be seeing my friends. Forgive me?" I replied, a touch annoyed.

"Doesn't matter. Just remember, you can't have much contact with them after you leave. The less people who matter to you, the less likely they'll be hurt—"

"I know, I know, when Beira's warriors come after me for the Amulet," I cut in. To be honest, I only half-believed anyone else besides Deidra was after me. We hadn't seen any warriors, fighters, or militia since the big reveal a few months ago.

I pulled the necklace from underneath my shirt collar and stared into the moonlight.

"I can't believe you still wear it. What a stupid thing to do."

"What else am I supposed to do? Mom doesn't know that I found it, and I can't risk leaving it in the house. At least this way, I can always protect it," I answered.

"But who will protect you?" Cay retorted.

"I can protect myself," I said simply. The car locks clicked as I opened my door. "Need a ride?"

"Sure." He got in and buckled his seatbelt. "You know, I won't be in Switzerland with you. I can only protect you here right now."

"You told me you and Logan were going to Switzerland," I reminded him as we pulled away from the curb. "To find Andrew's family."

"Yes, but I can't do that without you. You're the Cuardaitheoir. I can search the ends of the universe hunting the Amulet down, but ultimately, it will only respond to you." He paused. "Don't you feel it?"

I didn't give him the satisfaction of an answer. It was true that when I took the Amulet off, a part of me went cold. When it was pressed against me, my blood sang with joy and comfort, and without it, I felt sick and weak. Honestly, the reactions I had worried me, but I chalked it up to being the Seeker. If this blood bond happened to all the descendants, then what the hell was I needed for?

"Bridget, I know you're scared about the next step of training, but I promise you, the trainer you get will be the best. Our family doesn't do second-string," Cay said, interrupting my thoughts. "Well, most of the time."

I groaned, exasperated. "Are you ever going to let my dating history go?" I turned toward the high school, just blocks away from Cay's house. "I don't even miss him anymore."

"Don't you? You think you're so sneaky, but I see you. I know you've been obsessing over your emails to see if he messaged you."

"I'm completely over him."

"Are you really?" Cay asked as I pulled into his driveway. "Because we can't let anything distract you from this mission. It's the single most important event of your life."

"Why bother graduating, then?" I snapped. I was tired of this argument, and Cay was wearing thin on my patience.

He turned to face me. "Listen, Bridget, I know Logan and I have been driving you insane with everything lately. And I know the dick meant the world to you, but I have to know you're completely focused on your job. If you aren't... well, it could mean your death."

So overdramatic. I hated it when he brought up my mortality. I always thought that if I got hurt, Cay would just heal me, but he's been making it explicitly clear I would have to rely on myself. That was what scared me. I still felt like the new kid on the team, and I was getting shoved into playing the game alone in front of a crowd.

"I'll be fine," I responded.

He opened my door and got out. "Are you sure?" Cay asked.

"Yes," I said firmly. "I'll see you tomorrow."

"Goodnight," he said, closing the door.

Was Trip still a distraction for me?

No.

Was I lying to everyone, including myself?

Hell, yes.

"One more picture of my graduate," Mom chirped cheerfully the next morning as I stood in front of our fireplace in my graduation gown. I smiled and froze for the flash.

"Last one, Mom," I said. "I need to get to school to check in." The last thing I'd want is to be late for graduation.

"Just one more! Put your cap on," she replied. Dad moved from his perch on the arm of the couch, handed the mortarboard to me, and I put it on. I almost didn't care if it looked right.

"It's crooked," Mom pointed out. I sighed loudly.

"Sam," Dad jumped in, "she has to go. You can get more shots afterward."

Maybe I wouldn't be late to my high school graduation after all.

"Fine," she said, relenting. "We'll see you later."

"Bye!" I grabbed my stuff and dashed out the front door, my gown flapping in the summer breeze.

I unlocked my car and dumped my stuff on the passenger side. The interior was sweltering when I got in. The worn, black leather seats threatened first-degree burns on my legs as I sat. I sighed. This was my doing. I'd only been practicing my powers with Cay or Logan (which felt like every waking minute). When I was alone, I slacked off, giving my powers the freedom to wreak some havoc. Doing anything else was a lot more fun than the consistent reminder that I may have warriors, dragons, or whatever else to potentially slay.

I closed my eyes and focused on the mental image of sinking my feet into the cool ocean as it lapped against the shore. I practically felt the gentle caress of the wave as it dragged itself over my toes and back out to sea. The image proved worthy, and the sun dimmed from a cloud passing over. There was immediate relief, and I opened my eyes again.

Too bad my seats were still on fire. I checked the dusty clock on my dashboard. Noting the time, I backed out of my driveway and hightailed it to school.

I wasn't sure what I was feeling when I pulled into the parking lot, surrounded by most of the seniors, dressed in red and white gowns. This place had been my home for four years. I was somewhere between excited and scared, but I was ready for the next step in my life. Fellow graduates walked past my car to meet in the gym and say their last goodbyes.

I wouldn't be seeing these people again.

A wave of sadness and nostalgia washed over me. Part of me would miss my classmates, the people I'd interacted with for the past twelve years. I felt lost knowing they wouldn't be back come the fall. Then again, neither would I.

"Hey!" Bri said through my open window. I jumped.

"Sorry! Are you coming out, or are you planning on melting in there?" she asked. I closed the window and grabbed my purse.

"Sorry, feeling a little…" I trailed off as I got out of the car.

"Yeah, I feel it too," she admitted. "It's weird knowing I won't be seeing Dan Zachariah shoot spitballs in math anymore." We headed across the lot toward the gym where the graduates were assembling.

"Or George King dating a new girl practically every week." After the Halloween dance last year, Annabelle and George dated for a few weeks, but they called it quits before Thanksgiving. "Bri was right. He was a drooler," she had confirmed after they broke up.

I thought about the people I'd kissed in the past year. My heart ached for a little romantic attention from a certain rival Seeker, but I knew that would never happen.

"You know, I'm going to miss this place," Bri exclaimed as we piled into the gym. I took her hand and gave it a squeeze.

"I'll see you afterwards?" I asked. She nodded and went to find her male counterpart. The principal had us stand in alphabetical order by last name, so it was a bit chaotic trying to find our partners among the sea of red and white gowns.

I stood next to Matthew Monroe, Dina McMillan, and Cay, drowning in the noise of the conversations bouncing off the gym walls.

"No, I didn't do my hair this morning. Why bother? It's just going to get flat anyway," I heard one girl say to her friend.

"I know. You're so lucky. I wish my hair straightened," her friend replied as she pulled on her own corkscrew curls.

"Did you bring it?" Chris Jacobs' voice boomed. I looked up, mildly interested in the topic.

"Of course," Krish Patel said, pulling out a stash of silly string from his sleeve. I shifted my gaze, having expected harmless pranks like that.

"Okay, seniors, line up! We're walking down in three minutes!" Principal Sharpe announced through the microphone in the gym. In a flurry of polyester, my classmates and I stood in line and headed toward the football field, where our families and older friends were sitting, grinning goofily with poppers, ready to document the momentous event with cameras.

"Pomp and Circumstance" blared over the loudspeakers, and we waded through the grass and onto the bleachers. We stood, waiting in the sun, until our last peer reached their spot.

"Thank you, parents and teachers, for joining us in celebrating the graduating class of Ocean City High School!" Mrs. Sharpe began. "Please stand and join us in the national anthem, sung by Leah Young, next year's senior class president!"

The audience clapped as she took the stage. Leah sang slowly, her voice filled with thick emotion.

I zoned out. I was too busy scanning the crowd for anyone who might be coming to kill me. The Amulet was heavy on my chest, glued to my skin with sweat. I shifted a little, trying to dislodge the metal with no luck. Leah finished the song to everyone's cheers and applause. Both the crowd and the students were instructed to sit as the next presenter walked up the steps to the podium. We'd just begun, and I was already bored.

Instead of listening to speech after speech, I looked for my parents. I found Natalie Draper's parents and little brothers, Nathan and Neil. Nathan was a sophomore, and Neil was in fifth grade. I remembered when Neil was born. Natalie had brought blue iced cupcakes to our Girl Scout meeting to celebrate.

I shook the memory from my mind. I saw other families I recognized before finally finding my parents. Mom was wearing a pair of white shorts with a light-blue tank top while Dad wore khakis and a green golf shirt. They looked like members of a country club instead of my parents. Mom snapped a few shots of my class, and Dad fanned himself with the paper program the school had handed out. These were the two people who loved me most in the whole world and did everything they could to protect me.

I felt guilty for not telling them I took the Amulet. The necklace weighed heavier than before. But if I put it back, I couldn't keep it safe and away from any descendants. No, the best way I could repay my parents was by keeping the Amulet close and keeping the world—and, in turn, them—safe. It was the least I could do for all they'd done for me.

"Andrea Kalling," Mrs. Sharpe called out. I blinked a few times as the sounds and smell of the newly cut grass came rushing back. I'd zoned out long enough to nearly miss the names being announced. My row stood. We slowly made our way to the podium as each student had their name called.

"Dina Marie McMillan!" There were a few cheers and claps for her as she walked up to get her diploma.

"Bridget Gwendolyn MacNamara!"

Smiling proudly, I looked up at my parents and gave them a little wave as I crossed the field, mentally patting myself on the back for not wearing spiked heels. I didn't know how sturdy the cloth walkway would be and if it could withstand heels on soft ground. Reaching the podium, I shook Mrs. Sharpe's hand as my family and friends applauded and whistled for me.

"Congratulations, Bridget," Mrs. Sharpe said, handing over my diploma.

"Thank you!" Grinning, I walked across the field to stand with my row. The plan was to walk around the back of the bleachers and sit on the hot metal. I looked at the paper in my hand as I welled with pride.

Suddenly, screams rang out, and shouts of "Fire!" were called.

"Quick! Someone get water!" Another voice yelled. I whipped around and saw Dan Zachariah's gown go up in flames. Nearby students fled as Dan screamed and clawed at the melting material. Parents were scrambling toward their kids, trying to leave the field.

"Bridget!" Cay yelled as I saw him rushing at me, his gown flapping behind him.

"Do something!" he yelled again. I stood there, dumbfounded. Do something? Me? What could I do? I looked at Dan again. A teacher had grabbed the tablecloth with the diplomas on it and tackled Dan. He seemed burned and scared, but he was no longer on fire.

Cay caught up to me.

"Behind him," he said. Then I saw it. The fire had spread to the banner that hung on the side of the bleachers. It ran down the strings, which touched the ground and lit the straw-colored, parched, flammable grass. Flames were moving quicker than people, and the tiny bottles of water people were passing around weren't enough to douse the ever-growing blaze. Kids were fleeing in every direction, making it difficult to put out the fire. Fire alarms echoed into the now cloudy sky. I looked at Cay and blinked. Was I even allowed to use my powers in public?

If you couldn't, what would be the point of having them? a little voice in my head said.

Closing my eyes, I allowed some of the sadness I had tucked away in the empty core of my soul to reach out and consume my heart. I was grief-stricken instantaneously, and the sky darkened as buckets of rain poured down on us. Now the screams were about hair being ruined, shoes getting stuck in the mud. I concentrated on my pain from the breakup, the fear of what I'd encounter as a Seeker. Harder and harder, the rain pelted us as the flames fought to stay alive.

"Come on, Bridget! You can do this!" Cay yelled over the ruckus. The rain morphed into something slushier and colder: sleet. I opened my eyes, confused and faltering a little.

"Focus," Cay demanded. I glared but did what he asked. Slowly, the fire died down, leaving nothing but cold, wet ashes of what used to be grass. The devastation around us was horrible. Pieces of soggy, burned banner and cloth walkway lay scattered around the scorched field. I looked over at the emptying crowd, searching for my coconspirator.

I saw him. Blonde hair, tall build, tanned skin, and those piercing, green eyes. I'd recognize him in a blizzard.

Trip.

"Bridget! Why are you still out here!" Annabelle ran over to me. She threw a blanket she always kept in her car over my shoulders. Still searching for Trip, I glanced at the soft material covering my drenched gown.

"We need to get you warm and dry," she said, pulling me away. I scanned the area where I saw him, but he wasn't there. Not even a whisper that he was ever there at all.

I allowed Annabelle to lead me inside, partially amused by the fact that she kept rescuing me when that was to be my job.

"Where's Cay?" I asked, not seeing him when I looked back.

Annabelle frowned. "I didn't see him when I ran over." She blinked. "Was he standing with you?"

I didn't get a chance to answer her because the fire department had arrived and evacuated the space.

I found out the next day from a flurry of texts that Chris Jacobs had sprayed silly string on Dan Zachariah, who had been lighting illegal sparklers, causing him to turn away from the spray. When the sparks hit the banner and the ties holding it down, all hell broke out. Bri even emailed an article she found on the front page of the *Ocean City Gazette*. It was big news when it sleeted in the middle of summer as a fire caught at a high school graduation. While everyone was focused on the fire, I was focused on one student in particular.

What had Trip been doing there? Was he there to see me, to make sure I was still in Jersey? Had he found the Amulet? Was he back for mine? I had so many questions only he could answer.

I headed into the kitchen and grabbed a granola bar. We'd be leaving for the airport in the next twenty minutes, and I needed to eat something small before flying. Being a nervous flyer and having a large breakfast did not go well together.

"All packed?" Mom asked as she plunked her purse on the table. She opened it up and stuck her cell phone in a pocket.

"Yup. Just grabbing the last little things," I said, throwing the wrapper in the trash.

"Go do that now, so we can leave," she replied. "I'm going to go put our carry-ons in the car. Please bring yours out when you're ready."

"Okay," I said.

Since yesterday, Mom had been lukewarm to me. We'd never talked about it, but I knew she'd figured out it was me who put out the fire. Though Mom wasn't against me using my powers in small doses, she absolutely wasn't a fan of me using them in public.

I headed into my room to double-check my backpack. Gum to prevent ear pressure? Check. Dramamine for airsickness? Check. Music? Check. My phone was chock-full of new music to keep me entertained for the nine-hour flight to Zurich. I looked down at my white, double-zippered bag, which was practically overflowing with stuff. I was a touch concerned it would be over the weight restrictions. I looked at my "Pack List," and everything on it was absolutely needed.

"You ready to head out?" Dad asked, sticking his head into my room.

"Yeah, just give me a minute," I said before he left. I slung my backpack over my shoulder and took one last look at my room. Who knew when I would see this stuff again?

My phone buzzed from my pocket.

[Cay: Are you still wearing it?] The Amulet.

[Bridget: Of course. I never take it off.]

[Cay: Be careful going through airport security. L & I are here now, and things are tense. Can't risk exposure.]

[Bridget: Tense? What do you mean, tense?]

Suddenly, wearing a large necklace I was trying to hide seemed like a poor decision.

[Cay: I mean, watch your back. Who knows who's a BD.]

Beira's descendant.

It had been hard getting used to the idea that every person I met could be after me. But that was only working under the assumption that Trip and his family hadn't told everyone they had ever met about me and where I lived. I sighed. Moments like this made me wish I was normal.

[Bridget: Aren't they always lurking in the shadows?]

I turned my phone to silent. Being that same nervous flyer, I didn't need another reason to swim to Zurich.

After promising my friends a million times that I would text them when I landed, no matter what time it was, I turned on airplane mode and tried to get comfortable in the cramped plane seat. Dad left me the window seat, which was a mixed blessing. I loved looking out as we flew over clouds, but I hated watching the plane land. I always imagined it crashing, *Final Destination* style.

"You settled in yet?" Mom asked. She was sitting next to me in the ever-unpopular middle seat.

"Yup. Got my music, headphones, gum, drugs. I should be okay," I replied. A young girl in front of me kept bouncing around in her seat, causing my table to shake. If she kept this up, I refused to be held responsible for tying her to her seat with my shoelaces.

"This is your captain speaking. Welcome to Swiss Air, Flight 1304, direct flight to Zurich, Switzerland. We'll be ready for takeoff in just a few minutes, folks. Please direct your attention to your attendants as I explain the emergency procedures," the voiceover speaker said.

My eyes were glued to the hand movements of the flight attendants. It was important I knew all the safety rules in case the plane fell out of the sky and crashed into the middle of the Atlantic.

"Please turn off all electrical devices, including laptops and iPads, and store them under your seat or in the overhead compartments until we are in the air. Smaller devices like cell phones must be on airplane mode for the duration of the flight and stored in the seat pocket in front of you during takeoff and landing. Thank you," the speaker said. The attendants left to take their seats as the plane taxied toward the runway. I popped a piece of gum into my mouth and took my nerves out on it.

Mom patted my hand.

"It'll be okay," she comforted me. "In less than fifteen minutes, we'll be in the air, and the worse part will be over."

I smiled tightly. "Thanks."

"Just remember, it's like a roller coaster. You love those!"

My knuckles were white against my armrests. The plane lined up on the runway and idled for a few minutes, waiting for the green light to fly. As soon as that happened, we took off, driving down the paved road as the plane lifted. It tilted toward the clouds and began its gentle incline. Mechanics whirred beneath me as the wheels were tucked inside the body of the plane. I clenched my jaw and squeezed my eyes. The roller-coaster portion of the flight had started, and I squished my gum through my teeth, giving me something else to focus on.

Once the plane leveled out after what felt like an eternity, I could breathe a little easier. A baby two rows behind us was sneezing and crying.

"Oh, you poor thing," the mother cooed. "Let me wipe your nose."

Images of the seat behind me and the kid covered in snot ran through my head. Ew.

"You may now turn on your electrical devices," the captain announced. I plugged my earbuds into my ears and blasted my favorite song to drown out everyone around me. Leaning back against the seat, I closed my eyes and let the music wash over me. The first song that played was house music, something Cay had insisted I listened to when I trained.

Training was what Cay called a "care package," one more brutal than caring. Cay, Logan, and I had been spending most nights and certain Saturday afternoons strengthening my powers and physical prowess. Thankfully, Cay's intense training kept my mind focused on everything else but Trip. My favorite sessions were the nights that Neit, Cay's German shepherd, tagged along, especially for the obstacle course Cay had set up on the beach back in early spring. Running through the sand was hard enough, but running through the sand while competing against the dog through tunnels, jumping over hurdles, and dodging Nerf foam bullets made the Spartan Races feel like a game of tag.

Someone kicked the back of my seat, jarring me from my memory. Looking around to see if everything was okay, I rolled my shoulders out and leaned back, closing my eyes again.

"Bridget," Mom said, tapping me on the arm. I opened my eyes and pulled out one earbud.

"Are you hungry?" she asked.

"Pringles and ginger ale?" I asked. Mom nodded and called for the flight attendant. He appeared, and Mom ordered our snacks. Within minutes, I was chomping on a deliciously salty chip.

"How're you feeling?" Mom asked me.

"I'm okay. Music helps," I responded, biting into another chip. The crumbs tumbled down my T-shirt, landing in my lap, and I brushed them off.

"Bridget, we should discuss what happened at graduation," Mom said.

"Now?" I looked around me, nervous someone would overhear us.

"We're on a nine-hour flight. No time like the present." She dropped her voice lower. "What happened at graduation shouldn't have happened. I thought we'd discussed that we'd keep that to ourselves."

"Mom, I had to do something, or it could've been a bigger problem," I argued quietly. "Plus, Cay was yelling at me to do something."

"Cay isn't the boss of you," she pointed out.

"I know that. But what would you have done if you were in my spot?"

Mom hesitated. "I don't know," she admitted. "But it's harder to keep you safe when you go … flaunting it."

"Flaunting?"

"Now with the added…" she trailed off.

"Abilities?" I suggested.

"Yes, abilities. It's clear things are growing faster than you can handle them," she said.

"What are you talking about?" I asked, confused.

"The sleet. I know all about it."

"I think you're missing a few notes on that because I had nothing to do with it," I responded.

Mom blinked at me. "Bridget, I was there. I saw everything."

"Me too, and trust me, none of that was me."

"Then who was it?"

I pictured Trip standing behind the bleachers. "I wish I knew."

"Well, I wish you'd be more careful in the future."

"Isn't that why we're going to Switzerland? So I can learn to be more careful?"

Mom smiled. "Yes."

"Then don't worry. I got this." I gave her a reassuring smile and closed my eyes again. I felt as assured as I sounded. Turning on my playlist once more, I drowned out the din of the other passengers. My mind drifted back to the last moments I'd spent with my friends. It was hard that I wouldn't have my last summer before college with them. I focused my thoughts on my last session with Cay and Logan before I left.

We'd been out on the Tuckahoe Preservation at twilight, working on calling my powers. Bittersweet memories of my first time here with a boy nipped at the edge of my mind. I blocked them out and paid strict attention to Cay.

"Bridget? Were you listening?" Cay yelled.

"Closely," I nodded. *"Very closely."*

"Okay, good. Are you ready?"

I paused. "Yes," I said slowly. "Just that last part confused me."

"Which part specifically?" he asked, arms crossed.

"Um, all of it." I looked sheepishly at him.

He rolled his eyes. "I knew it."

"Redirecting your emotions," Logan whispered from behind me. Lately, whenever I zoned out with training, Logan was right there to bring me back to Earth and give me encouragement in the form of a hug or a smile.

"Aren't I cheating since it's almost summer? Because that's when I kick ass?" I called to Cay.

"This isn't about how easy it is to call your powers. This is about you learning to do it without the use of your emotions. To control them without a second thought, making it second nature."

I gave him the thumbs-up.

"Let's give this a shot," I replied. Without any warning, Cay launched a baseball-sized rock at me. My body tensed. A voice in my head screamed to duck, but my body didn't flinch. I waved my hand, and a strong gust of wind blew the rock off its course.

"Not bad," Cay approved. "Try again." He threw another rock at me. I tried calling for wind again, but nothing came. Worry seeped into my veins. I tried again. Still nothing. The rock sailed closer. I ducked out of its trajectory and waved my hands in the process. A tornado formed and sucked the rock into its cone, then disappeared, dropping the rock softly onto the ground.

"Not what I had in mind," Cay said.

"Not what I had in mind!" I shot back, a little stunned.

"Where did that come from?" Logan asked.

"No clue," I said, my eyes bouncing between the rock and my hands. "That's completely new."

My eyes fluttered open as I felt Dad gently nudging me with one hand.

"Hey, sweetheart," he said.

"Hey, Dad," I said, rubbing my eyes. "Where's Mom?"

"She went to the bathroom, which is called a restroom in Switzerland for us Americans." He closed his guidebook. "She'll be right back."

"Okay." I closed my eyes again and snuggled back into the seat.

"Before you fall back asleep, I just wanted to say that I'm proud of you."

"For what?" I faced him.

"This whole..." his voiced dropped, "Seeker thing. I know how scary this is, and you jumped in without hesitation. I'm proud of you."

I smiled and gave him a giant hug. "Thanks, Dad," I said, my voice muffled by his shirt.

"You don't have to do this, you know. Say the word, and Mom and I will come get you."

"You just said you were proud of me for going through with this." I leaned away from him.

"I know, I know. But I'll be proud of you even if you don't want to."

"You know what will happen if I don't."

Dad looked at me straight on. "Yes, but you need to know that you have options. Being the hero doesn't have to be one of them."

I studied Dad. His face showed his true age, the lines a map of what he'd been through. Dad's eyes were dark and serious; there wasn't the hint of humor normally dancing in his eyes.

I hugged him again, tighter than before. "I know, Dad. But I have to do this."

He didn't say anything, but he kissed the top of my head and hugged me close. "I love you."

"Love you too."

I never went back to sleep after our conversation. The worry of the unknown kept me alert for the rest of the flight.

"Got everything?" Dad asked as the plane began to descend. Passengers all over were shifting in their seats, collecting items that were left out during the flight, shoving them into bags so as not to be forgotten. When the plane landed and taxied to the gate, everyone on board stood to grab their stuff. Mom, Dad, and I stood, waiting for the doors to open and for people to leave. I used this time to stretch and lift my arms over my head as much as I could. The line of people broke, and it was our turn to head out. We started down the aisle, and I looked behind me one more time at the seat that I'd snuggled into for the better part of nine hours.

"Yup, nothing left."

We walked out of the airport and into the bright moonlight. I shivered in the cool night air. Dad wrapped his arm around me as Mom flagged a taxi.

"Do you speak English?" she asked the driver.

"Yes, yes. Where can I take you?"

"Will you take us to Adelboden?" He nodded and got out to help with the suitcases.

"Is this your first time to Switzerland?" he asked me in a thick accent, loading the luggage into the trunk.

"Yes," I said.

"You'll love it," he said confidently.

"How would you even know that?"

"Everyone loves Switzerland."

"Everyone ready?" Dad asked, opening the car door. "Let's get going."

Nearly two hours later, my legs were cramping, and my butt was going numb from sitting for so long. I desperately wanted to sleep with all the jet lag, but my mind wouldn't shut off. I kept replaying my last moments with Trip in the library, finding out he was just using me like a chess piece. I was just a game to him. His desperate claim of loving me was nothing more than a last-ditch effort to manipulate me into giving him the Amulet. I rubbed my thumb over the cool stone, comforting the rising anger in my chest. The moon blinked in and out of view from behind the tall trees.

There was no way I could ever treat Trip the same brutal way he treated me. I hadn't been with him for sport; I'd loved him before I could even admit it to myself. His words replayed in my head over and over.

"*Were you dating me to find out if I knew about the Amulet?*"

"*Not ... completely,*" *he'd admitted, finally looking at me.*

"*I knew it. I called you out on that, and you blew me off!*" *I shook my head in disbelief.* "*I'm such an idiot.*"

"*No, you're not!*" *Trip took a step toward me. His hands were open, like he wanted to take mine into them.* "*Bridget, I was only supposed to find out if you knew about any of this. If you didn't, I was to back off. But I couldn't. You're a wonderful girl, and I just...*" *His eyes pleaded with me to believe him.*

"*What? You just what?*"

"*I didn't want to lose you.*"

I leaned my head against the back of the seat and closed my eyes, feeling them burn as tears welled up. God, I was so stupid. If I couldn't stop the scene from replaying, the least I could do was let it drive me slowly insane.

CHAPTER 2

"Thank you," Dad said as he paid the taxi driver. I looked up at the building ahead, which was partially hidden in the shadows of the trees.

"Where are we exactly?" I asked. I thought we'd be staying in the center of town. That there would be life there, crowds, restaurants, shopping. Instead, the taxi kept going, driving a few miles past the town to what appeared to be a large bed-and-breakfast in the middle of the woods. It was spooky in the moonlight.

"I'm not staying here," I said immediately.

"Come on," Mom said. "It's not that bad. You're just nervous because we're arriving at night."

"It looks like vampires live here."

"Bridget," Dad sighed.

"Werewolves probably hunt these forests at night."

"Not wolves, but we do have a few witches," a jovial voice called out from the house.

I nearly fainted from fright. I think even my parents jumped a little.

"I'm sorry about that," an older woman said as she walked carefully down the small pathway. "We expected you a little earlier today."

"Yes, we did plan on arriving earlier," Mom said, finding her voice. Mine was still in the cab, along with my heart and courage. "The driver got a little lost on the way here. We didn't expect to be so far out of town!"

The woman nodded. "Yes, the Danann Academy was built that way. Originally, there was no town, but as the colony grew, we made sure our land was never encroached upon. I'm Norah," she said warmly, finally reaching us. "The headmistress or caretaker of the Danann Academy. We call it the Academy for short."

Dad cleared his throat. "I'm Owen, and this is my wife, Samantha, and my daughter, Bridget."

"It's nice to meet all of you," Norah replied. "I'm feeling a bit of a chill standing out here. Would you like to come inside?"

She didn't wait for us to respond before she headed back up the path. Clutching my suitcase handle, I dragged it behind me as we followed Norah inside.

The front hall was large and echoed as we stepped inside. Dim lighting made it hard to see, but I could make out the staircase on the left side, pressed against the wall. Across from the stairs was a small table with a mirror hanging above it. Though the building may have been old, the inside felt fresh with crisp, clean air.

"Come in, come in!" Norah ushered us in. The door closed noiselessly behind me. I stepped forward onto a plush red carpet, soft and cushy under my sandals.

"You must be tired from your travels," she mused. "Let me get those bags for you."

"It's okay," Dad said. "We can take them. Just show us the way." He smiled at her.

Norah conceded and waved for us to follow her up the stairs.

It was a quiet walk, except for the creak of the stairs underneath our muted steps. We stopped at the end of a long hallway. Doors punctuated the aisle on either side with sconces between each frame. The lights cast eerie shadows on the carpet. I almost didn't take another step forward, but Mom nudged me with her suitcase. Norah stopped at the third door on the left.

"This is Bridget's room," she plainly stated. "Yours will be across the hall."

No one moved.

Norah chuckled. "Come on, then! I promise, in the daytime, this old house will be warmer and brighter." She flipped a switch next to the doorframe, flooding the hallway with overhead light.

Mom cleared her throat, and I forced my frozen legs to move. My room wasn't incredibly big. A small desk sat across from the closet on the right-hand side. A wooden chair with a frayed cushion rested in front of it, basking in the bright moonlight. There was a twin bed in the opposite corner of the doorway. One wooden dresser and a mirror were at its foot. Framed by the wall and a nightstand, the bed was covered in a fluffy, yellow comforter. I had to admit, the room looked very inviting.

"You can put your clothes in the dresser and your suitcase under the bed or in the closet," Norah offered. I nodded and dragged my stuff in behind me, leaving it sitting upright in the middle of the room.

"Shall we see your room for the night?" Norah asked my parents.

"Sounds good," Mom replied with a tired smile.

Their room was somewhat bigger than mine with a full-size bed and a larger closet. Everything else was the same.

"Why don't you leave your things here," Norah suggested. "I'll go down and make you some supper. I'm sure you're hungry after such a long trip."

At the suggestion of food, my father's stomach growled. He let out a hearty laugh. "Sounds like it!" he said.

"Let's get a move on, then!" Norah led us back downstairs, then grabbed a large pot when we got into the kitchen and filled it with water.

"I hope pasta is okay. Dinner has long been done."

"Pasta sounds wonderful," Mom replied tiredly.

"Bridget, would you grab a few glasses from the cabinet next to the sink?" Norah gestured with her head. "Fill them with lemonade from the fridge."

I sleepily obliged, grumbling internally that I had to do it. A long, nine-hour flight, a two-hour car ride in the middle of the night, and now I'm expected to do housework? Can't a girl sleep before she takes on the forces of evil?

Mom smiled gratefully as I filled Dad's cup. I placed the pitcher on the table and collapsed into the seat. No one said anything for a few minutes as we waited for the water to boil.

Norah dumped a fresh bag of pasta into the pot and then sat next to me.

"I don't want to jump right into the heavy details of what is expected of you," she said to me, "but we need to get into it before tomorrow."

I blinked at her as my mind whirled with what kind of "heavy details" she could be referring to.

"To start, not all students here are tasked with a quest related to the Amulet. I know you're the Cuardaitheoir, but that doesn't mean you're more special than anyone else here. You'll have a schedule similar to the other students—academics in the morning and, when the time comes, physical training in the afternoon."

She looked at me expectantly, like I would argue with her. Right now, I was willing to say anything to allow me to go to bed faster.

"I understand," I said. The pasta was boiling furiously on the stove, causing Norah to jump up and turn it off. She poured out the water and plated the meal for us with a little bit of butter and some parmesan cheese.

We dug in hungrily as Norah continued listing the rules I'd be following.

"While we do have staff to keep the building clean, you are responsible for your own room."

I wondered where the other students' dorms were, but I didn't have the brainpower to entertain that thought longer.

"Studying our history and the Amulet is most paramount on your journey," Norah explained. "The knowledge you will gain will aid you greatly on your hunt."

She sounded like Gandalf from *The Lord of the Rings.*

"As I had mentioned, some students aren't here to study the Amulet. That responsibility is only for you."

I took a gulp of my lemonade, suddenly feeling how real this whole thing was.

"You will train with one of our instructors, Eden. She will teach you how to call on your powers and how to control them."

"I already know how to do that," I mentioned, frowning at the thought of more obstacles.

Norah ignored me. "Eden will also quiz you on your readings from the *Book of Brighde.*"

"If Bridget is the only one studying the Amulet, what are the other students working on?" Mom asked, placing her fork in her empty bowl.

"Some students are here to learn how to use their powers, like Bridget, and others are here to train as Protectors."

"I thought that only the Cuardaitheoirs get Protectors," I said.

Norah smiled and shook her head slightly. "You have much to learn. You will have many different Protectors in your lifetime, assuming they all survive their post. All will be trained here."

I felt a little sad that Logan and Cay wouldn't be the only people on "my team."

Dad cleared his throat. "I'm sorry, Norah, but I think we need some sleep. It's been a long day of traveling for us."

Norah hopped up. "Of course! We can discuss more tomorrow at breakfast. Go on up, and I'll take care of all this." She waved her hand over the empty dishes.

"Thank you," Mom said, relieved. She looked as if she had been moving for weeks without sleep instead of just being jetlagged.

I placed our dishes in the sink, bid Norah goodnight, and left the room.

Exhausted, I forced my tired legs up the stairs and into my room. I clicked on the light and blinked in the sudden brightness. The room was eerily quiet, which was much different from the noisy river outside that I was used to back in Jersey.

I sighed, staring at my luggage, which was still in the middle of the room. It was the only vibrant piece in the room. Hauling it onto the bed, I dug out my pjs and toothbrush with the tired promise of sleep. Heading into the bathroom to change and brush my teeth, I heard a scratching noise on the window. I froze and turned around to see if I could make out a tree branch against the moonlight. Nothing was there. No other noises followed, and I left for the restroom.

When I got back into my room, I double-checked the window. There was movement in the trees just past the meadow. I strained my eyes, scanning the forest for an animal or one of Beira's soldiers. Only the stars and moon looked back at me. I closed the curtains, blocking out the natural light from the moon. My mind must have been playing tricks on me because there wasn't anything there. Rubbing my tired eyes, I willed myself to calm down and get back toward sleep. The jet lag kicked in, and I couldn't stop my body from melting into the bed.

Closing my eyes, I replayed the obstacle course training in my head to help my mind relax.

"Faster!" Cay had ordered as I hopscotched through tire rings on the beach. I ran up a huge mountain of sand I was assuming Logan and Cay had built. A Nerf bullet hit me in the ankle.

"Stop!" he called.

I collapsed on the dune, digging my feet into the cool sand. "What did I do wrong?" I panted. Cay waved me down. I trotted, then slid down the mound.

"What happened to your reflexes?" Cay asked as he handed me my water bottle. I took a long drink and wiped my mouth.

"They're shot. I'm exhausted." I took another sip. "Don't I get a break?" Sitting on the sand, I resisted the urge to fall over and nap.

"Get up. There are no breaks in real life, so no breaks now!" Cay practically barked.

"You can do it," Logan said to me, extending his hand for me to take. "I've been there. It's tough, but so are you. Push through it," he said, and turned to Cay. "How about Neit goes through it with her?"

I perked up. Clasping my hands, I gave Cay puppy eyes. He rolled his eyes and whistled as Neit came barreling toward us. The dog and I took our places at the beginning of the course, the staircase. It wasn't wide enough for both of us. In fact, the boxes were a little uneven: the first step was the biggest, and the steps became narrower as the staircase descended. I wondered who would pull back, Neit or me.

"On your marks!" Cay called. "Get set! Go!"

We bolted up the steps, and I unintentionally edged Neit out. Balancing carefully, I sped as fast as I could over the balance beam. Neit went under it and cut me *off at the end. He dove under the bales of hay, crawling faster than me. I had to keep my mouth and eyes closed, or I would've been eating sand. The tire patch was up, and Neit kept his lead. A foam arrow came at me and knocked me in my ear as my foot caught on the lip of one of the tires. I slammed my knee on one, scraping the first few layers of skin right off.*

"Son of a—" I winced. I grabbed my knee to stop some of the bleeding to no avail. Neit barked, and I saw him standing atop the sand mountain. Cay stormed over.

"How are you going to be the Seeker if you can't even stay on your feet!" He moved my hand and furrowed his brow. I watched as the blood stopped flowing freely, turning into a slow leak instead. The skin gently fused back together, cutting off all the blood. At first, I grimaced, expecting the sudden rush of extreme pain, but it tickled, like he was dragging a feather across my leg.

I stood and brushed off my legs the best I could. Sand was glued to the wet blood still, so all I had done was smear it. Lovely.

"But back on point," Cay shook his head. "Bridget, I'm worried Neit beat you on such an easy course."

Easy? He was kidding, right?

"I tripped! It's not like I didn't try!" I argued. Cay leveled me with a look.

"Please. I saw you out there. I hit you with the foam bullets more times than I can count! You need to improve," he said sternly. "You'll be off to Adelboden soon, and after that, it's all up to you!"

I stuck out my tongue at him. As much as I didn't want to be wrong, Cay was right.

"I know," I said. "What else can I say? I'll try harder."

He just shook his head. "Let's go."

Pining for Logan's comfort and Cay's support, I fell asleep quickly after that and wasn't disturbed all night.

The next morning, breakfast was quiet. My head was swimming with information from last night—the anticipation of what was to come, the sudden rush of newfound independence. My parents would be leaving soon, and I could barely form a word to say to them. I blinked, and then it was time for them to go. Mom and Dad were saying their goodbyes and heading down the mountain to travel for a bit before going back to America.

"If you need anything, just call us," Mom said as she hugged me tight. "We'll come right back."

"I promise," I said, squeezing her back. When she pulled away, her eyes shone bright, and her nose was red.

"Bye, kid." Dad grabbed me close.

"Bye, Dad," I murmured into his shirt.

"You can handle anything. Just keep your head about you, and you'll be fine," he whispered in my ear.

I nodded and pulled back, then looked hard at my parents. Their only daughter was about to venture off to save the world and, in turn, demolish any chance of a happy ending for herself. With red eyes to match her nose, Mom looked worn around the edges. Her smile didn't reach her eyes, and lines were popping up around her mouth. Dad didn't look any better. His shoulders were sagging lower than normal, and his curly, light-brown hair was speckled with gray. I choked back a sob, nearly drowning in remorse, nostalgia, and regret. This wasn't easy for them either.

The cab pulled up behind them and honked. I flinched at the harsh, foreign sound against the quiet chirps of the birds and the bugs all around us.

"I guess this is it," I said, swallowing the lump in my throat. Mom sniffled and kissed me on the head.

"Stay safe," she said. My own eyes welled up, but I didn't let them spill. Dad hugged us both for one last goodbye. I held on longer than usual. I didn't know when I'd see them next.

I watched as the cab drove off, my parents leaving me on my own for the first time. My chest clenched with sadness.

"It's always hard seeing them go the first time," a light voice said behind me. I spun around, startled at the company.

"I apologize. I didn't mean to surprise you," a young woman said to me. Standing next to her was Norah.

"Bridget, this is Eden, your teacher," Norah explained. I studied Eden. Unlike Norah, who was short, had white hair, and was a little hunched over, Eden was tall and had a delicate figure. Her long brown hair was tied into a neat bun on top of her head, and her glasses sat firmly on her face. She was wearing jeans with a blue top and sneakers, and she was clutching a large book to her chest.

"Hello," I replied, wiping my eyes.

"I'm sure you're overwhelmed with being on your own, but I can assure you that I'll do my best to prepare you for what's to come," Eden said gently.

What *was* to come? For once, I wished someone would just tell me about my certain death instead of hinting at it.

"Why don't you two come inside and get yourselves acquainted?" Norah suggested. "Later this afternoon, I'll introduce you to the other students."

I followed politely behind Eden and Norah, partially nervous about the unknown and partially ready to take it on.

Navigating the Academy didn't feel like it would be a challenge for me as I trailed the two women.

"How about we sit here," Eden offered, pointing to two cozy armchairs. She had led me into what I assumed was a study. There were a few small tables scattered about the room with a love seat and coffee table in front of a fireplace. Instead of wallpaper, bookcases lined the walls. I made a mental note to check out what was on the shelves later, though I was sure they would be something akin to encyclopedias and history books.

"So, I'm sure you're a little nervous about this," Eden said.

"That obvious?" I asked, giving her a sympathetic smile.

She blushed. "I read a little about you before you got here."

"Well, you're right," I admitted. "I mean, you read... whatever, a file or something, so you know Cay forced my ex-boyfriend to tell me everything. Now I'm halfway around the world, trying to catch up on knowledge that my counterpart has known about since he was in diapers. Nervous barely begins to cover it."

She smiled lightly at my outburst. "I understand; it's a lot to take on. Since this is your first day, we can start light, though I know Norah would want you to jump in with both feet."

I gulped thinking about how deep that pool would be.

Eden placed the book she was carrying on the table in front of us. "After today, this will be the book that you study. You'll live and breathe this book. You can take notes in the margins, fold over pages, and highlight whatever you want. This book will be your most important possession."

She held it up, so I could read the cover. The *Book of Brighde*. "Protect this book with your life."

I looked at the book with fervent curiosity. The only thing I'd ever been told to protect with my life was the Amulet piece sitting comfortably on my chest. Plus, the only person who made it seem like my life would end if I didn't save the Amulet was Cay. Hearing all this from Eden was a different story.

"So, what exactly is this?" I asked.

Eden grinned. "This book is the history of the Amulet. Much has been lost over the years, but thankfully, this book survived. It's one of the only things that did."

I flipped the pages, skimming the words. The first chapter mostly discussed Danu, Brighde and Beira's mother, and the Tuatha Dé Danann, her worshippers. Skipping ahead, I saw Andrew's name a few times, but there was nothing that gave a clear answer on how to find the other half of Amulet. I'd ask Cay later.

Except Cay and Logan weren't here. They were out traipsing across the countryside, doing my job, looking for the hardest artifact to find.

Internally, I pouted, but I kept my posture relaxed and my face neutral. I'd be with them soon enough.

"Do you have any questions so far?" Eden's voice broke through my thoughts.

"Not exactly. I don't know what to ask," I admitted.

"How about we get to know each other a little better? I know I read about you, but I have a feeling I was a surprise."

"Truthfully, a lot of this is a surprise."

"Well, I'm planning on fixing that. When you leave here at the end of summer, you'll be fully prepared, like everyone else is."

"By everyone, do you mean Trip?" I hadn't said his name in such a long time. It felt foreign on my tongue.

Eden smiled. "Not just Trip. Even though you two are this generation's Cuardaitheoirs, everyone before you had the same training as you will receive."

I paused. "So, how exactly do you play into all of this? I mean, will you train me on just the history, or are you going to test my powers?"

"My primary job will be making sure you understand your family history, which will aid you in your search. I will also supervise some of your warrior training and your power training, but as I am not gifted the same way you are, I won't be able to keep up with you, but I'll do my best."

"Who's my trainer?"

Eden smiled again. "You'll find out soon enough."

"Will I have any other trainings? Like math or science?"

Eden shook her head. "Technically, we are considered a boarding school, so the younger students are taking classes like that. I know you recently graduated from American high school, so these classes wouldn't suit you anymore."

A large grandfather clock in the corner started chiming as I mulled over who would be training me and rejoiced in the fact that I didn't have to take yet another math course.

"Lunch?" Eden asked. I didn't even realize that I'd spent my morning hanging with Eden. I hoped all our sessions were this quick. I walked into the kitchen behind Eden, looking for some food.

"Students eat in the dining hall with each other," Norah said, surprising me. I didn't hear her come into the room. I glanced at Eden, looking for some direction.

"It's down the hall to the left," Norah answered. "Across from the bathroom. That's marked as water closet or WC."

Scurrying out the room, I made my way down to the dining hall. The door wasn't marked, so I guessed from the sounds of forks and knives knocking against plates that I'd found it.

I opened the door and slid in, doing my best not to draw attention. The door slammed behind me, creating an echo that caused what felt like a million pairs of eyes to look at me. Fog spread around my feet, drifting upwards. Great. Besides the fog, I felt the blush crawling up my neck to my cheeks as a bundle of nerves coiled itself in my stomach.

"Food is over here," a student said, coming up behind me. I flushed, grateful someone had come to my rescue.

"Thanks," I replied, doing my best to dispel the fog. Following the savior student, I avoided eye contact with everyone. The flames on my cheeks subsided a little, but I couldn't uncoil the nerves.

"I'm Matilda, but you can call me Mat," she said. She had a gentle British accent, soft and pleasing to listen to. I immediately felt calmer.

"Nice to meet you," I answered back. I trotted after Mat, heading toward the buffet. My stomach growled at the sight of all the food. Lemon chicken, potatoes with cheese, salad, bread, and butter. Food that reminded me of home. The nerves relaxed completely.

"You can sit with us," Mat offered, grabbing a roll for her plate. Weighing my options, I quickly glanced around the room. Seeing only five tables with a handful of kids at each made me realize I'd been expecting a full room like back at OCHS. Either way, I could always use an ally in the lunchroom as well as on the battlefield.

"Sure," I said shyly.

"We normally sit together," Mat explained as we set our plates down. "This is Oliver, Franny, and Ginger."

"Hello," I said to each of them as I pulled out a chair to sit.

"This is..." Mat trailed off.

"I'm Bridget." I pulled my fork from the silverware napkin roll. "Thanks for inviting me to sit with you."

"It's no problem. We've all been new at some point here," Franny said cheerfully, her French accent very prominent. When she smiled, her face lit up, and her light green eyes shone.

"What brings you here?" Ginger asked with a British accent like Mat's. Hers wasn't soft but was more nasally and sharp. She kept stabbing her fork into the same piece of lettuce, trying to pick it up.

I looked at the people at my table. I didn't know any of them, and I didn't know if I should say anything. What if one of them was meant to kill me? I couldn't be sure they weren't Beira's henchmen.

"Probably what brought you here. To study the history and my powers," I said casually.

"Well, not everyone is here for that," Mat said, tucking a strand of dark-brown hair behind her ear. "Some of us are here to train as Protectors for the Seekers."

I internally breathed a sigh of relief. No one knew who I was.

"So, who's who around here?" I asked, nodding to the tables around us.

Oliver spoke up and brushed a curly mop of dark hair back off his face. "The table by the food is a mix of the Dagda's descendants, including Cernunnos and Aengus. The table to the right are kids who are strictly from Babd but are still training, and the table to our left is the Protectors. They think because they're training to guard the Cuardaitheoirs that they're the gods' gifts."

Ignoring the other tables, I peered at the Protectors, studying the few at the table. Two guys and three girls were each eating and laughing, like lunch was the funniest thing in the world. Not one of them looked threatening. One of the girls had bright pink hair, like cotton candy. I suddenly wished I was home eating junk food from the boardwalk.

"That's Natalia," Mat said, following my gaze to the pink-haired person. "She's the nicest out of all of them. She only sits there because of her sister."

I looked at the girl sitting across from Natalia, who was drinking water. Her hair wasn't so bright. Just a dark red that probably wasn't found in nature.

Natalia's sister caught me staring and shot me a nasty look. I flushed immediately and averted my gaze. I looked up again and caught all the Protectors looking at me.

"Rose," Oliver said, narrowing his dark-brown eyes. "Aptly named, as she has a thorny personality."

"I can already tell we're just going to be best friends," I said, silently praying she wasn't going to be my Protector.

"I swear, she's from Balor," Ginger chimed in, copying Oliver's look.

"She isn't that bad," Franny said. Four pairs of eyes blinked at her. "She's nice to me," Franny added, sniffing delicately.

"Rumor has it, she used to date one of the Seekers," Mat added. My stomach dropped, and I nearly blew my cover by blurting out his name. Instead, I looked down at my lunch and nodded my head, as if this information was of no consequence to me.

"What are all of you?" I asked, returning to my lunch. My chicken was divine, and I was debating about going back for seconds.

"Mat is a descendant of the war goddess, Babd, Franny is a Protector, and I'm still training in my powers of Dil." Ginger said.

"Dil?" I asked.

"The cattle goddess," Ginger replied. "And Oliver is—"

"Also still training," he said, cutting Ginger off with raised eyebrows. She frowned at him but didn't say anything.

"What's this table called?" I asked, respecting Oliver's privacy.

Franny shrugged. "No particular label since we're all training for something different. We all started here when we were younger, so we kept eating lunch together."

Before I could ask her to elaborate, my chair shook. I whipped around to see Rose's foot pull away from the chair's leg. She had a smile on her face and had her eyes on me.

"Do you need help with something?" I asked politely, silently wishing I could send a gust of wind to blow her away.

"I tripped over your chair, which was obviously too far away from the table," she said with the same fake voice I'd used.

"Look down once in a while, and you won't have that problem," I replied.

She stared down her nose at me and smiled before walking away. The rest of her table followed without another glance. Natalia passed and sent an apologetic smile.

Great. Four years of high school hierarchy, and I was right in the middle again.

My afternoon lessons resumed with Eden, but this time, we were outside.

"I thought we could use the fresh air," she said as we sat under the shade of a tall tree. I took a deep breath. The air tasted sweet, and my whole body, down to my toes, felt happy. Like my blood was singing.

"Now," Eden cut in, "I need to know where you are with your powers."

"What would you like me to do?" I was certain I could handle this, due to Cay's state-of-the art training sessions.

"First things first, we'll test you in the elements. Please plant a seed and urge it to grow." She opened the little notebook she was carrying and steadied her pencil over it.

I frowned.

"You haven't done this before?" Eden inquired.

I shook my head.

"Have you created fire?"

I shook my head again.

"Have you pulled water from the air?"

I shrugged.

"Have you lost your voice?"

I laughed. "No, I haven't lost anything. I wasn't trained on the basics."

"What was your training then?"

"I'm going to need a minute."

I pushed my curly hair from my face, wrapped it into a messy bun on top of my head, and closed my eyes. Thinking of the day we had discovered how my powers were controlled was what I had called a breakthrough.

Cay jogged over to Logan and me. "That was cool! Try it again," he said.

"I'll try, but Cay, I haven't done that before," I told him.

"How did you do it now?" he asked like I had a simple answer for him.

"I don't know. I tried calling up the wind again, but nothing happened. I panicked and ran out of the way. That's when it happened."

He smiled. "There you go! A new emotion equates to new powers."

"I don't know. I've felt panic in the past, and that hasn't happened before."

"Your birthday is coming up soon," Logan pointed out. *"Maybe that has something to do with it?"*

Remembering what Cay had taught me, I allowed sunshine to fill the cavities of my body until I couldn't hold it anymore, and I burst. The sun burned brighter than before, and the grass around us dried out. About a hundred feet away from us, a fire erupted and formed a perfect circle in the grass.

"Can you put that out?" Eden asked. I glanced at her. She didn't seem mad, but I couldn't get a reading on her.

I thought of my friends back at home, Annabelle, Bri, Cole. I missed them tremendously. My parents' faces danced through, but all I did was push a few gray clouds around. I reached deeper and unlocked the special chest just for Trip. A little of the misery he had caused me slipped out, causing the sun to be blotted out by a dark cloud as thunder and lightning struck. Rain poured down, dousing the fire as well as our clothes.

"Enough!" Eden laughed as she wrung out her hair. I remembered my sessions with Cay, Neit, and

Logan, the private jokes my friends and I shared. The rain eased, and the sunshine was back.

"Not bad," Eden said approvingly. "We do need to play catch-up, but you're not as far off as I had originally thought."

I sent a warm breeze to help dry us off.

"How are you able to do all this if you don't know the basics?"

"I wasn't training for basics. I was training for battle," I answered.

"Have you had to battle a lot?"

"Not a lot," I admitted. "But I did need to be prepared for any sudden attacks."

"Who trained you?"

"My cousin, Cailean mostly, and..." I didn't want to say who else taught me.

"And?" Eden prompted.

"Trip ... my ex."

"Ah, your competition. Well, they trained you well. Those were some impressive moves for someone who doesn't know the basics."

I smiled ruefully. "Cay was a formidable trainer."

"Do you miss him?"

"Terribly. He's not just family; he's my closest friend." I stayed quiet for a minute, realizing how badly I missed everyone from home.

"Let's take a break from this for now. I have some other stuff I'd like to talk to you about."

For the rest of the afternoon, Eden broke down the rules of the house and the classes, leading up to my eventual graduation from this place.

The rules were simple: Breakfast was at seven o'clock sharp. If you didn't make it, you didn't eat. Then we headed to our scheduled lessons, followed by a break for lunch, immediately followed by a round of afternoon classes, a break for afternoon tea, then homework before dinner. Curfew was ten, lights out by eleven, rinse and repeat.

"After you pass your basic trials, your second trials, and the finals, you can graduate," Eden said.

"How long does that usually take?"

She shrugged. "It depends on the person. Most students are out in a year, but since you're a little more advanced, I don't see you staying here longer than six months."

Six months! That would be loads of time for Trip to find the other piece. My skin crawled with anxiety for the hunt. The Amulet half on my neck sent little comforting pulses like it was saying, *It's okay! You still have the advantage.*

"Chin up," Eden said, "It'll go by faster than you think."

As I climbed into bed that night, my brain felt overwhelmed with all the new stuff I was going to learn. Snuggling under the covers, I forced myself to let go of the stress by focusing on how comfortable I was in bed and soon drifted off to sleep.

"Where is it?" I screamed, bursting into the room.

"I don't have it," Brighde said as the blizzard outside our window grew fiercer with each gust.

"Liar!"

She smiled, drawing the corners of her mouth up as she tilted her head down. "Now you see, now you understand what it's like to miss the one thing that could help."

Lugh yawned loudly from his chair in the corner. "Are you two done with this nonsense already?" He stood. "I've given you suggestions and ideas on how to fix your mess without the help of the Amulet, and you stupid cows refuse to kiss and make up."

I whipped around to face him and sent him a vicious look.

"Be careful, dear sister," Lugh said. "Your face may freeze like that."

Brighde didn't even bother hiding her smile.

"Get out," she told me. "You've already spent too much time in my presence, and I no longer wish to breathe the same air as you."

Snow and wind whipped at the window, rattling it with every hit.

"Be careful, Brighde," I threatened. "It's winter now, and I am in full power." I made the wind howl again to prove a point.

Brighde copied Lugh and yawned. "You be careful, sister. Lugh and I have searched all over this world for my Amulet piece. When you do the same and prove our innocence, who else will you be able to blame for your failure?"

I screamed in frustration, instantly coating the outside in the thickest layer of snow the world had ever seen. Storming out of her room without another word, I sent an icy blast into the window, allowing the blizzard to drift in.

I woke with a start and then groaned. The dreams were back and even darker and angrier than before. I felt the raw, vicious fury buried in Beira's chest, which made no sense. My dreams were normally from Brighde's point of view, so seeing it all from Beira's eyes left me confused and tired. Groggily, I dragged myself out of bed and to the restroom for a shower before breakfast.

"Trip!" I heard someone call from down the hall. I whipped around, wondering if my ex was standing behind me. No one was there, except a girl running around in soaked pjs.

"My ceiling is leaking! Water's dripping on my bed!" she told me, rushing past to head downstairs, leaving wet footprints behind her.

Shaking my head, I was confused as to how I kept thinking I was seeing him. First at graduation then here. *Girl, get a grip.*

Since there were no classes today, I was able to grab a small bowl of cereal before heading back upstairs to take it easy. A small stack of postcards was sitting on my desk near my homework. I took out my phone and pulled up my list of addresses. Mom and Dad were first.

Dear Mom and Dad,

Having the best time here at summer camp! Miss you terribly, but I'll see you soon enough! Hope you're having a great summer missing me, too.

Love you,
Bridget

One down, and I had what felt like three hundred more to go.

Chapter
❧ 3 ❧

I'd wished more eventful things would happen at school for the first week, but besides going over the basics with Eden, learning chapters from the *Book of Brighde*, and feeling slightly homesick, life was bland. I barely made it to Thursday but was incredibly grateful for the extra two hours of sleep I was able to grab before rolling out of bed to forage for breakfast.

I was more homesick than I'd first realized because the following week was filled with extreme weather. There were reports of flooding from the Engstligen River near us, roads were closed due to downed branches, and despite the rain gear, people arrived at their destinations drenched.

"This isn't your fault," Eden said to me one soggy Thursday. I had dropped my book on one of the study tables, eliciting a loud *thunk* from the walls.

"Isn't it? This is my season. I should be able to turn it off."

"Bridget," Eden said gently, "your sadness is amplified because we're in summer, but the Amulet is the truest form of control you can have."

"I guess," I mumbled, feeling more pity for myself than anything else.

"Is there a way we can cheer you up?" She looked so hopeful that I felt bad telling her no.

"Maybe?" I sighed. "I don't know anymore."

Eden moved to sit next to me on the loveseat. "What has you so down?" she inquired.

I shrugged. "I guess … I miss my friends."

"Haven't you made any here? I see you sit with Ginger, Franny, and everyone else for the meals."

"They're nice," I conceded, "but we aren't making pinky promises or anything. Mostly, I sit with them, so I have a place to eat."

"I'm sure they don't feel that way about you."

I shrugged again. I desperately missed my girls. Bri was always the first to know the best gossip at Ocean City High, and Annabelle was the first to remind Bri not to get caught up in others' business. They kept me sane and grounded when my life was a hurricane, which it sometimes literally was.

"I just miss my friends," I said, feeling bummed out.

"Have you reached out to them?" Eden asked.

"I mailed postcards out last week, but since they think I'm touring the country, I don't expect to hear from them any time soon. And I can't find my phone charger, so I haven't seen any texts or calls."

Eden didn't say anything but gave me a hug. Comfort and warmth radiated from her, seeping into me. I felt like I just wrapped myself in my favorite blanket. For the first time in two weeks, the rain outside lessened. She pulled away with a big smile on her face.

"I think you'll be okay," she said. "Things will change, but first, let's order you a new charger so you can reach your family and friends."

She grabbed a tablet sitting on a table and started shopping. I smiled. With Eden, I'd be able to survive this place.

"Thank you," I whispered.

After talking with Eden, I headed to dinner, unintentionally missing afternoon tea. I was starving and couldn't wait to see what was on the menu. Dinner was sweet potatoes with butter and cinnamon, roasted turkey with gravy, crescent rolls, and green beans. It was a callout to an American holiday meal. My heart and stomach were happy.

My favorite thing was their rolls, crunchy on the outside, soft and slightly sweet on the inside. It reminded me of Mom's baking and helped me miss her a little less.

Grabbing a plate, I got in line, inching my way to the dinner rolls. When I finally reached the end, the basket was empty.

"Sorry," Rose said, looking at me with a smirk.

I raised an eyebrow at her as she waved the last roll in my face.

"You should get here earlier," she said. "Maybe you wouldn't miss it."

I straightened my shoulders and kept my face as neutral as I could.

"No matter." I looked her in the eye. "I should actually be thanking you for taking on the extra carbs, so I don't have to."

Rose's cheeks flushed red, and she narrowed her eyes at me. She turned and stalked off but not before throwing out the uneaten roll.

The score was now tied, one to one. *Don't worry, Rose. I won't let you win.*

"I don't understand why she thinks she's so special," Franny said to me as I sat. She was nodding in Rose's general direction.

I shrugged. "The day I figure her out is the day the kitchen whips up a Sam's Special." A pang of homesickness stabbed me as I remembered how greasy and salty that New Jersey Boardwalk sandwich was.

Franny frowned and tilted her head, light-brown hair falling down her shoulder, as everyone else joined us.

"How's dinner tonight?" Oliver asked as he placed his tray on the table.

"Delicious," I said, digging in. We ate in silence for a minute, filling our stomachs. I lowered my fork to my plate when I saw something underneath my potatoes. Nudging the potato over, I saw a fat, white maggot squirm out. Trying to keep my cool, I snatched my napkin off the table and spit out what I was chewing.

"Ew!" yelled Mat as she put her plate down. My food was moving all over now, sliding left and right as more maggots popped up. I launched myself from my chair, knocking it backward, and ran to the garbage can. The room was quiet at my outburst, until the only sound was my violent retching. I willed the image of wriggling bugs out of my mind, hoping it would calm my rolling stomach.

"Are you okay?" Ginger asked gently, handing me a napkin.

"Not yet," I replied weakly, taking the napkin and wiping my mouth.

"Bridget," Oliver said, coming over. "Those weren't real."

"They looked real enough."

"That's the idea behind the spell. It's just a simple illusion trick. Anyone with basic magic training knows how to do that."

"Who would do that?" I made myself face the room full of people watching my performance.

My eyes landed on Rose. She smiled and winked at me. Anger surged, burning up the remaining nausea, and I stormed over to her table.

"What the hell was that about?" I asked, seething. Rose stood slowly as if she was in no hurry.

"You know what it's about," Rose said. I didn't, but at that point, I didn't care to find out. A flash of lightning cut through the air and landed at her feet. She jumped, landing in a graceful fighting pose. Of course, she would have the training and skills of a ninja.

I stepped back and flicked my hands in her direction, sending another bolt. She moved to avoid it, but it nipped her in the arm, singeing her shirt sleeve. Blood seeped through the material, confirming the hit.

"What is going on in here?" Norah yelled at the top of her lungs. Rose's face froze in fear, and I stopped. I wasn't afraid. I was on the right side of this.

Norah turned to everyone else and said, "Dinner is over. Early curfew is in place."

Chairs and tables scraped against the floor as people hurried to clean their places and rush to their rooms.

Neither Rose nor I had moved a muscle.

"Both of you, my office, now."

I followed Rose as she left the hall, steps echoing in the empty room.

Norah waited until her office door was closed before she lit into us.

"I am so disappointed in the two of you; I don't even know where to begin."

I sat in a chair, feeling petulant and pissed that I was getting the blame when I hadn't started this. Shockingly, Rose didn't speak up, either.

"I will not reiterate how inappropriate, disrespectful, and childish you two are being," Norah spoke sharply, which was a new level for her.

Her remark was met with dead air.

"You two have nothing to say for yourselves?" she pointedly asked us. I didn't look at Rose, but I had a feeling her face matched mine: stone cold.

"Incredible," Norah muttered. "Since neither of you can find your tongues, I'm sure kitchen cleanup will loosen them. Starting tonight."

Incredulous, my eyes flickered to her face. Me? What had I done wrong?

"Are you ready to speak now, Miss MacNamara?" Norah asked me.

"I didn't do anything wrong." I felt stupid saying that, as I clearly could have done differently, but I was at a loss. Still seething and fighting against the growing tantrum in my chest, I leaned back in my chair with my arms folded, as if keeping my wrists pressed against my sternum would keep the anger at bay. Thunder broke out in the sky above our heads.

Rose looked at me curiously, but Norah ignored my storm.

"The dining room will not clean itself." She stared us down as if daring us to breathe.

Rose and I stood together, not fully sure if we should leave.

"How long will kitchen duty last?" Rose asked suddenly and brazenly. Inwardly, I shook my head at her. If you kept your mouth shut, then there would be less punishment.

Norah nearly laughed. "That is all you have to say for yourself?" She waved her hand at Rose. "Leave now, and maybe you'll graduate without faintly smelling of rotten garbage."

Rose paled. We turned to leave as Norah said, "Not you, Bridget."

My shoulders slumped, and Rose practically flew out the doorway. I could hear her thoughts in the cadence of her footsteps.

Once we were alone, Norah addressed me directly. "Bridget, I know that this is going to take getting used to, but do not stoop to her level. Do not allow yourself to be distracted by silly things such as Rose Cameron."

"Silly?" I cried, finally finding my voice. "Silly! Norah, she tricked me into thinking that there were maggots in my food! I vomited at dinner, loudly and publicly."

"I can understand why you retaliated as you did, but we do not condone violence here," Norah warned sharply.

My frustration bubbled beneath my skin. "I didn't start this. But if it happens again, I won't back down."

Norah slammed her hand on the desk. "You do not understand, child. Do not engage with the

Camerons again. They are nothing but a diversion from what your true purpose is."

I resisted the urge to roll my eyes. I was just here to save the world at the risk of my own life. Blah, blah, blah. I was so over the speech.

"Yes, Norah," I dutifully responded. "May I go now?"

I saw a simmer of anger lingering in Norah's eyes. "For now."

I turned and walked away.

"But—" she started as I was two steps from leaving, "I will be forced to deepen your punishment if you do continue your methods of retribution."

I said nothing as I closed her door behind me.

Rose didn't say a word to me when I walked into the dining room. One half, Rose's half, was on its way to being clean, while the other side of the room was still slathered in messy dishes and uneaten dinner.

My stomach lurched at the thought of my own dinner, but thankfully, it did nothing else. I silently went to work, dragging the rolling garbage can to each table and scraping the dishes. I stewed in my own anger, mostly directed at myself. I shouldn't have taken her bait. I knew better. She was like a less evil version of Deidra.

Flashes of my first fight with Deidra jumped across my vision: her hands grabbing at my neck, drawing blood, and turning my thunderstorm into an ice storm. Instinctively, I touched the necklace that never left me.

What was I even doing with this? Why was I the chosen one? What the hell made me so special?

A loud noise behind me forced my brain to redirect its thoughts. I whipped around to see Rose dragging one of the last three garbage bags out to the dumpster. The eerie outdoor light that flickered above the doorway cast an orange glow on the pavement. Looking back at my own mess, I still had two more tables to clean and a pile of dishes to wash. I sighed.

Working quickly to end this first night of misery, I washed and dried the dishes, stacking them in the cupboards where they belonged. I gave the tables a perfunctory wipe with the cleaning solution and rag, only to discover I still had one more bag of garbage to take out. Grabbing it by the knot on top, I dragged it across the smooth floor to the back door. Surprisingly, it didn't make a peep as I swung it open. I let it clank shut behind me, knowing full well it wouldn't lock, and hoisted the garbage over my shoulder like Santa with his sack of toys.

"I thought I was going to die," I heard Rose's voice in a hushed tone. I froze, scanning the area for her. I thought she was up in her room, basking in the fact that I had at least another hour left of cleaning.

A different voice answered her, but I couldn't make out the owner.

"You'll be okay," the male voice said. I walked as quietly as I could on the balls of my feet toward the conversation, trying to muffle any sound I made. Rose was just behind the dumpster, close to the field of wildflowers that had practically bloomed overnight. I hid behind the shed that housed our sport equipment and peered around the corner to get a better view.

"Easy for you to say!" Rose's voice became clearer. "She didn't shoot lightning at you!"

My ears perked up, and I leaned forward to hear better. Who was Rose talking to? Unfortunately, I couldn't see her counterpart.

"Shhh!" he said. There was a pause. "Look," he started, "I know you're worried, but trust me, she's not as dangerous as she seems."

I knew that voice. It couldn't be...

Rose answered with a shrug.

"Believe me. It will all work out," he said, wrapping his arms around her and moving his face toward the light.

Trip.

My heart raced, and my stomach dropped. I would have thrown up if I hadn't lost my dinner earlier. My ex-boyfriend was standing less than two hundred yards from me. The curve of his jaw fit nicely in the dip of her shoulder. His arms flexed and pulled her to his chest. Protectively.

He was here. I hadn't been imagining him.

The hollow cavity in my chest ached for him. My skin itched to feel him. My fingers wanted to touch him, to hold him, to be with him. My brain kept telling me no, practically pushing itself back away from the danger, but my body wasn't listening. It continued to yearn for his lips pressed against mine. Logic didn't always win in a battle with the heart.

They broke their embrace, but Trip slid his right hand down her arm and placed the left one under her chin. I had no idea what Rose was doing because I was focusing so hard on what Trip was about to do.

He dipped his face down and kissed her.

I died a little. My firm grip on the garbage bag weakened, and the bag slipped, crashing to the ground.

"What was that?" Rose asked, turning around. I flattened myself against the back of the shed, not breathing, not blinking, desperately praying they didn't see me.

I heard gravel crunch underneath the footsteps as they got closer to me. I weighed my options—hide in a different place or face them—thankfully, I didn't have to use either.

"I don't see anything," Trip said, heading back toward Rose.

I gulped. He was a mere six feet away from me. I saw his shadow from the floodlight above the door.

"That's good." Rose released a breath. "I wish we didn't have curfew."

"Me either," he replied. I could hear the wet smack of their lips pressing against one another. "But you need to get upstairs before Norah catches you."

"You mean us," Rose said playfully. I was positive I heard his smile from where I was imitating a statue.

"Yes, us, but I know Norah, and you should get back. I'll come back."

"I know." They kissed again.

"I'll see you tomorrow?" Rose asked.

"Maybe. You know I can't always get away."

Get away from where? What was Trip doing while I was stuck dealing with teachers, books, and tests all over again?

He kissed her one last time and said, "Now, go before we're caught."

I waited until the sound of the dining room door shutting was a distant memory before I dared to move.

Chapter 4

Closing the door to my room quietly, I slipped off my shoes and collapsed into my bed. Trip was here. And he was with Rose.

Clearly, she knew he and I had dated, but was that the only reason why she'd been giving me such a hard time? What if she was a spy sent to steal the Amulet? My hands flew to my neck, where the Amulet, like always, sat against my skin. It warmed underneath my touch, like it was trying to comfort me. It helped, a little.

I shook my head, and my thoughts returned to Trip. Why was he here, and what did it mean? I wished I could tell Cay, but he was off hunting for the Amulet.

An icy thought popped into my head: If Trip was here, did that mean Deidra was close? I sat up with a start. Was I even ready to take her on again? Who knew what she'd been doing out there?

Entirely creeped out, I closed and locked my door. I double-checked the window before climbing into bed again.

I yawned, feeling the weight of everything pressing down on my body. I forced myself to blot out all the thoughts of Trip, Rose, Deidra, and my self-doubt in order to get some sleep.

"What are you doing?" Lugh asked me. Stuffing items into a pack, I had destroyed my room.

"What do you care?" I muttered, not turning to face my brother.

"You're going to look for it, aren't you?" I heard the disbelief in his voice.

"Yes, dear brother," I said, rolling up a pair of breeches. "I can't trust that, if you two find it, I'll see my half."

Lugh sighed loudly, as if he was exhausted from explaining something to a small child for the fifteenth time.

"Beira, sister," he started, "despite what you may think, you and I both know Brighde would never take your Amulet half."

I barked out a laugh. "You can think such foolish things, but I know better. Our sister believes I have her half, so she steals mine for revenge. But where is her proof?" I gestured to the screaming snowstorm outside. "Even this is on the verge of being beyond my control."

I turned my back to Lugh and finished stuffing my pack. "If I had both halves, this would be a lesser storm."

"Beira," Lugh said gently. "If you and Brighde combined yourselves, the weather, and our family, would steady and be strong once more."

"Forgive her? The thief?" I snorted and faced him, grasping my bulging pack. "Lugh, you have lost your sanity. I will never trust her, and in return, she will never trust me."

I jumped, still lying fully dressed on my bed. My head hurt from the churning combination of anger and frustration from the dream and the personal fear that someone knew I had Brighde's Amulet. I waited for my heart to settle and my body to relax before I pulled off my pants and climbed under the covers.

My mind was a swirling vortex from Trip, Rose, and Beira, so that night, sleep was not easy to come by. Lugh kept teasing Beira about where the Amulet was, which always felt just out of reach.

I had a hard time dragging myself out of bed to the shower in the morning. Thankfully, it was quiet when I padded into the restroom, dangling my shower caddy loosely next to me.

I bathed in peace, brushed my hair and teeth in silence, and got dressed in the stillness of the morning sunlight. Feeling a little better after last night's shock, I was ready to focus on my lessons with Eden, study hard, and get the hell out of here, so I could live up to my family's legacy.

I found Eden waiting for me outside in the field behind the kitchen, where I'd seen Trip and Rose the night before.

"What's on the agenda today?" I asked, walking up beside her.

She placed the notebook she was writing in on the grass in front of her.

"Pop quiz!" she said cheerfully.

"On what?" I asked. "We haven't done much reading."

"I'll ignore that, as you're meant to be reading on your own, but it's on what you've learned of the basics so far."

"Which really isn't much," I muttered, plopping myself next to her. Of course, Eden heard me. Her hearing rivaled that of parents everywhere.

"So, you haven't been reading, and you haven't been practicing?" She sighed. "Missing your friends and family won't help you save them in the end."

I frowned. "I know. It's not that."

"What's going on?"

I chewed on my lip, unsure if I should tell her about my dreams. I sighed. What did I have to lose?

"I keep having dreams," I said, playing with a blade of grass. I twisted it in my hands and smoothed it out.

"What kind of dreams?"

"Recently, they've been violent, angry." My mind flashed back to Beira tearing into Brighde's room, screaming about her missing Amulet. I felt the fire in my chest again, like I was the embodiment of her fury.

"Angry about what?" she asked.

"Mostly the Amulet." I resisted the urge to play with the half that was around my neck.

"Mostly?"

"Yeah, the Amulet and Brighde, and Beira, and Lugh. The twins are fighting because each of them thinks the other stole their half of the Amulet."

A small group of students came out with their teacher and settled across from us.

"Come," Eden said, popping up. She brushed the grass off herself and grabbed her notebook. I followed suit. We walked a long distance away from the other students, toward the tree line at the edge of the meadow. A bug buzzed in the woods, creating a scenic atmosphere.

"You were saying each twin thought the other stole the Amulet?" Eden said.

"Yes. I usually dream I'm Brighde. Now I'm Beira, keeping my cool while Brighde came running into my—" I paused, *her* room, demanding the Amulet. But Brighde feels satisfied that Beira lost her half, too."

"Did the dreams start when you arrived?"

I shook my head. "No, I've had them since I found out I was their descendant."

"Do you think they mean anything?" She looked at me inquisitively.

"Probably, but I try to shake them off right when I wake up because I hate the way I feel. It's a lot, you know? The hatred, the fear, the anger..." We stopped at a bench a few feet away from the edge of the forest. I sat, staring into the cluster of moss, trees, and vines that appeared mysterious even in daylight. Eden faced the school.

"I think you should start keeping a journal of the dreams," Eden suggested. "It could help you decipher why you're getting them."

"Isn't it obvious?" I asked.

"Is it?" She pushed her glasses up her nose as I turned to look at her.

"Well, I think so. I'm seeing snippets of what happened to the Amulet pieces."

She shrugged. "It could be as simple as that, or it could be something more. A dream journal would help you."

I looked toward the trees again. Maybe it would help, though I wasn't sure how exactly.

"I guess." What else did I have to lose?

"Now, about that quiz..."

I scrunched my nose. I hoped she had forgotten about it. Sighing, I gestured for her to continue as I mentally prepared to face the sudden quiz.

It wasn't easy, and I didn't do as well as I'd hoped. She sent me off with more homework and a study schedule, which I planned on starting right after dinner. Pushing my door open, I slung my bag onto the desk chair and fell into my bed. I glanced at the clock on the wall. Dinner was in about an hour, which left me plenty of time to plan out what I wanted to say to Trip if I saw him again. Not if, when. I snatched my notebook and jotted things down. Trip was clearly dating Rose. She clearly didn't know how terrible he was. Or maybe she did, and she didn't care. She was kind of evil, after all. Trip was in Switzerland, which meant he could know where to find the other Amulet half. Or he was here for mine. I took a deep breath and continued.

On the one hand, Rose was afraid of me. On the other hand, Trip felt extremely confident I wouldn't kick his ass.

To be fair, I didn't know if I would. He was at full strength.

I was still mad at him for the bullshit we'd been through, the lies and betrayal. How he'd played me to find out my secrets. The pain took a fresh stab, and I blinked back tears. Sadness swirled through the anger, reminding me of the good times: the smiles, moments of closeness, intimacy, first kisses, first hand-hold, excitement when the new boy had wanted to date me. Betrayal popped up again because he hadn't really wanted me in the beginning. It was the first time I could say a boy had liked me for my mind. But my mind had been blank with information about the Amulet he was hoping to find.

I looked down at my notebook. The few words I'd written were blurred blobs of ink from the tears that had escaped. Not wanting to sit in my room feeling sorry for myself, I grabbed my stuff and ventured downstairs toward the lounge common room where everyone hung out during breaks. There were couches, a huge flat-screen TV currently playing a blockbuster superhero movie in the background, gaming systems, board games, and beanbag chairs. I scanned the room for Oliver, Ginger, Franny, or Mat, but they weren't there. Natalia was, but I didn't want to interact with her. I was trying to keep my distance from her family after last night. I turned and left, heading toward the library.

A few kids were inside, but no one was sitting at the small table in front of the picture window that faced the Lohner Mountains. I loved looking at the slope of the mountain range. The lush greenery that blanketed the trails leading up the side and the inviting cool colors of snow offered relief from the scorching heat outside. Each curve or crack appeared to be cut from the sky behind it, like a sewn design on a quilt. It calmed my nerves and helped control my anxiety from my Seeker destiny. I pulled out my notes to help distract me and reviewed them under the peaceful scene of the mountains.

"Hey," Oliver said, sitting across for me. I jumped a little, not expecting anyone to join me.

"Hey, yourself," I said, closing my notes. I still didn't know who knew what about me, and I didn't want to endure the wrath of Norah if something got out.

"How was your lesson today?" he asked, resting his hand on the table. His accent seemed more pronounced than before, and I noticed for the first time he was Scottish.

"Eye-opening," I replied, making him raise an eyebrow. I shook my head and smiled. "I guess I've been coasting and not taking the work here as seriously as I should."

He smiled. "Yeah, we've all been there."

There was a moment of silence before he said, "Rumor has it you got kitchen duty for the fight with Rose."

I sighed. "Yeah, from now until the day I die."

"For what it's worth, I went to speak to Norah on your behalf. To see if she would listen to reason."

I was touched and a little hopeful. "Really? What did she say?"

He shook his head. "Nothing I said would get her to lighten up."

I slouched. "Thank you for trying. I appreciate it."

"No problem. Rose is the devil incarnate, and Norah just doesn't see it."

"Is that who Balor is?" I chuckled a little too loudly. I expected a librarian to come and shush us, but when I looked, we were the only two left in the room.

Oliver smiled, "Maybe. He was evil for sure, enjoying torture like Rose does."

Glancing around again, we were still alone. "Where did everyone else go?"

Oliver looked around and shrugged. "No clue."

I looked at him quizzically, hoping for more information, but didn't say anything. No one else had gone to defend my honor, and I didn't see anyone else sitting with us. I didn't want to jinx the only solid friendship lead I had going.

"How long have you been here?" I asked.

"Since I was twelve. I'm seventeen now."

"Why so long?"

Oliver stayed quiet for a second. "Norah and my mom felt it was best if I stayed here until I could really control my powers."

I didn't want to press him for more details. Something about his hesitation told me to move on.

"And what do you learn?"

"Lots of stuff. I had to learn how to control my powers. They didn't develop until I hit puberty."

"Is that because you only have one magical parent?"

"Had. And yes." Frowning slightly as if he was composing himself, he seemed a little sad confirming this.

"I'm sorry."

He shrugged. "It's okay. My dad was the magical one in the family, and he passed from natural causes when I was eight. My mom didn't know how to manage my powers anymore, and she found Norah through the magic of the Internet. I was sent here."

"Wow. That's ... rough." I was barely surviving on my own here; the loneliness was crushing my soul. I missed my family and friends back home. I couldn't imagine how a twelve-year-old had managed.

He shrugged again. "It is what it is. My mom and I talked a lot about it, and I don't blame her. She comes to visit me, and we write to each other."

I didn't know what else to say, so I changed the topic. "So, what is your power?"

"Fire." He held out his hand, palm facing up, and a little flame flickered to life. It pooled into a circle, little embers jumping off into the air. The shape grew and thinned out, legs formed, and a flaming horse appeared. The horse reared back and kicked. It was so lifelike; I thought I heard neighing. Oliver closed and opened his hand to reveal the shape of a girl. Her hair was long and curly. Subconsciously, I played with my own hair. Then, it hit me.

"Is that meant to be me?" I asked, not taking my eyes off the dancing flame.

Oliver closed his hand, extinguishing her, and blushed, light pink dusting his umber skin. "Yeah," he said sheepishly.

"That was extremely cool."

Oliver grinned wide. "Thanks. I have Brighde to thank for my power."

It's not surprising I didn't know Brighde could offer that. I guess over time, descendants' powers morphed into new abilities, meaning Beira's side could probably do the same. I held back a sigh, as I mentally added another worry to my repertoire.

"What will you do with it when you leave here?"

He shrugged. "I'm still figuring it out, but I think Brighde's Seeker could use someone like me on their side. I may try to help with the search."

I smiled, knowing he was making that connection right now. "I'm sure they would appreciate it."

"What's your story?" He rested his arms on the table and leaned in. I tried to play it cool, but I didn't have a clue about what to say.

Thankfully, I didn't have to say a word as the door opened and in burst Ginger.

"There you two are! Come on, it's time for dinner, and trust me, you don't want to miss it!"

"Why?" Oliver asked.

Ginger couldn't hold back her giant grin. "Rose has extra kitchen duty. She's going to be serving us!"

Not giving us a full chance to react, Ginger bounced, her blonde hair flying behind her, from the doorway and down the hall. I felt my skin prickle with concern as Oliver looked extremely pleased.

"It sounds like Norah did listen!"

I offered a weak smile in return. I wasn't as thrilled as everyone else with our new chef as I kept picturing her poisoning my food.

I shuffled out behind Oliver and followed the droves of students reporting for dinner. Sure enough, Rose was there, dressed in a standard lunch lady uniform, down to the stained white coat and hairnet. If looks could kill, the whole school would be dead.

"I don't think I'm that hungry," I said to Oliver as I stepped away from the line.

"Come on, you can't show fear to the beast. She feeds on that," he said, grabbing my arm and pulling me back in.

"I'm not afraid of her," I said indignantly. "I just don't find the idea of her touching my food, or even breathing by it, appetizing."

"Then you go sit at the table, and I'll get your food since you're so worried."

"If she asks, I'll take my hamburger without a side of spit." I walked away from him and found my table. Mat and Ginger had already claimed their seats.

"How great is this?" Ginger asked, staring at Rose. I looked at the Protectors' table. Natalia didn't bother a glance in her sister's direction while her tablemates reeked of boredom and disinterest. I think Natalia and I were the only two who didn't find Rose entertaining. Suddenly, she looked over and locked eyes with me. Neither of us moved, yet she bore an expression that was hard to read. I dared not look away, mostly because I couldn't. Something about her was entrancing.

"Here you go," Oliver said, placing a plate in front of me. I blinked and leaned back, startled by the interruption. I quickly looked back at Natalia, but she had already turned around, her back facing me.

"Thanks," I said to Oliver, taking a sip of water. He smiled and took a seat. I didn't say much at dinner, as I was working out why Rose and Trip were together, how I was going to fit in all my studying, and how I would decipher my nightmares, per Eden's request. The only one who really paid any attention was Oliver, but I avoided his concerned glances as I nibbled on my food.

The dining room cleared out slowly, leaving a few stragglers. My friends left me as I bussed the tables around us. Once everyone was gone, Rose quietly emerged from the kitchen. I was too busy cleaning to really pay her any mind, only keeping half an ear out to see if she would have another midnight rendezvous with Trip.

I tried not to think about them. It wouldn't help my quest to find the Amulet half if I spent my time wondering about what they were doing together. In fact, it made me sick knowing he'd kissed her like he'd kissed me, held her hand, shared clandestine secrets in the blanket of darkness. A stab of nostalgia sliced through my memories and colored them rose red. I couldn't tell if I missed Trip or the mystery that surrounded him more. I missed Cay and Logan, and I wished Cay was here to crack a joke, or Logan was here to say something sweet and encouraging. They were the only two I could truly trust in this world right now.

I looked up, noticing the only sounds were coming from me moving the mop bucket across the floor. Rose wasn't in the room, but the back door was ajar again. I abandoned my post and stepped carefully to the opened door. I didn't see anyone or anything out there when Rose popped up in front of me.

"Spying?" she asked in a cool tone.

"On who? You? No. Why would I do that?" I stuttered, moving away from the door.

"Who knows? I don't spend my days decoding your brain." She pushed past me into the main dining room.

I took a breath and counted to ten while remembering Norah's warning. Taking the opportunity, I slipped through the door and into the cool night air. I immediately looked toward the field where I last saw Trip. Of course, he wasn't there. It's not like he'd be outside waiting for me or anything. I scanned the area one more time to confirm he wasn't there and then headed back inside. As I grabbed the handle, I heard something rustling in the bushes, and it wasn't like a gentle breeze caressing the leaves. I tugged on the handle, but the door was stuck shut. Shit! Rose!

I heard the noise again, and the hair on the back of my neck stood. I gulped and turned around. There was nothing behind me, much to my relief. *Walk toward the bush*, my brain commanded. *No, don't!* A panicked voice argued back. Outwardly, I rolled my eyes. I'd been told I'm some badass. It was about time I proved it to myself by taking down whatever was in the bushes. Which was probably a rabbit.

Baby steps.

I walked shakily toward the bushes, reminding myself I had powers I could use if needed. The rustling stopped, but I didn't hear or see anything escape from the thicket. After what felt like forever, I scrounged some courage and moved the branches. Nothing was there but silhouettes of the undergrowth. Relief poured through my veins, and I headed back into the building.

CHAPTER 5

Another week of studying with Eden, having nightmares, seeing things in the dark, and following Rose for another glimpse of Trip passed. By Friday, I felt like I had made the whole thing up.

I woke up Saturday morning, feeling rested after a nightmare-free sleep. The sun was shining clearly through my window, and I swore I heard the Jersey Shore from thousands of miles away. I missed my home, but the lonely ache was less dreadful than usual. I lay in bed a few minutes until needing to use the restroom forced me up. I grabbed my stuff and padded down to the hall.

The steam from the shower was refreshing, like a day at the spa, and I reveled in comfort as I toweled myself off. Heading back to my room, I saw my door was left slightly ajar and not closed, like I thought I had left it.

I swung the door open, hoping to catch someone in the act of doing something, but no one was there.

I checked the few places someone could hide, but I was alone. Maybe I hadn't latched my door after all.

I headed to the dining room to see Ginger sitting at a table, reading.

"Anything good?" I asked, nodding toward her breakfast of what looked like porridge and fruit. She looked up at me and smiled.

"It's not bad. They have some gipfeli left if you're hungry."

I grabbed the Swiss version of a croissant she'd offered and some tea with milk, then joined Ginger at the table.

"How are your studies going?" she asked, closing her book. I saw the title had the name Dil written in cursive on the cover.

I chewed thoughtfully. Should I tell a nearly perfect stranger just how I'd been: paranoid, lonely, and sad?

"Not too badly," I finally replied. "I failed a pop quiz the other day, but I'm planning on practicing more today, so I don't get caught off guard again."

"I haven't worked with Eden, but I hear she's good."

I smiled. "She is awesome."

"Do you want to practice together today?"

"Absolutely. I will take any help I can get," I said.

"Let's go," Ginger said, grabbing her book.

We walked out into the bright sunshine and into a handful of students scattered across the front fields.

"I guess we weren't the only people who need a refresher," I said.

"How about over there?" Ginger squinted and pointed to a far corner toward the main road, a good distance away from our classmates.

"Sounds good."

"What's your power?" I asked as we trudged through the tall grass.

"My ancestor is Dil."

I frowned. That didn't really tell me anything.

Ginger caught on to my silence and said, "She's the goddess of cattle. I'm good with animals."

"Cool. Can you talk to them like Dr. Doolittle?"

She smiled and shook her head. "Something like that. They don't speak to me, but I can understand them on a deeper level than most other people."

"Are you planning on being a veterinarian with those powers?"

"More like an animal rights activist and working for a nonprofit. We're here."

We reached our destination, and Ginger dropped her book in the grass. "What do you want to work on?"

I wavered between telling her and keeping my mouth shut. As far as I could tell, no one knew who I was. Should I bring her into the biggest secret of my life? The Amulet flashed heat, like a warning.

"I just want to work on my elementals," I offered casually. Eden said it was important for me to understand the basics of nature before I could truly understand my powers.

"Which one have you been struggling in?" Ginger asked. "I passed all my elemental tests, so I can show you anything."

"All of them," I admitted. "But earth has been trickier for me than the others."

"Okay." She sat on the grass and crossed her legs. I sat across from her.

"The first thing you need to do is clear your mind."

Why did that always have to be the first step? Closing my eyes, I inhaled deeply and released the breath slowly, allowing as many thoughts as possible to flow out of me.

"Imagine what's going on underneath the soil we sit on. The ants moving through their tunnels, worms wriggling under the layers of dirt as they keep their skin moist to breathe, the tiny bugs nibbling on the blades of grass around us."

My skin tickled, as if the bugs and worms were crawling all over me. I shuddered and opened my eyes.

"Can't do it. I'm getting creeped out. New image, please."

Ginger shook her head but started a new description. "Take a breath again and picture the grass swaying in the gentle breeze. Hear the bugs in the distance, chirping like a tiny choir. Feel the sensation of the cool soil underneath you."

This time, I was able to empty my mind of all other thoughts. I felt the sun gently beaming down on us, wrapping around us like a hug. I was at peace.

"Can you try to grow a flower from a seed?" Ginger asked. She picked a pansy in the field next to her and pulled the seed out.

"I tried once before but was unsuccessful. I know in my book, it says I have to connect with the seed, but I don't understand how to do that." I let out a sigh. I'd barely begun, and frustration was building.

"Imagine how the seed would feel if it was human. Small, full of bright potential, excited and anxious to show the world how wonderful it can be, to grow into something breathtaking..." As her voice trailed off, I pictured a little seed. I breathed deeply, inhaling the rich oxygen from the trees, bushes, and grass around us. I visualized the seed first waking in the warmth of the sun, sprouting a little tail, and sunning itself to absorb all the nutrients it needed. As it grew, it broke through its outer shell, pushing the tail up and away, and its leaves began to bloom. Using the newly grown tail, the seed gently pulled itself onto a patch of thick grass. I pictured it sinking roots in the ground and growing into a mature plant, sprouting petals as it became a full-grown flower, being visited by new friends, like bees or insects, and constantly embracing the sunbeams and rain showers that helped it stay strong and healthy. I was melancholy when I thought that the flower missed being a little seed and suddenly wished there was another flower there with it.

I wrinkled my nose as a splash of water dropped on me. I opened my eyes and saw the clouds had darkened a little, and a light sprinkle of rain was misting everything.

"Weird," Ginger said, looking up at the sky, "the forecast didn't call for rain today."

I hid my face, not wanting her to see my secret.

"Should we go in?" I asked her.

"Or we can switch gears and work on water elementals?" she suggested.

"Okay, what's first?"

Ginger cupped her hands in front of her. "Usually, you would use a bowl or cup, but I'm improvising." I watched as she collected water in her hands. In a nonmagical person, water would leak through the tiny gap between their hands. Ginger was able to hold the water and stop it from leaking. She swirled it around and sloshed it, but not even a drop slipped out.

"How did you do that?" I asked, perplexed.

She released her hands, and the water fell into the dirt. "A lot of the teachings all start with 'Be one with the element,' or whatever," she explained. "But for me, I thought of that feeling I get when I swim in the lake. Floating, free, airy. I feel powerful yet delicate at the same time."

I slowly nodded my head in understanding. I knew what power felt like, even if I couldn't truly control the elements. I knew how to demand them when it mattered.

"Let me try," I said, holding my hands out like she did. I collected an amount of water in my hands and watched as it dripped through the space between my fingers.

"Try again," Ginger said gently. I furrowed my brow in determined frustration. I knew how to command water. I wouldn't let this get the better of me.

I collected the water in my hands again. This time, I squeezed my fingers shut and yelled in my head at the water to stop moving. At first, nothing happened, just water droplets adding to the collection in my hands. I yelled once more, and the water stilled. No droplets, no drips. Nothing moved.

"Try moving it," Ginger urged.

I pushed the water with my mind in a gentle circle. It swirled lightly in my hand, but it was nothing as severe as Ginger's demonstration. I pushed it faster and faster, watching it spin until a small whirlpool appeared. In a moment of pure satisfaction, I pulled the water in the opposite direction, keeping the spirals tightly wound. Instead of spilling over the edges of my fingertips, the water slowly lifted into the air like a cyclone. Ignoring the echo of Norah's voice in my head cautioning me to be discreet, I pulled the cyclone higher and higher into the air, spinning it like an inverted V. The tip of the cyclone dissipated, evaporating with every turn, until there was nothing of the twisting water left. I looked down at my hands, expecting to see them moist, but they were bone dry.

"Whoa," Ginger whispered. "That was really cool."

I smiled, pleased with myself. One sign down, one to conquer, and two to learn.

"Ow!" Ginger rubbed her leg and looked up.

"What happened?"

"I don't know. I think someone threw something at me."

I looked around but didn't see anyone standing close enough to us. Feeling a sharp pinch on my arm, I saw a red mark grow on my skin.

"Ow! I felt something too!" I said, rubbing the sore spot. I saw the green grass below our bodies develop frost on their tips as small pellets of hail were falling from the sky.

Just as Ginger opened her mouth to say something, an obnoxious bell went off. I looked around and saw everyone outside making a mad dash for the school.

"Run!" Ginger said, and she took off. I didn't have time to ask what was happening before she was gone. I jumped and ran after her. The field felt much bigger than it had before as we dodged the increasingly larger lumps of ice. Students and teachers were filing in quickly, but there was still a backlog of bodies.

"Look!" someone shouted in front of me. "Up there!"

Heads turned upward as a large shadow zipped across the sky. We heard a crash, and an icicle the size of a boulder plowed into the shed, crushing the roof. Kids screamed as smaller icicles were pelting those who were still outside. The older kids were grabbing smaller kids and hauling them in the door, passing them off to someone inside before grabbing another. I watched, confused and help-less, as ice smashed into our dumpsters, spilling bags of rotten food and garbage onto the pavement. Familiarity slammed into me, and I knew exactly what to do. Just like at graduation, I closed my eyes and forced myself to take a deep, calming breath. I imagined the earth was enflamed, melting the ice before it could do any more damage. The heat from the sun warmed my face and arms, protecting me from the frozen water. My socks started getting wet, but I ignored it, thinking of my home, my friends, and my family, allowing the warmth inside me grow stronger.

"Bridget!" I whipped around and saw Ginger staring at me. Everyone else had been able to get inside, and we were left alone in the sunshine. Puddles pooled around our feet, the icicles melting. Ginger said nothing else and pointed behind me. I followed her finger.

The field was now on fire. I instantly turned down the sun and asked for a quick sun shower to come and put out the flames.

"I guess you won't need help practicing anymore," Ginger said, aghast.

I gave her a sheepish smile.

"Bridget." I jumped at the sound of my name coming out of Norah's mouth.

"My office. Now," she said, turning on her heel and storming away. Eden stood next to her, wringing her hands and biting her lip. I hoped she wasn't mad at me too, but she didn't meet my stare. I trudged past her, heading to Norah's office, dreading what punishment would be served.

When I went inside, I knocked on Norah's door.

"Enter," came the reply.

"Do you know what that was?" Norah asked before I even had a chance to close the office door.

"Ice," I replied.

"In the dead of summer?" She raised an eyebrow at me.

"It was really weird, Norah. One minute, I'm practicing my elementals, and the next I'm being nailed in the head with balls of hail."

She gestured for me to sit. "Bridget, I must confess something to you. This was the first time in many, many years that our defenses have failed."

"What do you mean?"

"I have talked with you about the perils that face you once you leave your studies."

I nodded.

"We have protocols and fail-safe plans in place to protect the students and faculty who reside here. Today, those protocols were weakened, and we were attacked."

Deidra. More likely, Trip.

"While I'm not exactly sure who the one person behind this is, I can confirm this comes from the house of Beira."

When I didn't reply, she asked, "Do you know about this?"

I shrugged. "I figured as much. At my graduation a month ago, something like this happened, but it wasn't Deidra."

"Who was it, then?"

"Her brother, Trip."

"Are you sure?"

"No," I reluctantly admitted. "But I swear I saw him there, and he's had his full powers since he turned eighteen last December. I don't get mine for another two and a half weeks. I don't know who else could create ice in the middle of my season."

"I see," she said. Norah remained silent for a minute. Not knowing what else to do, I shifted uncomfortably in my seat.

"Did anyone else see you use your powers?"

"When? At graduation?"

"No, today."

"I think Ginger did. She was behind me when I was melting everything."

"As well as setting the grounds on fire," Norah added.

I scrunched my nose up and hunched my shoulders. "I'm sorry! I was just trying to help."

Norah smiled grimly. "I know, Bridget. Thank you for your assistance on this, but I'm afraid we must be more guarded about your secret now that you've been compromised."

"Does this mean I won't be able to train anymore?" I asked, stricken.

"Of course not! It's more important for you to train now than ever before. But we have to be more careful. No more training openly. We'll have to find a hidden spot for you and Eden to practice."

I nodded in acceptance.

"You may leave, but be careful when you study. We cannot risk any more incidents like today."

I got up and left, slinking to my room to avoid conversation with Ginger or anyone else who may have seen.

Chapter 6

I flung my door open and stomped into my room. Defenses had failed... Had I caused it when I'd been practicing? Did I really have that strong of a power? I wish I had someone to talk to about this. I paced around my room, just a knot of nerves walking in a circle. How could I have known training for my elementals would send a flare to all my enemies?

There was a light scraping noise from my door that drew my attention. A piece of paper was stuck underneath my door jam. I threw open the door to find an empty hallway. Closing the door behind me, I picked up the folded paper and opened it. It was a note.

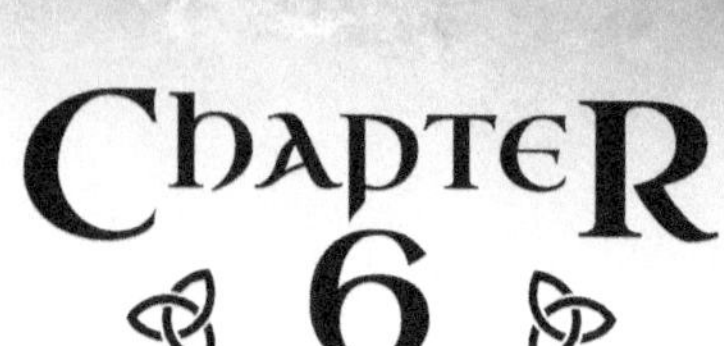

Well, this would be one heck of an awkward conversation. I sighed and sat on my bed, all energy suddenly zapped from my body. I hadn't even truly begun to fight, and I was ready to tap out. Being a Cuardaitheoir was the greatest and scariest thing I had yet to do. The training still eluded me most days, but it was cool being able to control water or create a sudden heatwave with a quick, emotional memory. I wondered what my life would have been like if I hadn't learned about my powers. What would I be doing right now, my last summer before college? Would I be spending it on the beach with my friends, or working a summer job to make some money? I smiled at the idea of having Jimmy's Hot Dogs while I soaked up the bit of sun I was allowed to have. Now that I knew about my powers, I didn't burn anymore.

I lay back on the bed, letting the nostalgia wash over me. Training with Cay and Logan, dancing with my friends at Homecoming, my first kiss with Trip. Nostalgia shifted to remorse as I remembered the good moments I'd had with Trip. The scavenger hunt was so sweet and thoughtful. It was one of the times I felt really connected. Then I flashed to our breakup in the library. He'd known I was ignorant of our destinies, and he'd preyed on my naïveté. I don't know what hurt more, the betrayal or the lies. I rolled onto my side and curled into a ball. Loving him had felt easy, even when Cay was shoving his lies in my face. I could look past that and still see the good in Trip. I had stupidly believed anything he'd said to me.

Shame rose to my cheeks. I couldn't control how much I didn't know about my family history, but I still should have seen through his crap faster than I did. I haven't been able to forgive myself for allowing Trip into my life so thoroughly and swiftly. Cay was right; I'd been stupid.

I sniffed as a tear rolled down my face. Now Trip was dating Rose, my new archnemesis, and was hell-bent on taking me down. Normally, I would be so frustrated and angry to be stuck here while he was gallivanting through Europe looking for the other Amulet half, but right now, I was just sad. Sad that I'd left my home, my friends, and my family. Sad that I'd lost Trip, even though he was mostly a sneaky jerk to me. Sad that Mom hadn't told me about my life sooner, costing me a fighting chance against the Findlays and every other descendant of Beira. And sad to be causing even more problems here, and I didn't know how to stop any of it.

Misery flowed through my veins as I lay in a ball on a foreign bed in a foreign country, feeling utterly alone in the world. The heavy downpour of rain outside was soothing as I fell asleep.

Sometime later, I woke up. The rain had stopped, and the sun was low in the sky, casting a pink shadow across my room. I blinked a few times, and the dried tears on my cheeks loosened. Looking at my phone—it was nearly six thirty—I realized I had to book it to dinner and then clean up the dining room. I stopped at the restroom to wash my face as I headed to grab a seat.

When I got into the hall, I saw Ginger, Mat, Franny, and Oliver sitting at our normal table. I didn't have the stamina to face any of them after today, so I grabbed my food and sat at the corner table with my back to the room. No one came to talk to me, which was a silent relief, and the room emptied as students finished their dinner. When the last person was done, I cleaned my spot and resumed my after-dinner duty with Rose.

After a bit of cleaning, she grabbed the trash and hauled it to the back door.

"Going to follow me again?" she asked, eyebrow raised.

It took every fiber of my soul not to say, "I know you're dating Trip and trying to sabotage me."

What I actually said was, "You aren't worth following."

She scoffed and headed outside. Ignoring the warning in my head that said, "Stay inside tonight," I slipped between the doors and slid to the shed, hoping to see Trip again. Sure enough, he was standing there with Rose. This time, they were in the pool of light from the lamppost.

I had the *pure joy* of watching them kiss for a minute. Every time I saw the flick of a tongue, I swallowed back bile.

Thankfully, they stopped and got to talking.

"Nothing?" Trip said, running his fingers through his hair. He'd let it get a little longer, and he looked like the long-lost member of a boy band. I forced myself to keep the pitiful swooning to a minimum.

"Nothing. She hasn't done anything else. I don't even know if she really knows how to use her powers."

What a shock: Rose thinks I'm an idiot. I rolled my eyes.

"Don't underestimate Bridget," Trip warned her. "She may come off as innocent, but she is much smarter than you know."

My heart leaped at the compliment and then fell at the insult. I didn't play innocent! I *was* innocent. Sort of.

Rose sighed. "Do we have to talk about her every time? I'm not here just to stalk your ex-girlfriend."

That took me by surprise. They spent their time together talking about me?

It was Trip's turn to sigh. "Rose, you know I have a complicated history with her. It's important that I know where she has the Amulet piece."

"You mean *if* she has it."

I watched him shake his head. "No, I know she has it, and that puts us in the red. Brighde's lineage is closer to finding the second half and I... I barely know where to look!" He sounded exasperated. My heart began to race, and my breath caught in my throat as I played with the Amulet around my neck, even more determined not to lose it now that I knew Rose had been in my room looking for it. I made a mental note to install a lock.

"It's important to find out just what and how much she knows."

"Well, you heard what happened today. With the hail."

"Obviously." Was that a confession?

"She melted it without breaking a sweat! She *set fire* to the grass!"

"Hey," he said, pulling her close to him. He rested his hands on her arms. "She doesn't have her full powers yet. You can still take her if you needed to."

Rose frowned but didn't say anything.

"Bridget's tough and resourceful," Trip continued, "but she's no match for a trained Protector."

"You sound like you still love her," Rose said pointedly. Butterflies popped up in my stomach, like they had when I'd first met Trip. I thought I'd killed those little suckers.

Trip smiled at her and tilted her chin up. "How can I convince you that isn't true?" He kissed her lips firmly but not as deeply as he had a few minutes before. Rose didn't fall for his charm and pulled away after a second.

A set of footsteps drew closer to the couple, and Trip looked past Rose to see the figure coming into the light.

"Natalia," he said coolly.

Natalia knew he was here? I gently smacked myself on the forehead. Of course, she'd know about her sister's romantic relationships.

"Findlay," she responded, standing next to Rose. "Rose needs to come back now. Lights out is coming, and she needs to be in bed before Norah catches you two." Her bright hair was tied in a messy knot on the top of her head, but a soft breeze blew a few stray hairs around her face. She wrapped her arms over her chest, as she wore nothing but a tank top and pj shorts.

"I'll only be a few more minutes," Rose said to her sister. "Can you cover for me?"

"Always." Natalia looked at Trip again, "Don't forget, Seeker, we may be Protectors for Beria's side, but I'll protect my sister over any one of you."

He narrowed his eyes at her as she walked away from them and slipped quietly back into the building.

"I really wish she'd get with the program," he muttered.

Rose pointed a finger at Trip's chest. "Don't toy with me, Findlay. Our families have been bound together for centuries, but that doesn't mean I'll follow you blindly. I want proof of the things you say about Bridget." She crossed her arms over her chest. "As for my sister, she's my family, and I've got her back the same way she's always had mine. This," she gestured between them, "is not my priority if you can't get along with her." As much as I disliked Rose, I could learn a thing or two from her about boys.

He took a deep breath and let it out slowly. "What do you want? More training time with Zachary? You know he's the best Norah's got. If he can't get you ready to fight Bridget, no one can."

"I want something definitive that will defeat her."

Trip shook his head. "Even finding the other half of the Amulet will only weaken her, and once she turns eighteen in less than two weeks, all bets are off. We have to act fast."

"Then give me something else because I haven't been able to make her break a sweat or shake in fear since she arrived."

Trip smiled so quickly; I almost thought I imagined it.

"I'll think about it and get back to you," he promised, moving closer to her and placing a hand on her cheek. "In the meantime, keep whatever you're doing up. And don't stop looking for the Amulet."

Rose nodded and lifted her head up for a kiss. I turned away and snuck back into the dining room before I saw their lips touch. I'd had enough of that for one night and headed to my room.

I tried to sleep, but it was difficult with thoughts of Rose standing over me in my sleep, reaching for my necklace. I kept a firm hand on it, and I jammed the desk chair under the doorknob for an added layer of security. Tossing and turning for what felt like forever, I finally passed out.

Lugh sauntered into the library where I lay in the only patch of sunlight that streamed through the heavy blanket of snow. Since Beira's Amulet half went missing, neither of us had had an easy time controlling the seasons.

"Hello, brother. Care to join me in the only warmth in this castle?" I gestured to the pillow next to me.

"No, dear sister. I've come to share with you the news you've been waiting for."

I sat up, excitedly. "Beira's death?"

Lugh rolled his eyes. "You would have known of her death way before I even thought about telling you."

I shrugged. Our twin intuition had been less intense since the Amulet halves had gone missing.

"Perhaps. But if it's not that, will you ever tell me what you're so gleefully keeping a secret?"

Lugh pouted. "It's not fun when you don't guess."

I sighed. "Lugh, this is the first time in nearly a year I've been able to keep a moment's peace. Please, just tell me."

He smiled. "Well, you must remember this peace a little longer, as this is the last time you will have it."

"Why is that?"

"I think I know where your half is."

I woke up the next morning feeling both unsettled and excited. Maybe these dreams would finally be good for something besides a helping hand in my current costume as a zombie. I dutifully wrote the dream in my journal, noting I was dreaming as Brighde again, as Eden had suggested, then closed the book. My chair was in the same place I'd left it the night before, giving me a sense of relief. That was one night Rose hadn't been snooping in my room. I padded down the hall to the restroom, brushed my teeth, and came back to my room to start my day.

Breakfast was a sleepy affair. I wasn't the only one who couldn't sleep solidly through the night anymore. I grabbed some coffee, a roll with butter, and a couple pieces of fruit. I stared at my breakfast for a minute, wishing the roll was a Jersey bagel with pork roll, egg, and cheese. I sighed and made my way to the library to continue studying the *Book of Brighde*.

Strangely, the library was full of life as students were talking softly about what had happened yesterday.

"I swear, the ice was the size of the building!" one girl said to her friend.

"No way. That's not possible," her friend replied. *Oh, it's possible!* I thought.

"Forget the size of the ice! What is going on with the weather? Hail in summer? What's next? Surfboards in snow?" Another random kid chimed in.

"They have that already. It's called snowboarding," the first girl said.

I smiled and sat at a table by the window. The view of the mountains helped me feel less stressed as I jumped into the history of Brighde.

The morning passed quickly enough, and I needed to stretch my legs. I gathered my stuff up and threw away my garbage from breakfast.

"Hey!" Franny said as she and Mat walked into the room.

"Hey, yourself," I said warmly. They placed their stuff on the table I had just deserted.

"What are you up to today?" Mat asked, sitting in the chair and pulling out a green notebook. "Anything fun?"

I waved my own book at them, making sure to cover the title. "Just trying to stay ahead."

"How can you be studying when we could be attacked at any minute?" Mat mentioned excitedly. I immediately tensed.

"Years of practice?" I suggested weakly.

"You've spent a lot of time around hail the size of cars and spontaneous fire?" Franny raised an eyebrow. I tried not to avoid her stare.

"You know, in the morning in Jersey, it could be sixty degrees, and by dinner, you're shoveling snow."

"No, I wouldn't know that," Franny answered, her accent clipped and pronounced.

"But we do know other things," Mat teased, lightly taunting me.

I kept my cool as my insides were doing the samba all over my stomach.

"Like what?"

"Like... who started the fire on the field."

I nodded my head. "Cool. I know stuff, too."

"Like what?" Franny asked this time. It was my turn to smile.

"Like I really need to get back to studying," I replied.

"About how to start fires?" Mat asked.

"Anyone who camps knows how to do that," I said, shrugging my shoulders.

Franny rolled her eyes. "Ginger told us," she confessed.

"Told you what?" I frowned slightly.

"We know, and we wanted you to know we won't tell anyone anything," Mat said. She lowered her voice and said, "You're a Firestarter, like Oliver."

I didn't have anyone holding a mirror to my face, but I was pretty sure it was painted with surprise. A Firestarter? That wouldn't have even crossed my mind as a cover story.

"It's okay. You don't have to say anything," Franny chimed in. "We just wanted you to know we're cool." She gave me a reassuring smile. Without another word, the two of them grabbed their stuff and left, leaving me speechless.

Two more days passed, thankfully uneventful. My bones and muscles twitched with the rise of my powers as my birthday crept closer. I was humming with anticipation all the time, like my ligaments were tightropes.

Every night, Rose and I had kitchen cleaning, and every night, I followed her outside. We were like this old cartoon I used to watch with my grandparents. There were two dogs, Sam and Fred. Every morning, Sam would go to work protecting the sheep from the wolf, and say, "Mornin' Fred," and when they'd switch places, Fred would say, "Mornin' Sam," and leave. No surprises, just run of the mill.

My routine with Rose felt the same way. She would walk past me, clutching a bag full of garbage, leave it right by the door, and go outside. I would wait about two heartbeats, grab the bag, and follow her outside.

By the fifth night of our daily routine, Rose and I were cleaning up the dining room again when I saw her pull the usual "I'm going to throw the garbage out" ploy without a garbage bag. I gave up my own appearances and followed again. To no one's surprise, Trip was outside in their usual spot: the light of the lamppost.

They kissed, like normal, and like normal, my body fought against itself either to shoot them both with lightning or crumple into a ball and cry. Right on schedule, they stopped kissing, but it was Rose who stopped it this time instead of Trip.

"I don't know if I can keep this up anymore," she said. "She isn't doing anything, and I'm going crazy trying to find something that isn't here!"

"It's here," Trip said firmly. "She had it with her when she left Corbin City, so it has to be here."

Goosebumps pricked my skin. Trip had been following me a lot longer than I'd thought, beginning before I'd even gotten to Switzerland.

"Well, I'm at my wits' end," Rose said. "No luck finding anything, and I don't know what else to do."

She turned away from him, almost remorseful. I blinked, just in case I was losing my mind. I'd never seen the softer side of Rose.

"Hey." Trip put his hand on her shoulder. "Hey."

Rose turned around. "What?"

"I know this is hard, but you're doing great work. I wouldn't put so much trust in just anyone."

Rose must have believed him because she sighed and dropped her arms. "What else can I do?"

Trip smiled softly, a smile I'd only seen on him one time, during our scavenger hunt date. It was his secret smile, the one he saved for me. The smile that erased the tension and stress from his face and gave him an angelic look.

My heart broke all over, and I let the tears roll down my cheeks in my dark corner.

Trip handed Rose something, but from my angle and through blurry eyes, I didn't get a clear view.

"We're resorting to this?" Rose said in disbelief.

Trip nodded. "It's our contingency plan."

Rose looked down at what was in her hand and nodded her head. "I'm in."

Chapter 7

The next morning, the sky was a murky gray, and I talked, walked, chewed, and moved as if trapped in a web of molasses with my brain full of cotton. Sticky, slow, and unproductive. Heading to breakfast, I practically fell down the stairs. Once there, I nibbled on a roll and had some tea but couldn't shake the feeling.

"Bridget?" Eden asked in my added Saturday lessons. Norah felt an extra lesson a week would help harness my powers now that my birthday was just days away. And she probably wanted to keep me out of trouble. "Are you feeling alright?"

"Just tired," I said, pretending to stifle a yawn.

"Are you sure?"

"Yeah, totally."

Eden regarded me warily. "Look, it's okay if you're feeling worn out. We've done a great deal of practice and studying, and your test is coming up, but I need you to be honest and upfront with me if something else is bothering you."

I blinked a couple of times, not because the sunlight in the field was blinding but because my sight was a little blurry.

"I'm good," I reassured her.

"If you're good, show me a microburst."

I took a steadying breath and closed my eyes. A headache was causing a nuisance in the back of my skull, but I did my best to ignore it.

"Anytime you're ready!" Eden yelled through the loudspeaker, safely out of distance.

I called upon the air around to me circulate, moving it faster and faster to create a cyclone in front of me. With my mind, I pulled the cyclone up toward the clouds and slammed it down to earth over my body, forcing it to break and pull apart. I pushed the wind away, keeping it in a tight formation as it spanned out around the field. Grass was pressed to the ground as rocks lifted into the air and spun toward the edges of the microburst. I didn't flinch in the eye of this storm. Its power coursed through me, and in turn, I fed its power back.

"Wrap it up!" Eden's voice cut through my concentration.

"Yes, please, this wind is messing with my hair," a new voice said. My eyes flew open, and I stared at an unknown human directly in front of me. Her face was narrow and sharp, as if she could slice me with her cheekbones alone.

Alarms went off in my head, and I immediately jumped into action. I pulled my microburst back into a cyclone to draw my opponent up into the spiral. She smirked as she moved a step away from me and drew the water from my cyclone, reducing it until the air was arid. I frowned and called upon the thunderclouds that were perched over the Lohner Mountains. With speed and ferocity, the clouds clapped and sent something like a sonic boom straight on top of my adversary. I hoped this would shake her up a bit, but she deftly moved out of the way as I sent a bolt of lightning to stun her.

"Is that the best the little Cuardaitheoir can do?" she sneered. Without missing a beat, she dropped the temperature and created icicles out of thin air. They dangled for a minute before they shot at me. Muscle memory kicked in, and I tucked and rolled out the way. The icicles missed me as others popped up next to my face and plunged straight into the earth. I stood and looked around at the cage of icicles trapping me. I called upon the sun to send heat and melt the frozen water.

As the icicles melted, I set a circle of fire around her, hoping to slow her down, but she grabbed a pocket of air, and snow fell out, dampening my fire.

My eyes went blurry again, but I wasn't sure if it was from the smoke or the affliction from before. I resisted the urge to surround us with fog, so as not to lose sight of her.

Suddenly, she stopped and looked away from me. I glanced over but didn't see anything around us. She looked back at me with dark eyes.

"Next time." And then she vanished.

"Bridget!" Eden called as she ran up to me. "Are you alright?"

I panted a few times before I could answer. "What the hell was *that!*"

"Beira's kin," she replied as I carefully stepped over the puddle at my feet.

"I got that much, but ... how?"

Eden frowned as she shook her head. "I don't know, but I'm sure that won't be the last time."

I was interrogated by Norah, which was followed by assurances we would set up more defenses, and I was given instructions to grab dinner and head to my room. I felt like I was being punished for something I didn't do, but I obliged. I didn't have the energy or interest to socialize anymore that night anyway. Though my body was tired, my mind was spinning. If Deidra could reach me in here, she could absolutely reach me out there. What could I do? My powers were feeble in comparison to her warriors. Was I ready to get out there and fight? I grabbed the Amulet under my shirt, feeling the bumpiness of the stone under my fingers. If I couldn't fight off a minion of Deidra, how could I fight the enemy herself?

I wished Cay was here. He'd know what to do. He was much better suited for this battle than me. Since his healing power alone was one of the more useful things, I thought of our obstacle course training again, when he'd healed my injury after an incident with the course.

Cay and I collected Logan, and the four of us—Neit included—headed back toward Cay's house. Cay and Neit stormed ahead, leaving Logan and me to our own devices.

"How's the knee?" he asked. I looked down at my mess of a leg.

"Healed, thanks to Cay," I replied. "I'm sure he's tired of cleaning me up."

"Cay would do anything to protect you," Logan said a little too seriously.

I looked at my right hand. When I'd rolled out of the icicles, I'd slid a little and gotten a gash on my palm that was bleeding through the dressing. I watched the red liquid bloom into a misshapen flower on the bandage as I imagined what my life was like a year ago, before I'd met Trip Findlay.

Happy.

Healthy.

Hopeful.

I slept in that Sunday and refused to be active in any way. I allowed the doubt and negativity to nestle into my heart and didn't do a damn thing about it. My birthday was a week and a half away, and I couldn't defeat a fly, let alone the mysterious warrior. I sighed and rolled over onto my side. My room was silent except for the steady rhythm of the curtain banging on the windowsill. I heard scuffling outside my door but ignored it until it disappeared. Thinking back to my training session, I recalled one of the last conversations I'd had with Logan.

"Cay would absolutely protect you," Logan insisted. "You're the Seeker, the most important person in the world at this moment."

"Well, one of two," I muttered.

"Wrong. You're the one who has the Amulet. The rest should be easy!"

"Easy? I only have half the Amulet!" I clarified. "The search is only the beginning."

"Half still puts us ahead. Bridget, stop being so pessimistic. You're a bright person; you can do any-thing you put your mind to."

"Stop the after-school special. I get it, but it's hard sometimes feeling so cheery about all of this.

Especially when Cay keeps reminding me that I could die any moment."

"Hey!" He grabbed my arm and pulled me back, allowing more space between us and Cay. "Yes, at any moment you could die. But so could I, or Cay, or anyone else, for that matter. We're human, fragile. And we would die protecting you. It's our job."

I blinked. "You'd really die for me?"

"Of course. That's what I'm here for." He flashed me a grin, looking like he'd enjoy the work.

"It's just... I feel fallible. Even Neit beat me." I crossed my arms over my chest and pouted a little. I couldn't help but feel a little sorry for myself.

"Bridget," Logan started, "you're being silly. Trust me, once you accept your fate, it'll be easier to handle." He wrapped his arm around my shoulder.

"I warn you; I smell. Really badly," I said. "Hug at your own risk."

"I'll chance it," he said, winking at me.

The next morning, I walked down the stairs to see half of the school crowded around Norah's office. A few teachers were there trying to keep the crowd contained.

"What's going on?" I whispered to Ginger.

"We got a new kid," she whispered back. I got goosebumps. Last time we got a new kid, Trip appeared and opened a whole new world for me.

"What's the big deal?" I asked.

"He came in the middle of the night. No one knows who he is, but the rumor is he's connected to the one of the Cuardaitheoirs."

I gasped. Straining to see above everyone else, I stood on my toes to get a better view. Suddenly, an icy shock pumped through my veins. What if it was Trip? My heart sped at the thought, and I started planning what I'd say to him.

The crowd around me surged backward as Norah's door opened.

"There's nothing here as important as your studies," Norah announced. "Everyone back to your classes."

Quickly, we scurried our way back to the classrooms, not wanting to be caught dawdling.

"Miss MacNamara, a moment, please," Norah said. I stiffened and turned as the hallway emptied.

"Relax," Norah said, more gently. "You're not in any trouble. There is someone here for you."

A tall figure emerged from Norah's door.

"Logan!" I cried, then pushed past Norah and threw my arms around him.

"Hey, yourself," he said. His arms tightened around my waist and held tight. He felt strong and familiar, a feeling I haven't had in a long time. He felt like home.

Norah cleared her throat. He dropped his arms immediately, but I couldn't let go. Not just yet.

"There will be plenty of time for reunions," she said. I pulled away from my friend but kept close to him.

"But for now, let's go into my office to discuss why Mr. Carter is here."

"I'm guessing it's not for my birthday?" I whispered to him as we entered Norah's office. Logan gave me a sad smile as we sat.

"Bridget, you're aware things are starting to get a little ... tense outside these walls," Norah said, closing the door behind her.

I frowned slightly and nodded, not wanting to admit I was totally naïve to the outside world.

"There have been reports of skirmishes between Beira's and Brighde's kin. Some lives have been lost, but that is the hefty price we pay when engaging in war."

I swallowed hard. Death. War. People had lost their lives because of me. I stupidly thought because I wasn't ready, nothing would happen. Like the world would be in suspension waiting for me.

Logan must have noticed my reaction because he grabbed my uninjured hand and gave it a squeeze.

"In these trying times, we can't take any chances on the house. I've made the final decision to call in your Protector," she indicated to Logan as she rounded the corner of her desk, "to keep you safe beyond what I can do. His room will be next to yours to ensure he can keep a close eye on you."

Logan and I glanced at each other, sharing a look that apparently Norah misread.

"Not that close of an eye," she said sternly. We both blushed.

"I didn't realize I had a Protector assigned to me already," I said, switching the conversation. "Why didn't you tell me, Logan?"

"You didn't know who you were. I couldn't openly do my job," he replied.

"Head back to your lessons," Norah interjected, "and Mr. Carter will see you at dinner. Remember to keep a low profile. No one knows Bridget is a Cuardaitheoir."

"I will," Logan replied. Standing, he gave Norah a curt nod, and we left.

"I am so glad you're here!" I said as we headed into the hall. I gave him another hug and held on longer this time. "How is everyone? How's Cay and Neit?"

"Neit is with Alec at college. As for Cay, I haven't heard from him in a few weeks," Logan said into my ear as we embraced.

I let go. "Why not?"

He shrugged. "The last time we talked, he said he was going offline. Something about preventing the Findlays from following him. I call him every day to make sure he's alive, but so far, there hasn't been any credit card activity, no social media, and his phone stays off."

I gnawed on my lip as we passed the dining room. "I hope he's safe."

Logan gave a slight smile. "You know Cay. He'll be fine."

"Oh, Bridget, there you are," Eden said, stepping out of the study. "Let's go; we have a lot to catch up on."

"See you tonight," he said as I waved goodbye. I didn't care that Eden looked slightly perturbed that I was late. Being on time didn't matter as much as a piece of home being here at the Academy with me.

Logan was the big talk at dinner. Naturally, I invited him to sit with us at our table before Rose and her group could stake their claim. She glared at me, but now I wasn't sure if it was over Logan or that I was her boyfriend's ex.

Unfortunately, Logan and I didn't get a chance to talk because everyone came over to meet him. The girls were either fawning or asking probing questions about his relationship status. Guys were asking what it was like being a real Protector. They probably didn't realize that he wasn't fighting as much as searching for a hidden family. Even Franny wanted his sole attention.

"To ask him about Protector things," she said when I asked why she kept bothering him.

"My, you're super popular," I said as we headed outside to sit in the gazebo on the side of the house. Curfew was at ten o'clock, but we had a little more time before we had to be in our rooms.

"Yeah, so it seems," he replied, plopping on the bench. I stayed quiet for a minute, thinking of the first time I'd been in a gazebo with a boy. Many of my firsts happened with Trip.

"How are you?" Logan asked, pulling me from my memory.

"I'm okay, I guess. I like my friends here, and I love learning about my powers and my family history."

"But?"

I took a breath in, tasting the sweet, calm air around us. The temperature was mild, perfect for a night to sit in the moonlight with an old friend.

"It just sucks sometimes because I feel held back," I blurted out. "I should be out there trying to find the Amulet, not Cay. It's not his job. It's mine." I sighed and leaned back, the nest of tension in my chest unwinding. I'd been holding onto it for a while.

"You'll get there." Logan spoke softly, his words carried to my ears by a gentle breeze.

"I don't feel like it," I replied.

"Bridget, give yourself some credit. You've taken on such a huge responsibility with little to no information. You're mastering your powers, which is a far cry from where you started, and you finally know more family history than Cay was able to give you. You've got this."

I looked at my friend in the moonlight. His face radiated with vigor and passion.

I nodded slowly, my head feeling cumbersome. "Okay, I'll try. But I still wish I was out there."

"I know." Logan wrapped his arm around me and pulled me close. I sighed and leaned my head against his shoulder, giving in to the quiet moment. He was so warm and familiar. My eyes felt heavy, and they drooped.

"Bridget," Logan whispered, "You should go to bed. You're falling asleep."

"No, I'm not," I said drowsily.

He chuckled. "Liar. Let's go." I sat up and blinked a bit from the bright light of the motion detector.

"I usually don't fall asleep on people," I said, stumbling toward the front door. It was hard to talk with a swollen tongue.

"It happens to everyone," Logan said, practically carrying me inside. My head was swimming, and my feet didn't want to walk.

"Whoa, there." Logan caught me as I tripped inside the front door of the building.

"I feel weird," I slurred. Doubling over, I vomited up dinner, sour and chunky, all over the foyer carpet I was desperately holding on to. The slimy feeling of saliva caused my stomach to heave again, and I emptied more of the contents of my stomach.

"Bridget!"

Logan's voice was the last thing I heard before I passed out.

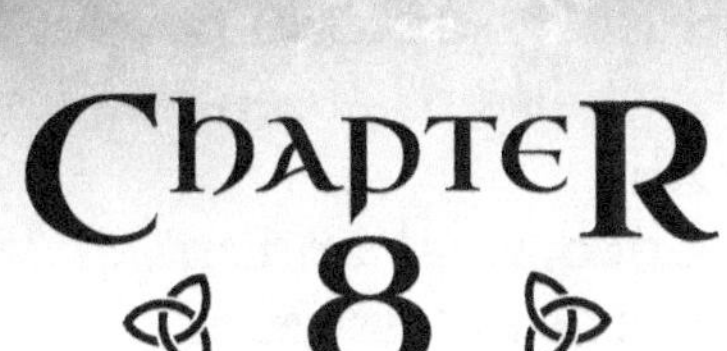

CHAPTER 8

I woke up in the hospital with a cold compress to my forehead and Eden, Norah, and Logan looking worried, angry, and sick—in that order—at my side.

"What happened?" I croaked.

"Someone drugged you, it seems," Norah said, angrily.

"Drugs?"

"More like poison," Eden explained. I went to scratch an itch on my nose and noticed the wires sticking from my arm.

My stomach churned as I tasted my mouth, coated with slippery spit, and I leaned over and heaved. Nothing but bile came out, landing on the floor next to me. Beeps were going off everywhere from the machines I was attached to, and a nurse rushed in.

"It's okay; you'll be fine," she said to me in a soothing tone. I took a raspy breath in and gagged again.

"Water," I croaked. The nurse poured me a glass of cold water, and I swished it in my mouth before spitting it into the little bucket she held under my chin. I noticed Norah's frown deepening as Logan turned a slight shade of green. He kept breathing out of his mouth.

I lay back in bed, weak and shaky. "Sorry," I apologized as the nurse sidestepped the mess I left on the floor.

"It happens." She smiled and left to grab cleaning supplies.

"The doctors confirmed it was a very mild dose of wolfsbane. Thankfully, the dose wasn't strong enough to kill you," Eden continued, circling the bed to the other side.

"Thank Brighde for small favors, but this sucks too," I whispered. "How did it happen?"

Logan looked guilty and avoided my gaze. I frowned.

Norah spoke after passing Logan a stone-faced look. "We can only assume it was put into your food at school. The kitchen staff, as well as the students, are being interrogated as we speak. The food has been sent to the lab for further investigation to determine what you ate."

"Is anyone else sick?"

"No," Norah finally said.

"They targeted me specifically?" I asked.

"We can't say for sure," Eden replied gently.

"That's crap," I said. "If no one else was sick, then someone must be after me. They know I'm the Seeker."

I looked away as tears pricked my eyes. I'm not even safe at school.

"There is no way to know that for sure, at this time," Norah firmly said, kindly ignoring my sharp tone.

"Bridget, everyone at school came to our table at some point to introduce themselves. We can't narrow it down right off the bat," Logan said finally.

I ignored him and spoke directly to the one in charge.

"What happens now?"

"Now, you get better, get stronger, and find that Amulet," Norah replied. "Leave the poison to me. I'll make sure the perpetrator is punished severely."

I nodded and yawned.

"We'll leave you to get your sleep," Eden said. "Someone will check on you tomorrow. In the meantime, Logan will stay at your side."

"Goodnight," Norah said as she and Eden headed out. I groaned a goodbye to them and drifted off to sleep.

Logan stayed with me for the rest of the time I was in the hospital. He kept bringing up memories, trying to distract me from being stuck there.

"Remember the time Cay had you, me, and Neit race around the OCHS track to see if we could beat the dog?"

I smiled. "Of course, he won. Besides the fact Neit's a dog, I couldn't stop laughing."

Logan grinned at me. "You were so happy to not be shot with Nerf bullets."

I rolled onto my side, being careful of any remaining IVs stuck in me. The knowledge of the needle in my skin made it crawl, and I did everything I could to ignore it.

"Who wouldn't be happy not having things thrown at them?"

Logan shrugged. "I guess I'm used to it, so it doesn't faze me anymore."

I giggled. "No?"

I had some ice chips in a cup, and while most of them had melted, a few pieces remained. I dipped my hand into the cup and gently threw a chip at him. Logan didn't flinch.

"See? Doesn't bother me."

I threw another one. "I'll have to try harder."

He remained stoic as I threw the last ice chips at him, leaving wet patches on the floor.

"I'm all out," I pouted. "Will you get me more?"

Logan laughed. "No! As much as it doesn't bother me, I don't want stuff thrown at me."

Just then the nurse came in for my hourly vital check. He eyed the wet spots and drew his gaze back up to me.

I blushed as I gave him an embarrassed smile. "I had a point to prove."

"Did you prove it?"

"No," Logan cut in. I narrowed my eyes at him as I rolled onto my back for the nurse.

"He'll clean it up," I said to the nurse while looking at Logan. He narrowed his eyes back at me but grinned again.

"Fine, but only because you're stuck in bed."

Two days later, I was back at school and nowhere nearer to discovering who poisoned me, though I had an inkling as to who would. I know Trip gave Rose something, but I didn't know what it was. Poison could fit the bill. Eden had a rigorous schedule set for me to catch up on my missed work. Logan stuck to me like glue, less inconspicuous than Norah would've wanted. Mat, Franny, Ginger, and Oliver avoided me, like they were afraid to catch the mono Norah had told everyone I had.

I was not holding it together very well. My body tensed whenever I passed the dining room, and I was only eating food prepared in front of me, even if it was just chicken broth and crackers. I staked out the kitchen staff and followed their every move.

"Bridget," Norah said to me a few of days after my release, "How are you doing?"

I was sitting in a chair in the kitchen watching Chef Abby slice up zucchini for tonight's dinner.

"I'm fine," I replied, not taking my eyes off her knife.

"Let's take a walk, dear," Norah said. I sent her a panicked look. "It'll be okay. I promise."

She pulled me from the chair and into the empty dining room.

"Bridget, Eden tells me that you've been avoiding studies with her."

I cleared my throat. "Yes, that's true."

"May I ask why?"

I looked down. A combination of shame and disappointment swirled in my chest. How was I supposed to tell her I was nervous about what I ate?

"Are you still worried about the poison incident?"

I sighed heavily. "Yes. I should be over it, but I'm not."

"Don't be ridiculous!" Norah exclaimed. "I wouldn't be over it, either. But I also would know when to ask for help."

She cast a long look at me from the side, and I blushed.

"I also know you aren't sleeping," she said. This time I peered up at her. "And I can see that you've lost some weight. More than what could be expected from your hospital stay."

I looked down at my shorts sagging around my thighs. I used to have beautiful thighs, thick and strong, but now, they seemed foreign to me. Not how I know them.

"I try!" I cried out. "I just… I keep seeing it happen, and my brain keeps playing it on repeat, trying to sort out who put something in my food. The next thing I know, the sun is up…"

Norah motioned for me to sit.

"Logan told me he's heard you awake at night."

"He's not sleeping either?" I asked. She smiled ruefully.

"No, he's not." She paused. "Would you like to take something to help you relax?"

"Like what?"

"It's a mild sedative that the doctor prescribed. It'll calm your mind so you, and maybe Logan, can sleep."

"I don't know," I shifted uncomfortably in my seat. My head hurt from lack of sleep, copious amounts of stress, and I'm guessing, a lack of proper food.

Norah rested a hand on my shoulder. "I think it will help you. I've also arranged for you to eat meals in your room to ease some of your anxiety."

I nodded.

"Furthermore, no more stalking the staff when they prepare meals."

"How can I feel safe if I don't know what they put in the food?"

"Bridget, we've eliminated the kitchen as those who poisoned you. They've all been cleared."

"But that doesn't mean that someone couldn't sneak in!" Like Rose.

Norah chuckled even though I was stewing in my fury. "No one could sneak in with you sitting there like a hawk!"

I cracked a smile. She did have a point.

"Take the rest of today off and recuperate a little more. I've also told Eden you won't be taking lessons tomorrow. I think you need an extra day before jumping back in."

I smiled lightly. "Thank you."

"Go on and head upstairs."

I nodded again, left Norah in the dining room, and started for the stairs.

When I got to my room, I tried to rest, but a movie of my life was playing on the back of my eyelids. Logan chatting with everyone coming over to our table, me chewing the salad served with dinner, drinking from my open glass of water. I rolled over and stuffed my face into the pillow. The movie just kept scrolling, keeping me awake. Frustrated and sleep-deprived, I closed the curtains. The window was open, and the sweet smell of the meadow below drifted up. I closed my eyes and took a deep breath in, filling my lungs to their capacity. Opening my eyes, I let the breath out and looked down below.

Something moved in the tree line. I rubbed my eyes and looked out again to see the figure still there.

It was just far enough for me not to know exactly what I was looking at, but I was able to make out that it was tall. While deer are commonly found playing out there, this wasn't something on four feet. Straining, I could have sworn I saw blonde hair. My blood quickened in my veins. There was more movement, and then the figure was gone. I placed my hand over my chest to steady my breathing.

Who had been out there?

I closed the window, locked it, and shut the curtains. There was no way I could sleep tonight.

Norah came in a couple of hours later with some chips and a prepackaged sandwich from a local shop. She left a bottle of water and the sleeping pills on the dresser before she headed back downstairs. I ate gingerly, worried about having heavy food in my stomach, but I knew I needed it if I was taking any meds. As I toyed with the idea of taking the drugs, the blonde figure popped into my brain. I contemplated if I was a reliable witness, given the stress I was under. I threw my trash out and peeked out from the curtains again. No one was hiding in the trees that I could see, but I still felt creeped out. I downed the pill to hopefully get a good night's sleep.

"Where is it?" I nearly jumped out of my skin with excitement. I haven't felt whole since the Amulet had disappeared.

"Oh, sister, please," he said, as if this wasn't the most important thing in the world. "You think I would keep this secret from you?"

I leveled him with a look, but he didn't flinch.

"You didn't even guess," he pouted.

I resisted the urge to roll my eyes, such a childish response. Some days, Lugh was my best friend, and some days, he was worse than Beira.

"Brother, you know I love playing the juvenile games, but right now, I don't have the temper nor the time to waste engaging in amusements."

He plopped on the couch next to me, playing with the tassel on the pillow.

"Fine," he said finally. "But I just want to say, Beira played along."

It took all my restraint not to rip him to shreds as I seethed, knowing Beira was given a head start.

"Lugh, dear, why would you tell Beira about the Amulet before me? Your favorite sister?"

Lugh just looked bored. "To be fair, neither of you are my favorite." He popped up off the couch and held out his hand to me. I took it, and he pulled me up.

"Beira knows that we searched the whole of this world for the Amulet."

"Yes," I replied.

"And we have turned over every rock and searched the deepest of seas?"

"Yes," I said, growing more impatient.

Lugh smiled. "Have you not solved the puzzle yet?"

I debated on what instrument I would use to disembowel my brother.

"Arwan."

"Our cousin, Arwan?"

Lugh nodded.

"What does the god of the Otherworld want with my Amulet?

"Let's ask him, shall we?"

The next day, after writing the dream down, I stayed in bed and watched some videos on my phone. The air outside was so humid; it oozed through the crack in the window. Even the air conditioning couldn't cut through the heat. I was hot and sticky, but I felt better after the decent sleep I'd gotten the night before. I dozed off again at some point because, when I woke up, the room was dark. Feeling more refreshed, I turned on my light, grabbed some chips, and started on some homework so as not to fall behind.

"Hey," Logan said, knocking on my cracked bedroom door. I was reading another chapter in the *Book of Brighde*, as per Eden's schedule. I closed my book and placed it on the nightstand.

"What's up?" I asked, throwing the empty chip bag away.

"Not much. Just checking in before I head to bed."

"All is fine on the Western Front," I joked. He looked at my dresser. My pile of granola bars, chips, and peanut butter crackers that my parents had sent in a care package were scattered across the top. I wrote home asking for comfort food without going into detail about why I needed the comfort.

"Is it, really?" he asked, concerned.

"What do you want me to say? I'm not eating the food here."

Logan sighed. "I get why you don't want to, but the chefs, Norah, and I are taking extreme precautions to make sure the food's safe for everyone, especially you."

"That's great, but I don't trust anyone here. Logan," I sat up, "I don't feel safe. I barely can eat what Norah has shipped in, but I'm doing what I can, so I can at least keep up my strength. The sheer fact that I'm at almost full power is what keeps me functioning on some basic level." Thankfully, my birthday was three days away, and I'd been feeling a taste of what was to come.

Logan sat at the edge of my bed and gazed at me with red eyes. "I feel so guilty for putting you in this situation."

"What do you mean?"

"It's my fault. I should've done a better job. I should've seen them do it. I… I failed you." Logan put his head in his hands and shook his head.

I didn't know how to react. I'd never seen Logan act like this before, and it kind of unnerved me seeing my Protector break down like this. I didn't know he cared this much.

I sat on my knees and wrapped my arm around him.

"Logan, this is not your fault. This was bound to happen at some point. Even Cay knew—he spent every waking moment reminding me."

He lifted his head and looked at me. "You've lost so much weight."

"What?" Not the reaction I'd anticipated.

"I heard Norah and Eden discussing it before. Because you can't eat the food here, the processed crap isn't helping your nutrition, and you're losing too much weight. Your fear is my fault."

I took his face in my hands. "No, it's not. I don't blame you."

He pushed my hands down. "I blame myself."

"Logan, that's not—"

"What? Fair? Bridget, I am here to protect you in all capacities. I am here to make sure no one hurts you, which includes physical, emotional, and mental harm. I dropped the ball, and now you're sick."

My heart hurt hearing the guilt and sadness in Logan's voice, feeling it pour out of him.

"How can I make you feel better?" I asked quietly.

He raised his eyebrows. "You can't."

I didn't know what else to do, so I hugged him. Hard. And I didn't let go for what felt like forever.

CHAPTER
9

The next morning, I woke up feeling more rested than I had in a while. The pill I'd taken gave me the silent sleep I'd so desperately craved, and I was able to recuperate. Stretching, I knocked the *Book of Brighde* on the floor, forgetting that it was there. My limbs were loose and relaxed, ready to take on the day. My spirits were up, the sun was shining with warmth only the burning star in the sky could provide, and my birthday was two days away. I was determined not to let this sunniness disappear under my anxiety and fear, though they lurked just under the surface. I made an effort to regain my normal schedule and face my nerves, starting with getting back the strength I'd lost.

"Good morning," I said as I sat next to Franny at our breakfast table. Four pairs of eyes stared at me. "What?"

Ginger swallowed what she was chewing and spoke first. "We thought you were still sick."

I shrugged. "Modern medicine is a miracle." I took a bite of bread that was still warm from the oven. My stomach turned a little sour from the heaviness, but I wasn't going to let that stop me from living my life again. "For the record, I'm not contagious, if anyone's worried."

Franny still seemed wary of me and subtly moved her chair away from me. Ginger didn't say anything but nodded and kept eating.

"Glad you're feeling better," Oliver said, giving me a bright smile. I smiled back, feeling less trepidation.

"Did I miss anything good since I was out?" I nibbled on another bite.

"Nothing exciting besides Logan and you," Franny said, shrugging. "Seriously, this place would be boring as hell if it wasn't for you."

"Thank you?" I asked.

"Well, one good thing did come out of your sick holiday," Ginger piped up. She smiled an impish grin. "Rose has had cleanup duty all to herself."

I smiled back but internally wondered if that gave her the freedom to see Trip without my snooping. I looked around to see her sitting with her table, chatting and eating, completely ignoring my return. My mind spiraled with all the things she and my ex could have discussed that I'd missed. I placed my bread on my plate since my stomach was clenching.

"It's nice hearing she got what she deserved," I said, ignoring my body. I breathed carefully to keep my stomach at bay.

"Are you sure you're okay?" Mat asked, noticing my uneaten roll. I nodded.

"Stomach's not back to full strength yet."

"Hey," Logan said, grabbing a chair next to Mat. I saw excitement in Franny's eyes, but I couldn't tell if it was from how handsome Logan was or because she thought he was bringing more drama.

"What brings you to our humble little table?" she asked him, her voice coy. She took a sip of water from her cup.

He gave her a half-smile. "Since Bridget is really the only person I know here, it just makes sense I would hang out with her and get to know her friends."

"You can ask us anything," Franny breathed. Oliver choked on his water as Mat hid a smile behind her hand. I rested my elbows on the table, head in hands, dying to see how this would play out. Logan flashed a look at me, but it was Ginger who came to his rescue.

"Franny, I think Logan would rather grab some breakfast before the group interview." Ginger shook her head slightly.

"Of course! We'll be here when you get back." She blushed lightly as she took another sip of her water.

"Bridget, do you want something?" Logan asked, nodding to my roll. Oliver eyed Logan up and down before sliding his glance over to me. I sighed and stood.

"I should have something else besides bread, I guess."

I felt their eyes on us as Logan and I headed toward the buffet table. I grabbed a little plate, unsure of what to get. Logan, on the other hand, grabbed a large plate and was filling it up with gipfeli, various cheeses, and a spoonful of yogurt. I took a couple slices of cheese, some butter for my abandoned roll, and a bit of granola. I was trying to get food that would settle my stomach. I poured myself a cup of tea as Logan was spooning granola over his yogurt. I sighed a little wistfully, wishing I could eat like that again.

"You okay?" Logan asked, pouring himself a cup of coffee.

"Better question is, are *you* okay?" I replied. He picked up a utensil roll and grabbed his plate before looking at me.

"Yeah. I'm feeling a lot better now. I'm guessing you are too?" He nodded toward my plate.

I shrugged. "I feel much better than I have in a while, but my body is still recovering from the poison. I hope they find out the culprit soon."

"You and me both," he said as we headed to the table.

After breakfast, my morning dragged by. I was still catching up on missed work, and Eden was pushing me as hard as I could tolerate.

"Bridget, you have two days before your basics test. I know you're ready, but everything needs to be in tip-top shape." I was surrounded by colorful bowls filled with random things to represent the four elements. I was attempting to fill the empty bowl in front of me with water from a rain cloud. The cloud needed to be only as large as the bowl, and it wasn't going well.

"Try again."

Weary, I closed my eyes and pictured a small, dark cloud hovering over the bowl. I imagined the cloud overflowing with water droplets, threatening to burst, before the clear liquid dripped from its brim. I concentrated on the water falling only into the bowl while keeping the cloud from drifting away.

I heard a soft *plonk* and opened my eyes. A single drop was in the bowl, but it hadn't fallen from a rain cloud. Eden peered over the bowl and frowned.

"Maybe we should come back to this one," she said, switching the empty bowl to one filled with dirt. Next to me was a smaller bowl of seeds.

"For your earth test, you will be expected to plant and nurture a seedling into a matured plant. You may begin at any time."

I plucked a couple seeds from the bowl next to me and buried them in the dirt. I sprinkled some water from my own bottle on top and placed my hands over the seeds. My tired body swelled with warmth from the sun above me. I absorbed more than just its heat. Its light shone within me, and I channeled that energy from my chest, down my arms, and into my hands, radiating heat into the dirt. After another round of water and sunlight, a little sprout of green poked through the top, followed by a stem. I released the breath I was holding and focused harder, providing the little plant with more food and water. I watched as it bloomed in front of me, growing taller and stronger, its leaves unfurling to reveal a dark green. Finally, a bud appeared at the head of the stem. I gently nudged the flower with my mind, and it blossomed into a light-purple flower with a yellow circle in its center.

"Alpine aster," I said, smiling. The flower was the first right thing I had done in a while. Eden returned my smile and moved the flower next to her.

"Very good. Take a few minutes to regroup before we move on to wind." I got up and stretched my legs, shaking out my limbs. Picking up my water bottle, I sipped on it as I carefully stepped over the bowls around us. We were in the back field, sitting just outside the forest line in the shade of the trees. Eden said the best place to practice was surrounded by the elements, and this was the perfect spot for it on the property. I stepped outside the hard line of the shade into the sun, and I immediately squinted. It was too bright for my taste, but I was still tired from my testing and my week of not sleeping to do anything about it. I heard the snap of a branch behind me, but I ignored it, seeing as the forest always had something to say. I turned to face the trees, standing in a pool of sunbeams and letting the warmth penetrate me. Eden was rearranging some of the used bowls, moving them out of the way of the ones I still needed to work with. Taking another drink of water, I felt more refreshed and was ready to work on my next test. As I headed back toward our spot, I noticed a flash of red in one of the bushes. I shielded my eyes from the sun as I peered over at the bush. The red was still there, but it didn't look like a flower or plant I could see. Frowning, I moved toward it as a gentle wind came through, softly shaking the leaves. The red didn't move with the breeze.

"Bridget, are you ready?" Eden called from behind me. I turned to face her when I heard more branches snapping and leaves rustling. I whipped around to see the red fading quickly into the woods.

"Eden!" I yelled as I ran for her. "I saw someone!"

"What do you mean?" She looked around us, but no one else was visible.

"In the woods, over there," I pointed, trying to catch my breath. I didn't run far or long, but the excitement and fear worked together to take my breath away. "I saw the color red in the bushes, and then it ran away."

She rushed over to the spot I was pointing at and searched through the bush. I collected myself and headed over there. We scoured the area but didn't come up with anything. Unfortunately, we hadn't had rain for the past couple of days, and the forest floor was hard and dry, allowing our spy to escape without a footprint.

"I'll let Norah know of this immediately, but you still need to finish your elementals." She pulled out her cell phone and texted someone. "Let's head back and complete today's lessons as we wait for Norah to come out."

We walked back to our bowls and resumed the spots we'd had before. Eden's phone chirped, and she looked at it. "Norah will be here shortly." She placed her phone in her pocket and moved a bowl away from me. "You are to pick this bowl up with a breeze and have it flip three hundred and sixty degrees three times before you bring it to rest in front of you."

My mind didn't want to move a bowl; it wanted to find out who the person in red was, but I acquiesced. A soft wind tickled the back of my neck. I reached out with my mind and grabbed onto it, pulling it around in front of me. The breeze danced around my face, brushing against my cheek. As I encouraged it to grow, the breeze pushed away from me and expanded. I directed it toward the bowl. The wind flew up in the air and then swooped down, collecting the bowl in its hands. I gave the bowl a flick with my mind, and the wind flipped it around three times. Carrying the bowl away from me and then turning it around, the wind leaped up and dropped itself down in front me, quietly placing the bowl on the ground. I silently thanked the wind as it encircled me, then disappeared.

"Impressively done!" Eden exclaimed. She marked something down in a notebook she had brought with her.

"It feels good to flex my magic again," I said, grinning.

"Hi!" Logan said as he ran over to us. His footsteps were muffled by the thick grass on the field. "Norah sent me ahead, but she should be here any minute," he told Eden. To me, he asked, "Are you okay?"

"Yes, I'm fine. Nothing attacked me." Logan grabbed my water bottle and took a swig, wiping his mouth when he was done.

"Can you point me to where you saw it?" I looked over at Eden, and she nodded as she prepared for my fire test.

"Over here," I said as we headed away from the collection of bowls. I relayed to him what had happened and how Eden and I had searched the area.

"Fresh eyes are always a good thing," Logan replied. He walked behind the bush and crawled inside, peering over every branch next to him. I looked around again but didn't look too hard, as I already knew nothing else was on the ground. I was running the toe of my shoe over the edge of the grass when Logan popped up.

"I found something," he said, holding a piece of string between his thumb and forefinger. I moved closer to examine it better. The string wasn't exceptional outside of the fact it was red. I felt justified in what or who I saw but a little nervous about who it could have been. Logan's body heat rolled off him, and I noticed him gazing at me.

"That looks like it matches what I saw," I said, taking a step back.

"I will find out who is following you," he said, soft but firm. Logan looked me in the eyes and held my gaze as my heart picked up its pace.

"What are you holding, Mr. Carter?" Norah's voice broke the spell between us, and I moved out of her way to see the thread. I heard Logan recount how he had found the evidence as I walked away from them. I had the sudden urge to get some air, even though I was standing in the middle of a field. I felt high strung and wrung out at the same time. Fear was constantly cascading through my body, and it left me gasping for breath when it dissolved. I wanted a break from it all, and I hadn't even earned my place in the war.

"Bridget?" Eden said, coming up behind me. I turned to see Norah and Logan still looking around the bush. "You can sit for your fire test tomorrow. Have some lunch and meet me in the library with the *Book of Brighde* when you're done."

"Do you need help with cleaning up?" I offered.

She smiled and shook her head. "No, you've already overworked yourself for today."

"Do you think I'll be ready in time for my birthday?"

She smiled again. "Of course. You were already strong when you came here, but you are studying, and practicing has helped you control your powers. I'm sure tomorrow you will figure out the water test before you sit for the official test in the afternoon.

Besides, it's common for a Seeker's powers to wane a bit before their eighteenth birthday."

I let the comfort of Eden's words wash over me as the worry and tension in my body melted away with her support.

"Thank you for saying that. I felt like I was doing something wrong."

Eden said nothing but stepped forward and hugged me. My eyes watered, but I blinked the tears back. I didn't want to show her just how much it meant to me. I wasn't ready.

Once Norah and Logan had completed their investigation of the forest, Norah decided Logan needed to spend nearly every waking moment with me, at least until my birthday. Thankfully, it was less than forty-eight hours until then, so it was completely bearable. Franny didn't complain at all when he sat with us at dinner. She even offered him her dessert, as she said she was full and didn't want to waste food. Logan kindly refused her offer. I'd never seen him eat processed sugar, so I didn't think twice about his refusal.

The morning after the incident in the forest, I opened my door to see Logan standing outside of it, his back to me. I blinked and rubbed my eyes as I padded past him toward the restroom. After I had showered and brushed my teeth, I headed back to my room, where Logan followed me. He almost walked in behind me, but I stopped him before it happened. A girl needed to change in peace.

We headed to breakfast, but this time, we sat alone. My friends were mysteriously missing, but I didn't focus on that. This morning was my last chance to nail my water practice test, and I wanted to succeed.

"Feeling ready for today?" Logan asked between sips of coffee and mouthfuls of yogurt. I took a bite of my toast with jam and nodded.

"Water doesn't want to be my friend lately, but I think I found a way to seduce it. I'm going to pass these tests with flying colors."

"I believe in you" was all he said. I smiled into my tea as I took a drink. I was finally starting to believe in myself, too.

I took my time finishing up my meal, but I didn't want to be late for Eden again. I hurriedly threw out my trash and rushed outside.

"Okay, Eden," I said, strutting into our practice ring, "what challenge can I defeat today?"

Eden was crouching over the water and fire bowls, placing them in their positions. She stood and wiped her hands on her pants.

"I'm happy to hear that confidence, especially since there has been a change." I furrowed my brow.

"What kind of change?"

Eden pushed her glasses up her face and blew out a sigh. "As it turns out, time is of the essence, and we need to test you sooner rather than later, at Norah's request."

"Soon, like..."

"Now." She grimaced a little.

I gulped and fingered the Amulet around my neck. It sang a little note of encouragement to me. I was ready. "Why?"

"Given everything that happened, Norah felt we couldn't delay these tests any longer. We're to expedite your trainings before we let you go."

Oh. Let me out into the real world, which I'd been hiding from since I got here. "Okay. What's first?"

She smiled at me and gestured toward the wind bowls that were set up. I took my place in the center of them and shook out my hands.

"You can begin whenever you're ready," Eden directed. Remembering the feeling I'd had over the wind yesterday, I pulled on a random burst of air around us and repeated the same actions I'd done for my practice test, flipping the bowl three times before placing it in front of me. I looked up at Eden expectantly.

She shot me a quick smile and motioned for me to move onto the earth test. As I plopped on the grass, I placed the seeds in the dirt, urging the little seedling to grow. While I'd had no trouble with this test yesterday, today was a bit more challenging. I was warm from my adrenaline rush of the tests and sweating from straining to direct the sunlight to the dirt. I had to nurture the seed with more water and sunlight than before. Finally, the stem peeked out, and things went more smoothly. The flower today was a beautiful blue spring gentian.

Eden then directed me to my water test, and my heart jumped at the nerves that danced in my belly. *Relax*, I commanded. I drew in a deep breath and released it slowly. I sat quietly and focused on the empty bowl, my hand covering the Amulet. I emptied my mind of all distractions and once again pictured a tiny rain cloud floating above the bowl. The cloud went from white to dark gray, and thunder suddenly cracked above me. I blinked, surprised by the thunder, but I continued coaxing the cloud to release its water. Another crack of thunder and a blaze of lightning dotted my eyesight as I heard water tinkling against the sides of the bowl. I sighed in relief as the bowl filled to the brim before the rain let up, and the cloud drifted away.

Eden made no show of my passing the water test but hurried me along to the fire test. I wasn't worried about the fire test, as I normally had no problems causing them. Today's test was different from just creating a spark. I had to light fires in five bowls and then extinguish them all at once. I focused my memory on the sun at the beach, blazing hot rays scorching the sand. I looked out to the ocean through a haze of heat drifting from the sand back to the sun. The bowl on my left side ignited. I shifted my sight to the bowl on my right, letting the fire burn in the other. I pictured the same scene again, and that bowl lit up, heat radiating off it. Sweat was dripping down my back from being surrounded by fire. The next bowl on the left side was up. I tried to summon the fire using the memory from before, but that didn't work. I frowned slightly and pulled up another memory. I pushed past the pain from the memory of Trip, back to our firepit date where we had shared s'mores and our dreams. I focused on the fire that night, burning hot with flames dancing in the air. The heat from the fire licked my cheek as it flitted away into the cool night sky. The bowl caught fire, and I moved on to the bowl on the right. Holding on to the memory, I dove deeper into the fire that night, entranced by the blue base. I watched as it swayed and moved within the pit, morphing into orange and yellow. As if I had channeled that fire, the bowl burned blue, unlike the others. I moved on to the last bowl, the one placed directly in the center of them all. Like a laser beam, I imagined a fireball exploding in the bowl, being contained within its walls. The last bowl ignited, and I released the fire memory from my mind, allowing the picture of Trip to go up in flames as it left. The five bowls burned for a minute longer while I readied myself to extinguish them.

The Amulet was warm against my body, and I wished I could use the breath from my own lungs. Closing my eyes and collecting the images of all five bowls in my mind, I imagined a candle snuffer covering each fire and putting them out at once. Unfortunately, that didn't work, and the fires remained ignited. I rolled my shoulders and tried again. This time, after keeping the image of the bowls in my head, I drew upon my worry and fear that I was a target again, sitting out here in the open. My fear and worry combined into a balloon filled with misery and confusion. I pricked it with an imaginary pin, and the balloon popped, splashing water over all the bowls. I heard hissing around me, and when I opened my eyes, I saw steam rising from each bowl.

"Wonderful!" Eden's voice broke the silence we were sitting in. She came over and gave me a hug. "You passed!"

I hugged her back and let out a sigh of disbelief. I passed my basics, making me one step closer to finding the other half of the Amulet.

CHAPTER
10

I helped Eden clean up the test and went to take a refreshing shower. As I climbed the stairs to my room, I wished I had a bathtub to just soak in and relax. To spend an hour without thinking about the end of the world or how someone is trying to kill me. To allow myself to just... be. I opened my bedroom door to grab my shower things, only to find Logan sitting on my bed.

"How did you get in?" I asked, opening a drawer for some fresh clothes.

"Did you pass?" he replied. I turned to face him.

"My question first." I placed my hands on my hips and waited.

He sheepishly looked away from me toward the closet, where a little bouquet of pink, white, and yellow flowers sat with a balloon that read "Congratulations!" floating in the air.

"Norah unlocked the door, so I could surprise you with that, but I wasn't able to get out fast enough when you came in. I thought I would have more time."

"My test was pushed up," I said, picking up the bouquet and breathing in the lovely scent. I faced Logan and smiled. "Thank you. I passed."

He grinned and stood to envelop me in a strong hug. I melted into him as he gave the best hugs. He felt more and more like home every day.

"I knew you could do it!" he said.

"Thanks." I blushed at his support, letting the feeling warm my heart. "I have to shower, but can you put those in water for me? I'll meet you downstairs in the library. I have the rest of the day off, so I was hoping we could go celebrate."

"I'm so proud of you," he said as he gave me a kiss on the cheek.

I stood with my mouth open as I watched him walk out with the bouquet in hand. Standing a few seconds more, I cupped my cheek that was just kissed, replaying how soft his lips felt against my skin. I shook my head. I needed to stop daydreaming and get ready.

I was dressed in jean shorts, a comfy dark-blue T-shirt, and sneakers. I wasn't sure where we were going, but seeing as we were surrounded by mountains, closed-toed shoes sounded like the best idea. I saw Logan sitting next to my favorite view of the Lohner Mountains in my favorite spot in the whole building.

"Hey," I said in a near whisper. Libraries always made me speak quietly. He looked up at me and brightened.

"Are you ready to go?" He grabbed a backpack sitting on the table.

"I'm ready, but I don't know where we can go."

Logan stood and motioned for me to follow him. We left the library and headed toward the dining room.

"I spoke with Norah, and we were granted permission to go off campus for the afternoon. I left the flowers on her desk, so she can confirm that we came back." The dining room was loud and full of hungry students. Logan bypassed the buffet line and walked straight into the kitchen. He popped out a couple minutes later holding two packed lunches and a couple of bottles of water.

"Please tell me we're going on a bear hunt," I joked as we left the dining room.

"I'm going to take you trottinetting."

We headed toward the front door as Logan was stuffing lunches and water into the backpack. "Trottinetting? What is that?"

"A trottinett is a scooter with bike brakes and wheels. Adelboden has plenty of trails we can ride on, so I thought we would spend the day riding down the mountain and having lunch."

"Sounds good to me. Lead the way!" We headed down the front path, weaving our way through the overgrown flowers that lined the lane. The weather was perfect for a walk. Not too hot, not crazy humid, just perfectly pleasant for two best friends heading toward an afternoon of fun.

We made it to the hotel and took a cable car up the mountain where we rented our trottinetts. Once we strapped on our helmets, we began our descent down the mountains. At first, we rode on smooth, paved roads, but the posted signs directed us onto a gravel trail. I slowed my speed to avoid crashing, with Logan following suit. On our right was a valley with dark-green trees scattered up and down the mountainsides. I wanted to look out over the valley, but I kept my eyes in front of me as a sharp turn came upon us, and we merged onto another paved road. As we passed wooden houses on our left side, I twinged in jealousy that this was their view every day. I trailed behind Logan, just enjoying the rush of air on my face, the sweet smell of the grass. We cruised through bundles of pine trees towering over the countryside. Logan slowed and made a sharp left. The road narrowed as we rode on, a steeper drop on our right side. I hugged the left side of the road, nervous about the height. Halfway through our descent, Logan pulled over and stopped his trottinett, so I did the same.

"Are you hungry?" he asked, pulling off his helmet. My stomach growled in response.

"Yes," I said, taking off my own helmet. My hair was glued to my forehead, and I used the back of my hand to push it back. I hated the feeling of hair sticking on my face. Accepting the water bottle that was handed to me, I sat on the embankment to move off the road and took a long drink, not realizing how thirsty I was.

"How are you liking it so far?" Logan sat next to me, holding out a wrapped sandwich and a bag of chips.

"This is amazing! I feel so small compared to these mountains." I unwrapped the sandwich and took a bite. Logan did the same, and for a few minutes, neither of us spoke. We just sat there, eating, drinking, and admiring the view of the valley below.

With food in my belly and the sun shining warmly upon us, I felt so calm and peaceful; I could have fallen asleep. Tilting my chin up to the sky, I bathed in the sunlight, feeling its heat wrap around me like a hug. I closed my eyes and smiled. A minute later, I grabbed my water and caught Logan staring at me.

"What?" I asked, taking a sip.

He shook his head and smiled. "Nothing. Are you ready to finish our ride?"

Collecting our garbage, Logan shoved everything into the backpack, including my empty water bottle, and extended his hand to me. I graciously accepted it, wiped the dirt from my palms onto my shorts, and strapped the helmet back onto my head. This time, I took the lead as Logan followed me down the hill.

Returning our trottinetts back to the rental place, we headed back toward town. I took out my cell phone and saw we had a couple hours before we really needed to get back.

"I had fun. Thank you," I said to Logan as we walked down tulip-lined lanes.

"I'm glad you had a good time," he grinned. "That last time I did that was... wow, maybe ten years old."

Looking at him in surprise, I said, "I didn't realize you've done this before. Did you use to live here?"

"No." Logan didn't elaborate. I let my mind wander, remembering how Tomas was pretty much adopted by the Findlays. Knowing what I knew now, I wondered if Logan had been adopted into Cay's family. The question sat on the tip of my tongue, but seeing how he'd just answered, I didn't want to pry.

"What do you want to do now?" he inquired. My legs were a little tired from pushing the trottinett over some gravel roads and through town when we were nearing the hotel.

"Is there a place where we can just sit somewhere and soak in the sun?"

He eyed me carefully. "Do you mean the beach?"

My face fell when I realized that was what I'd been craving: the simple activity of putting on sunscreen, sitting on a beach chair, and digging my toes into the sand.

"Yeah, I guess I do, but I know that's not around here."

"We could just head back and sit under one of the trees out front. I'll even grab a blanket or a chair," Logan offered. Part of me didn't want to go back just yet, but that sounded too nice to pass up.

"Sounds good to me."

As we entered the Academy's grounds, the smell of smoke hung thickly in the air. I didn't look at Logan as I ran toward the small crowd gathering outside.

"What happened?" I asked Mat as I rushed up to her.

She shook her head. "I'm not completely sure. I know there was a fire, but that's all we know right now."

"Did everyone get out?"

"As far I know, yes." I gave her a thankful smile and went to look for someone who had more info. I didn't see Eden or Norah, but I did see another trainer, Zachary. I hesitated now that I remembered Trip name-dropping him to Rose. I didn't know if I could trust him because I couldn't be sure he wasn't working with Beira's side, but I didn't see anyone else around who I thought could help.

"Hi," I addressed him. He looked down at me, clearly recognizing who I was. It seemed my identity wasn't a secret after all.

"Students are meant to be on the other side." He uncrossed one arm to point where everyone else was standing.

"Yeah, I was just wondering if you knew where Eden was," I replied.

"She is still investigating with Norah inside." The finality in his voice indicated that was all I would get from him. I nodded in acceptance and headed back toward Mat, who was joined by Franny and Oliver.

"Hey," Oliver said. "I was wondering where you were. I didn't see you."

Logan responded as he walked up and stood close behind me. "She was with me."

I rolled my eyes at his territorial tone. "We went scootering down the mountains to celebrate passing my elementals. Are you all okay?"

"Yeah! It was so crazy," Franny cut in. "One minute, I'm working on my homework, and the next, I hear the fire alarms go off. I was holding my work, so I just got out of there." She pulled a folded piece of paper out of her pocket. "This may be all I have left."

I gave her shoulder a sympathetic pat.

There was a hush among the chatty students. Norah had come out the front door and stopped.

"The fire has been smothered, and we have been told the damage is minimal. Everyone may enter the building. Please go collect your belongings if they aren't in your room, and head to dinner early. The kitchen is preparing the meal now." She moved out of the way to allow the throng of people past.

When I made it to the door with Logan, Norah motioned me to step aside and not go in. She waited until everyone was back inside before breaking the news.

"Bridget, the fire was in your room." I panicked, thinking about my clothes, the little trinkets I'd brought from home to remind me of my friends, the *Book of Brighde*.

Norah rested a hand on my shoulder.

"The book is safe," she said, reading my thoughts.

"Can I go see?" Did I lose everything?" I asked, looking at the door.

"I want you to be forewarned: your room is pretty damaged."

I didn't wait for her to say anything more as I took off for my room, Logan hot on my heels. I thundered up the stairs, getting hit with a pungent smell of charred cloth and singed wood. Eden was standing outside my room, waiting for me.

"Remember," she said as we reached her, "things can be replaced."

My room was gone.

The curtains were burned halfway up, my bed was black, the dresser drawers were pulled open, and some of my clothes were stained from smoke. The floor was charred but stable as I stepped gingerly inside. The walls had scorches reaching toward the ceiling, as if they'd been desperate to escape this prison.

"Because your door was closed and the sprinklers went off, the fire was able to be contained," Eden said gently. She carefully walked to me and handed me the *Book of Brighde*. "I was able to save it before the fire got to it."

I couldn't stop the tears from escaping. Everything overwhelmed me. Not only was I sad I had lost most of my stuff, but also Eden had walked into fire to rescue the book needed for my powers to save the world. I was both touched and heartbroken.

"What do I do now?" I asked her, letting my tears fall. I hadn't felt like a little kid in a long time, but this broke me. A soft rain fell outside the open window. Eden hugged me and let me cry. Logan stood back, allowing me the space to grieve.

"Don't worry," she said. "There are other beds for you to sleep in, and we can go to town tomorrow to replace what is lost."

I pulled away and wiped some of my tears. "Thank you."

"Let us give you some privacy. We'll be in Norah's office when you're ready to move into your new room." They left, leaving me alone.

I nodded and looked around, not wanting to fight this alone. I didn't know if I had the emotional energy to sort through my stuff and determine what I could keep. Standing in the middle of my room, alone, I sighed and let the weight of the world sink on my shoulders. I wanted to lie on the floor and let it crush me, but I didn't want to sit anywhere in this room, and I needed to pull myself together to move forward. I could mourn the loss of my things later, after everything was done. The Amulet warmed my skin, offering comfort. I wrapped my fingers around it as I figured out where to start.

My closet door was shut, so the outside exterior had taken the brunt of the flames. A lot of the stuff in there was saved, minus the smoke lingering on things. I picked up my duffel bag that was originally on the top shelf—it had fallen to the floor—and sorted through my clothes. If they were destroyed, I left them on the bed, but if they were salvageable,

I packed them. After going through the rest of the closet, I was able to save two more pairs of shoes, a few pairs of leggings, and a light sweatshirt. Everything else was gone. My dresser was next. As I examined every drawer, I discovered that I was luckier than I'd thought. The top layers of clothes couldn't be saved, but the clothes underneath were only smoky. I was more than grateful when my underwear drawer was basically untouched, except for the smell. I'd lost all my toiletries, most of the items I'd brought to remind me of home, and my favorite pair of jeans. *It's only stuff*, I thought as I blinked back tears. Stuff is replaceable, and the two most important things were rescued. The Amulet practically vibrated, and I took that as a thank-you for saving its life.

After cleaning, I carried my duffel down to Norah's office and raised my hand to knock.

"Bridget," Franny said, rushing down the stairs. "I just heard it was your room."

She wrapped me in a hug, duffel and all.

"Thanks." I hugged her back, letting her kindness wash over me.

"Did you lose everything?"

I shrugged. "Nothing that can't be replaced." *Deep breath.*

"That's wonderful. I'm glad you had your most important items rescued or with you already. If you need anything, let me know. I have clothes I can spare," she said with a sympathetic smile.

"Thank you, I will." Franny hugged me one more time.

"Do you know how it happened yet?"

I swallowed back some tears and shook my head. "No. I'm sure it will take some time to sort all of this out."

"It must be hard, not knowing. At least it will be sorted at some point; I'm glad."

Looking down at the floor, avoiding her eyes, the tears began to well.

"Oh, no!" Franny exclaimed. "I didn't mean to upset you. I'll let you talk to Norah and leave you be." She took my hand and squeezed it before heading back up the stairs.

Knocking on Norah's door, I braced myself for another conversation related to the one I'd just shared with Franny.

"Come in," Norah said from behind the door. I opened the door, noticing that the normally-spacious office felt cramped. While Norah and Eden aren't relatively large people, Logan's anger took up the remaining available space.

"Would you like a cup of tea?" Norah offered, gesturing to the tea tray on her desk.

"Thank you, but no. I just want to wash my clothes, take a shower, have dinner, and go to bed, in that order." I dropped my bag on the floor and took an open chair by the window.

"I can help you with all of those things," Eden volunteered. "You have a new room assignment, which is closer to the toilet, and dinner isn't over yet. As for washing your clothes, I'm sure we can take care of that after you have something to eat."

I slumped a little in the chair. "I lost all my shower stuff. I'll need to replace everything." I was glad I'd had my wallet on me when I was out with Logan, or I would need to replace a lot more.

"I have an extra toothbrush, and you can borrow my shampoo and soap for tonight," Logan offered.

I smiled gratefully at him.

"Well, now that those things are settled," Norah interjected, "tomorrow we can work on replacing all your items. As for your new room, I have put you on the floor under Logan's, and your room will be right next to the stairs. It's our last available single room, so if another fire breaks, you may get a roommate."

"Can I go there now and get myself sorted before I come down for dinner?"

"I think you can have dinner in your room tonight, if you would like," Norah said. "Just so you can rest for the evening."

"Thank you. All of you." I looked at each one of them, hoping they understood the deep appreciation I felt, even if I couldn't say it just at this moment.

"Come on," Logan said, picking up my duffel bag, "let's get you some dinner."

As we entered the dining hall, I grabbed a plate of food and some water while Logan waited outside the room. We headed up two flights and opened the door to my new room. It was the mirror opposite of my old room, with the bed on the right side instead of the left. I set my dinner on the dresser across from the bed. The room smelled a little musty from being closed, so I opened the window for some fresh air. Logan placed my stuff on the floor next to the closet.

"I'll be right back with the shower stuff," he said. I gave him a thumbs-up and started to eat my dinner. It was chicken in a cream sauce, and it was delicious. I felt more nourished and rejuvenated with every bite and sighed in appreciation. By the time Logan returned, I had finished eating and was ready to wash my stuff.

"Here you go," he said, leaving everything on my dresser. Besides a toothbrush and shampoo, he brought down body wash, conditioner, toothpaste, a towel, and gym shorts with a shirt.

"Thank you so much," I said. I was excited to bathe and put the rest of this evening behind me. Logan stood for a second before enveloping me in a hug.

"I'm sorry for hugging you without asking, but I think I needed it more than you," he whispered in my ear. I wrapped my arms around him and squeezed.

"It's okay this time. I understand." I rested my head against his chest and let him support my weight. It felt nice to have someone to lean on, literally.

"I think I should shower," I said, breaking our embrace. "It's still early, so I'll probably throw a load of clothes in the washer first. Want to come with?"

He raised an eyebrow, and I blushed. "I mean, to do laundry, not to join me in the shower."

Logan's face was heavy with severity. "Bridget, I can't leave you alone anymore. Shower and everything else. Today's fire proved that."

"But you were with me when the fire happened. You were technically protecting me," I pointed out.

"Norah has asked me to increase my presence even though she wanted me to keep a low profile. I'll be waiting for you outside your room, and there has been discussion that my room should be next to yours."

I raised my eyebrows. I knew I was the Cuardaitheoir, but breaking floor rules seemed extreme.

"I'll be fine, but if it makes you feel better, you can clear the restroom before I go in."

Logan rested his hands on my shoulders. "I know you think this is a joke, but I'm doing what I'm meant to do."

"Do all Protectors act like this?"

"Only when their charges are being attacked the way you are," he replied simply.

True to his word, Logan checked the restroom and even searched my room before I went back in. I had changed into his set of borrowed clothes, so I hung up my towel and grabbed my smoky stuff before heading to the laundry room.

Dumping everything into the washing machine and feeling grateful there was some detergent left, I sat on the folding table across from the washer. Logan leaned against the doorway, scanning for anyone or anything that may pop up. We didn't talk. I didn't have the energy to engage in any more conversation about my safety.

When we got back to my room, I made him promise he would get some sleep tonight and hurried him out the door. Tonight, I wanted to be alone.

I started to put my clothes away. Seeing as I didn't have my full wardrobe, it didn't take long. As I climbed into the fresh sheets, my body relaxed against the softness of the mattress. So much had happened today that passing my tests this morning felt like years ago. I curled my fingers around the Amulet again, seeking some clarity. In the time that I'd been here, I'd been attacked by Beira's kin, poisoned, and nearly set on fire along with my room. Trip was canoodling with Rose, my new enemy, and I had yet to face my true nemesis, Deidra. I flopped back onto the pillows. Would I ever catch a break? Thankfully, I had Logan, who could be overprotective, but that was his job. When I'd been told I would get a Protector while I looked for the Amulet, I'd imagined running down a football field with my Protector as my defender, pushing people out of my way and stopping them from tackling me. Boy had I been wrong.

Running my fingers through my hair, I caught a hint of soap. I smelled his scent on my skin, and I smiled, snuggling into the bed. I fell asleep, feeling safe and protected.

Chapter 11

Clipping my helmet to my head, I took my place on the trottinett and waited for Logan to do the same. We took off down the paved road with the soft tickle of fresh air on our faces. Gliding around the sharp curves, I took in the sweeping beauty of the valley below and the mountain ridges around us. Logan looked back and grinned as he started a free fall down the hill in front of us. I tried to match my pace to his, but gravity was on his side, and I lost him as we entered a pine tree grove. Not worried, I slowed my descent and took my time through the trees, enjoying their sweet smell.

Not sweet, smoky.

I looked around and saw some of the trees on fire! I stopped and tried to call my powers, but all I got was a trickle, enough to put out one tree, not five burning ones. Hiding under that tree was a bear, and I froze. I hadn't dealt with wild animals enough to know what to do. The bear ambled out of the tree line as if everything was fine, and came over to me. I wanted to run, but at the same time, I felt safe. Intrinsically, I knew this bear meant me no harm. It waved its snout in the air and motioned for me to try again. Taking a cleansing breath, I focused on conjuring a rain cloud, dark and full of water. One formed, large enough to cause an eclipse of darkness.

The bear whimpered softly.

"Okay, I'll try," I said and willed the cloud to dump its contents. It shivered under my power, looking like a tree shaking in the breeze. I pushed it harder, and it burst like a popped balloon. Within minutes, the bear and I were surrounded by soaked wood, and the cloud dissipated. My new friend made a purring noise, signaling its contentment, as it brushed against me. I put my hand on its back and stroked it like I would a dog. Its fur was bristly and rough to the touch. I remembered I still had to find Logan—he was probably wondering where I was. The bear waved a paw in the air, but I wasn't sure what it meant.

Motioning me to follow, the bear meandered down the path. As we left the grove, a field dotted with purple and pink flowers appeared around us. A baby cub rolled down a small hill and landed in front of the bear. The cub cried, excited to find its parent. I assumed my bear companion was the cub's mother, and the three of us continued on.

We walked along the path, seeing more trees and fields. As we traveled, more cubs came out and joined us. By the time we'd made it to a lake, there were roughly seven of us in this party. The mama bear stopped at the lake, and the little cubs ran into it. I remembered from third-grade science that bears could swim, so I wasn't worried. We watched them for a bit before the mama let out a bellow and hurried toward the lake edge. I looked out and saw one of the cubs *had stopped swimming and was facedown. Without thinking, I called upon the wind to scoop the cub out of the water and bring him to shore. The mama rushed over to him and rolled him over to see his face. The cub wasn't moving. I used the wind to press down on the cub, mimicking chest compressions. The mama bear turned to face me, and I panicked, thinking I was doing the wrong thing. Finally, the cub rolled over and flipped onto his feet, making a coughing noise. Its mom wrapped her arms around him and licked his face, both of them purring. She called to the other cubs, and they joined me back on the path.*

As we walked on, I had a sense of us coming to the end of the path, but we were nowhere near the rental place. I looked over at my companions, and all I saw were smiles and calm bodies. I felt peaceful despite everything that had happened, and I was okay with the journey ending.

We stopped at a crossroads, and the bears looked toward me as if asking which way we should go. To my left were more trees and a path that headed deeper into a forest. I couldn't tell if it went down the mountain or up. On the right was a clear path down the mountain. With what I knew, the darker path was usually the choice to make, but my internal guide was pushing me to the right. Turning right, the pack of us headed down the mountain and nearly made it to the bottom toward the valley. The mama bear abruptly veered off the path and headed toward a group of stones. I followed, and as I got closer, I saw the stones formed a throne. Next to the seat rested a basket of grains and fruit. As the mama climbed onto the stone pillar where the throne sat, she shed her pelt and changed into a beautiful woman. Her hair was pale and braided, wrapped around her head with a lovely crown sitting on top, and she wore a bell-sleeved dress that brushed the tops of her bare feet.

I stared, not knowing what to do or expect.

"Come to me, little Brighde," she called, her voice soft but with a strong Scottish lilt.

I moved toward her and stopped at her feet. She looked down and smiled.

"You don't recognize me," she said. "I'm Artio, also known as the Bear Goddess."

She held out her hand to me, and I took it. Lifting me onto the pillar, she wrapped me in a warm embrace. Feeling the same comfort and safety as I had at the beginning of our journey, I returned the hug. She smelled like earth, sweet and fragrant with a hint of wild animal musk. It wasn't an unpleasant scent, and I breathed deeply.

"Brighde sent me here to guide you along this passage. She wanted you to understand how to use your powers to help as well as defend." A little cub clambered onto the pillar and nudged me with its nose. I smiled and petted him, feeling the rough fur and smelling the oily musk of his body.

"Did I do well?" I asked, looking up at the goddess.

She smiled widely. "Yes, you have." Cupping my face in her hands, she added, "Brighde would be so proud of you."

My heart broke at those words, releasing the worry and fear I'd been carrying for so long. It was the approval I'd never known I'd wanted but always needed.

"Thank you," I whispered.

"To continue on your journey, you must remain courageous, fierce, strong, and keep your wits about you. You do not have an easy path ahead."

I gulped, remembering the dark woods from earlier.

"Happy Birthday, little Brighde," Artio said as she took her place on the throne. The other cubs all gathered around her feet. I blinked, and she and her throne were gone. I stood in the field all alone.

I fluttered my eyes open to bright sunlight streaming through the curtains. The room was bathed in reds, yellows, and oranges as if I were lying in a field of colored tulips. I smiled and got out of bed, and as my feet hit the floor, I noticed a difference in me. I felt stronger, braver, and more than ready to face Deidra and the rest of Beira's army. I grabbed clothes and my borrowed toothbrush then headed to the restroom. As I brushed my hair, I noticed my skin looked different. It looked brighter, and the dark circles I had been getting used to were gone. I smiled, and my teeth were white enough to be in a toothpaste commercial. In fact, I was glowing. Grabbing my stuff, I left, not knowing if anyone else could see it.

I stopped in Norah's office on my way to breakfast.

"Come in," she said after I'd knocked.

"Morning," I said, closing the door behind me. She had a cup of coffee next to a plate of half-eaten toast and jam sitting next to her on the desk.

"Happy birthday," she replied warmly.

I smiled. "Thank you. I'm sorry for interrupting your breakfast, but I had a question about getting my full powers."

She motioned for me to sit. "If it's a question about your glowing, don't worry. That will fade in time as your body adjusts to the new powers."

I was relieved. "That's good to know. How do I hide it until then? So people don't know I'm the Seeker?"

"Concealer will help dull it for now."

I relaxed a little with that solution.

"I was planning on going into town to replace some of my items that were burned in the fire," I told Norah. "Is it okay if I go before my lessons with Eden?"

"Eden planned on continuing your education in the afternoon, so you may go after breakfast. But Logan needs to go with you. Now that you have all your powers, we want to be extra careful."

I nodded and smiled. "Thank you!"

As I was leaving Norah's office, I found Logan coming down the stairs.

"Hi!" I said cheerfully. "Norah said I could go into town if you come with me. Do you want to go?"

"Yeah, let's go," he said, reaching the last step on the stairs. "Let me grab a quick breakfast, and I'll meet you out front?"

I gave him a thumbs-up and headed outside.

It was still early, so the sun was behind the building. A small nip was in the air, and dew was still on the grass. I shivered slightly from the chill but welcomed it, as I knew the weather would get warmer soon. Walking slowly toward the main road, I felt every bit of my body, all my muscles tensing and flexing with every step I took, merging themselves with the earth. The energy from the ground beneath me traveled up my legs and into my body, connecting me with something bigger than myself that, while I couldn't entirely label it, I somehow now understood. I was a part of something larger, more than just a person, and it connected me with the heartbeat of the plants, the dirt, the water around me, the air I breathed, and the sky above me.

Logan came out to meet me, holding a travel mug.

"I need my caffeine today," he explained as he caught up to me. "I barely slept."

I looked over at him, and I saw the scruff on his face, the dark half-moons under his eyes, and the tired lines in his face.

"I've been there," I replied.

"Before I forget, happy birthday," he said, shooting me a tired smile.

I grinned. "I can't believe I'm finally eighteen."

"Really? That's all you're excited about?" His eyes sparkled in a way I'd never noticed before. It was like the stars were plucked from the sky and placed in his irises.

I blinked and averted my gaze. "The powers are super cool. Just have to get used to them all over again. I feel like I'm at full charge when I was dealing at fifty percent before. Or I got a booster pack, and I could fly to Mars and back right now."

Logan burst out laughing. "Mars, huh? Unless you can fly and breathe without air, I doubt that will happen."

I clucked my tongue. "I know, but I feel ... invincible."

He stopped walking and turned me to face him. "Not to harsh your buzz, but I need you to be serious for a sec."

I tried hard to sober up, but my blood was singing in harmony with the Amulet piece around my neck.

"You are not invincible. It's possible to kill you, and Beira's descendants will not hesitate to do so."

I inhaled sharply and smelled the manure. "I know. But I just feel so extraordinary."

"That will go away," he said, continuing our walk. I frowned, not wanting to lose this feeling. Elation dripped slowly from my body, and I was sure you could see a trail of shimmery gold behind me.

"Okay. But for today, I'm going to enjoy it, and then I'll deal with the rest of the world."

Our trip to town was quick, and I was able to replace most of the stuff I needed. Whatever was still missing, I could live without, or I could have my parents ship to me from the States. When we got back, Logan headed upstairs to his room, I guessed for a nap, while I dropped my stuff off and went back outside. There was an intense debate on our way home about whether or not he should leave my side, but I insisted. Even though Logan gave me a strict list of what I could do, which was basically limited to the library, I didn't want to be cooped up inside today. With this new power racing through me, I wanted to test what I could do before lunch.

I headed toward the back field where I'd had my basics test yesterday. Everything looked the same, minus the bowls, which had been brought back inside. My Amulet hummed against my skin and needed to release a burst of power. I lifted my hand to the sky, and a bolt of lightning erupted from my fingertips.

Eyes wide, I looked at my hand. That had never happened before. I only controlled the weather; I couldn't *create* it. I tried again, and this time, thunder boomed overhead, echoing across the valley. I held both hands above my head and clasped them together. Thunder and lightning split the sky in half, making the trees around me shake from the vibrations. This was new. I looked down at my hands, expecting to see electricity crackle from my fingertips, but they looked the same. Nothing was there but nails, knuckles, and skin.

Something caught my eye, and I saw the same red flash from yesterday. Not waiting a second, I took after it, chasing it through the forest. The red flash was very clearly human and in great shape because I was having a hard time keeping up, even with my new powers. Stopping for a second, I held out my hand, and lightning shot out, hitting the tree just to the left of the stranger. They faltered for a minute but didn't lose speed. I let out an exasperated breath and started running again. I ran through brush, leaped over logs, and slid through mud. Red was losing steam, and I was catching up, though the air in my lungs was slicing them open. In a moment of inspiration, I shot out two more branches of lightning, but instead of letting them fly freely, I held onto them, attaching them to two trees on either side of the person. I tilted my head to the side, and the lightning bolts connected in the open space between the trees, causing an electric spiderweb. They attempted to dive underneath, but the web grew to fill the entire space, and they were electrocuted.

"Oh, no, oh, no," I said, slowing down. Panting heavily, I dragged them by the feet away from the lightning and released the web. Electricity danced up in the air and disappeared. I flipped them over to see if they were breathing, but instead, I stopped breathing.

Trip was lying unconscious in front of me.

Chapter 12

I looked at him, watching his chest rise and fall. Thankfully, he was only knocked unconscious, but I wasn't sure if there was any internal damage. His eyes were closed, but his face was serene, given his situation. The hood had come off when I'd flipped him over, and his hair was disheveled and sweaty.

Should I help him?

Yes! exclaimed my conscience.

Why? If I don't, my competition could be slowed from finding the Amulet.

He would help you, it said.

I snorted but decided to help him anyway. He wouldn't help me, based on his track record, but I couldn't leave him there.

Remembering I could now heal people, I kneeled next to Trip. I copied how Cay used to heal me and placed my hands on his chest. Nothing happened. I unzipped his hoodie and placed my hands on the thin material of his T-shirt. My hands heated up, but not from the heat on Trip's skin. They glowed red, almost mirroring the color of his sweatshirt. I felt his heartbeat under my hands, strong and unrelenting. I moved my way down his chest, and his lungs inflated to a full breath. I hovered over his head, feeling the synapses in his brain firing off. Everything seemed to be working, so there wasn't more I could do. I stood and waited for him to wake up.

While I waited, I looked around to take in how far away from civilization we were. I couldn't see the building anymore, but I did see a path that wasn't properly made. Someone had traveled this same way all the time, crushing down plants and packing down the soil. Was this the same path Trip took to visit Rose? Since kitchen duty had ended, I didn't know how often they still met up. I turned to look in the direction behind me, away from where I came. The unofficial path continued on. The pull of the path taunted me to follow it, but I couldn't pass up my chance with Trip after not seeing him for all these months.

I'll come back for you, path.

I heard stirring behind me, and I looked down at Trip. He was groaning and trying to sit up.

"I wouldn't sit up just yet if I were you. You were electrocuted," I said, crossing my arms over my chest.

"How did that happen?" he asked.

I shrugged. "You ran into my lightning web. Well, more like you dove into it headfirst, like it was home base."

Trip sat up slowly and looked at me. "I know I deserved something, but I didn't deserve that."

I laughed in his face. "After all you did... What do you think you deserve?" I asked, calming down.

Trip frowned. "I didn't do anything that would get me electrocuted."

I shook my head. "You are..." I started, annoyed, but I really wanted to know his endgame. "Why are you here?"

"What do you mean?"

"Stop it. I know you know what I'm talking about." I gestured to the forest around us. "Hello? You're sitting in mud in Switzerland, where I just so happen to be."

He stood slowly, wiping the dirt off his pants. "I'm here for the same reasons as you."

"Which are...?" I raised an eyebrow.

"Do I need to spell it out for you? The Amulet halves."

"I just needed to hear it from your mouth this time, not someone else's." He glared at me, so I took my chance to continue.

"Why are you spying on me?" I smiled sweetly at him.

"I'm not here to spy on you," he scoffed, stuffing his hands into his pockets.

"Sending people to search my room?" I raised both eyebrows, waiting for his reaction.

His face darkened. "I did what I had to do."

"Like always," I said flatly. "The dutiful little Seeker."

Instead of taking my bait, his face softened.

"You know, I wish I could change what happened between us," he said quietly. My heart gave a little jump at that, and I quickly cursed it. *Traitor.*

"Your actions are saying something completely different." I crossed my arms again and shifted my weight.

"What do you think they're saying?" he countered, mirroring my pose.

It was my turn to scoff. "What they've always said, that you're only here for the Amulet you think I have." The necklace I always wore nearly burned my flesh for that, as if warning me.

Trip shook his head. "You know nothing. Yes, I'm here for the Amulet, but I'm also here for you. I ... want to apologize for how I left everything."

I blinked at him. In all my dreams, my pining for him for months, did I ever expect to hear an apology from him? Inwardly, my heart did another little jump. Ignoring it, I narrowed my eyes in disbelief.

"I mean it, Bridget," he continued. "I messed up. I shouldn't have left without telling you, I should have told you everything from the start, and I should've stopped Dee from trying to—" his voice hitched on the words, "kill you."

My face relaxed a little at his honesty. I still felt the lines of a frown drawn on my face, but appreciation was blooming in my chest from his confession. Closure was finally coming around.

"Should have, would have, could have," I replied. "Your apology changes nothing."

"I don't expect to erase what happened, but I wanted you to know how I felt." He sighed and chewed on his lower lip, looking at me hopefully.

"If you're so regretful of what you did to me, why do you have Rose searching my room?" I asked without sarcasm or attitude. I genuinely wanted to know.

Trip stared at me, his eyes shining and his lips pressed together. He blinked and looked away. "You know I have to find the Amulet. I was just doing everything I could think of."

"We both have to. I don't go through your room."

He smiled teasingly, answering, "You don't know where my room is."

Before I could chew him out on that, he jumped in, "Why don't we work together?"

My mouth fell open, and I gaped at him. "What?"

"Yeah," Trip said, stepping toward me, laying his hands on my upper arms. "We could work together and find the Amulet."

"Once we do that, who wields it?

"We both could."

For the second time, I burst out laughing and pulled away. Trip frowned.

"Trip, you can't be serious!" He raised his eyebrows at me. "Trying to share the Amulet is how you and I got here in the first place."

"So? We can do better and fix it for future generations."

I shook my head. "It's not better or progressive if we do the exact same thing as our ancestors."

"What do think we should do then?"

Trip was still standing close enough to me that I could smell the mustiness of his sweat.

I looked up at him thoughtfully for a minute. "Only one Cuardaitheoir wields the Amulet."

"It didn't work out so well before."

I remembered the story about Danu, who was sick of her daughters' fighting. She split the Amulet in half so they both could wield a part of it.

"So, we're stuck in the same rut we were in before. Nothing changes," I said.

Trip looked crestfallen but nodded. "Nothing changes."

The silence hung awkwardly in the air between us, thick and sticky in the filtered sunlight.

"I ended it with Rose," he said suddenly. I didn't say anything, so he went on. "I was only using her to find out where the Amulet half was, but she was getting jealous that I spent my time talking about you. She demanded I give up the hunt for the Amulet or give her up."

His hands were stuffed back in his pockets, and he moved toward me again.

"I know I messed up," Trip repeated, "but I still miss you." He took my hand and held it gently as I stood there, my mind desperately trying to process everything.

"Please, tell me we can at least be friends." Trip spoke so softly; I wasn't sure I heard him. I pulled my hand out of his and shook my head.

"Time to go," I said, turning away from him. I felt his eyes penetrating my back. I gulped and turned around.

"Don't come here anymore."

Then I left.

My heart was aching as I walked through the forest, following the path Trip had created. He missed me. The butterflies I thought were long dead fluttered in my stomach. Did that mean I missed him? I fingered the Amulet half around my neck. I didn't know any more than I had before, except that I wouldn't be sharing my responsibilities or the Amulet with anyone. Taking a deep breath and holding it, I pushed forward through the woods, letting my lungs burn from the lack of oxygen. I released the breath slowly and stopped walking, a thought drifting into my head. Maybe we *could* make this work. What if he had changed? What if he really was different now? I shook my head and continued. Before anything could happen, I needed to know if I could trust him.

I opened the main door to the school and was greeted by silence. It was early afternoon, just after lunch, and no one was around. Closing the door behind me, I waited a second for my eyes to adjust. The plush carpet absorbed my footsteps, leaving no trace of my being there. Suddenly, I stopped. The air was different, like the particles were electrically charged in some way. Though I was made for summer, I had always been able to sense when snow was coming. A specific scent came in a winter wind, a warning that snowflakes were right behind it. A chill skittered down my back, and I sensed I was being followed. I whipped around just in time to catch Rose's fist with my jaw. I stumbled backward and fell over. *Ow!* I rubbed my face, standing. With my back turned to Rose, I laid my hand on the sore spot and let my red heat do its thing.

"What is your damage?" I faced Rose, moving my jaw, testing for any soreness.

"You took him from me!" She took a step toward me, but I sent a blast of air at her feet.

"That's close enough." Adrenaline snaked through my body, and I felt the growth of my powers thrumming under my skin. "I didn't take anyone from you."

Rose sneered, her face distorting, but she didn't move. "He was mine before you popped into his life."

"Are you telling me you and Trip were together before we were?" My nerves twitched at the force of the power I was keeping down. I swallowed and willed myself to focus on my breathing.

Rose rolled her eyes. "Before and after you." She smirked and crossed her arms over her chest. At least one piece of gossip was proven right.

I smiled and shrugged. "As long as it wasn't during." I kept a cool exterior, but it was getting harder to ignore the buildup of power. I needed to release it soon.

Her nostrils flared before she took control of her features. "I know what you are."

I clapped and got a confused response. "Sorry, I don't have a cookie to reward you, so a round of applause will have to do."

"The Seeker."

"Yeah, I caught that's what you meant before." I frowned. "I'm sorry. Is this part supposed to upset me?"

Rose growled and charged at me. My power flared and stood at attention, ready for the attack. I rested my weight on my back foot and got into the fighting stance Cay had taught me so long ago.

She leaped and attempted to land on me, but I was able to push her off with a blast of air. I left her hanging for the moment and then dropped her to the floor.

She landed with a *thump* but didn't let it stop her attack. She bounced, light on her feet, as if the drop didn't affect her at all. Grabbing a flag secured on the wall above us, Rose swung her body in the air, her feet headed toward my chest. I practically rolled my eyes at her and deftly moved aside. She swung back and let go, landing softly on her feet.

"While I'd love to keep this going, I have things to do," I let electricity crackle between my fingertips. "Rain check?"

Rose's eyes watched the bolts and hesitated.

"You won't win," I warned her.

Shooting me the nastiest glare, Rose straightened her shoulders and walked up the stairs, never once looking back at me.

Part of me was disappointed. I wanted to end this ridiculous fight once and for all, but I could wait. She wasn't really the person I needed to be after. Honestly, I was considering the spat with Rose to be practice for when I finally faced Deidra again.

"Happy birthday," Eden said as I met her and Logan inside the training gym. Other students were in there, sparring with one another, so the three of us weren't alone.

"Thanks," I smiled. "What are we working on today?"

"Now that you're at your full power, you'll be working toward your second test," she replied.

"When will I take that?"

"Soon." She grinned and gestured toward Logan. "Besides working on your supernatural powers, you also need to continue your physical training. You may not always be able to rely on your magic. Logan will be helping with this."

"This won't be like what we did with Cay," Logan added. I nodded and looked at the equipment in the room.

"What will we do first?"

"Stretch." Logan moved his thick arm across his chest and used the other to pull it closer to his body. He nodded at me, indicating that I should follow. I mirrored his actions and felt the sting of my muscles being stretched. The movement was familiar since this was the warm-up I'd done with Cay. I smiled to myself, remembering how it had been with Neit and him.

Logan switched arms, and I followed. We moved onto stretching out my hamstrings, ankles, wrists, hips, and thighs. By the time we were done, I felt like a wet noodle, limp and loose.

"I need to test your cardio first to get a game plan on what we should focus on," Logan said as he led me to a treadmill. "Start slow, and let's see how far you can go."

I shook my head. I was active enough in high school, but my cardio was nothing to write home about. Middle school track was torturous because I couldn't run the mile in under thirteen minutes, let alone the eight they wanted us to hit.

I climbed on board and adjusted my settings. Pressing start, I began the run. After three minutes, I was breathing heavily but holding my own. After five minutes, I was panting and wishing I was dead. By the time I made it to ten minutes, I was gasping for air, about to collapse, and sure I was dying.

Logan spared me and turned off the machine.

"Okay, that was ... not great."

I gulped the water Eden had handed me and ignored him. My racing heart needed my attention more than he did at the moment.

"Good news is, you'll only get better from here. Because we will be doing this pretty much every day."

I stared at him. "Running?"

He nodded. "To start. Then we'll add in some light combat training, and by the time you have your test, you'll be able to kick any butt you want." Logan gave me a sympathetic smile.

"I know it's a lot," he said. "But I promise, you'll get better. Just have to keep at it."

I gave him a thumbs-up, as I was still working on getting my breath back.

"Take another minute, and then we'll head over to the kettlebells for lifting."

I groaned, wishing I had let Rose get the better of me.

My shower after the workout felt amazing, and dinner was just as gratifying. As I got back to my room to read more *Brighde*, I noticed flashes outside my window. Turning off the light and pulling back the curtain, I saw lightning spark in the sky. My brow furrowed. No storms were in the forecast—I would know—and it wasn't hot enough to cause a heat storm. There was no pattern or organization to how the lightning struck; it was all over the place. I waited to hear thunder, but it never came. A strong wind pushed through, bending the trees and forcing their leaves to swirl in the air. I pushed open my window to get a better look outside, and I shivered. The temperature dropped, and I swore a single snowflake danced past my nose.

That was impossible.

I looked toward the woods, which were shrouded in darkness. If Trip was outside playing games with me, well... the game was on.

Chapter 13

I got up early the next morning to catch up on the *Brighde* chapter I hadn't read last night. I was up to the part of her life where she'd invented keening, the sound of crying and singing. Brighde created it to mourn the loss of her son Ruadán after he'd died in a battle against the Fomorians and was slain by their leader, a giant one-eyed god. He liked to torture people and encourage his supernatural followers to be just as vicious and malevolent as him. Reminds me of the conversation Oliver and I shared. I wonder if this is the same god he was talking about.

I was having a hard time keeping up with Brighde's life. Every time I thought I understood it, another family member or myth popped up, leaving me struggling to grasp their connections. A spreadsheet wasn't making it any easier. I'd created a list in the back of my dream journal to keep everyone in Brighde's family straight. The list included Lugh (cousin), Beira (twin sister), Danu (mother), Ruadán (son), Bres (her husband and Ruadán's father), Artio (cousin), Arwan (cousin), and now the Fomorians with details on how they were related to the goddess.

I trudged to breakfast and grabbed something before I plopped into my chair next to Franny.

"Rough night?" she asked, spooning sugar into her tea.

"Something like that," I said. The marmalade on my roll was sliding off the top, and I took a bite before I lost some of the jam goodness.

"Were you able to sleep with all that flashing going on?"

I nodded. "I'm a very sound sleeper, so it didn't even faze me." Clearly, I wasn't going to announce what my suspicions were, since no one besides Rose knew Trip was still around. And I was not having this conversation with her.

"I couldn't. It felt like I was watching a laser show in my room." Franny took a sip of tea before continuing. "I wish whoever made it happen would stop."

Pretending I didn't hear her remark even though my entire body wanted to tense, I took another bite of my breakfast to delay my reply. Thankfully, Oliver sat before I could say anything and provided a distraction.

"Morning, everyone," he said cheerily. He gave me a smile as he placed his napkin in his lap.

"Good morning to you," I said back. "What has you so chipper this bright and early?"

Still smiling, he said, "Did you see the lightning last night? That was incredible."

"We were just talking about it," I replied. "It kept Franny up."

She looked weary and said with a bite, "Not all of us can sleep through New Year's fireworks in June like we're dead."

I grinned and shrugged. Her snippy response reminded me of Bri, and my heart burst into flame and fell through my chest. A part of me was still sad I had to keep my life a secret from my friends back home. I made a mental note to text my friends or at least send them more postcards, even if they couldn't send me anything back.

"You slept through it?" Oliver asked incredulously. "How is that possible? You missed out."

I shrugged again, taking a sip of water. "I'll catch it next time."

Oliver just shook his head. "If you didn't hear it or see it, did you notice the deep frost covering our windows this morning?"

The blood drained from my face, and I hoped no one noticed.

"No, I didn't open my curtains," Franny answered. I shook my head, looking down at my half-eaten roll.

"My window was frozen shut," he said, and I frowned. A lightning storm was one thing, but frozen windows were a whole other story.

"That didn't happen to me. Was anything else frozen shut or unusual?" I asked.

It was Oliver's turn to shrug. "Not that I noticed, but I haven't talked to other people yet. Maybe they know something?"

Franny's eyes darted toward Oliver and then at me. I avoided her gaze as I took one more bite of my meal.

"I have to talk to Eden before lessons today. I'll see you for lunch?" I barely saw heads nodding as I dumped the rest of my breakfast into the trash and rushed to Eden's office.

"Come in," Eden's voice carried through the door after I knocked.

"Did you see the lightning last night? And the freeze this morning?" I asked, closing the door behind me. "Oliver said his window was frozen shut. Did anyone else mention that?"

"Good morning to you, too," Eden replied lightly as she wrote something on a piece of paper. I scrunched my nose at the subtle chastising.

"Good morning, Eden," I dutifully responded, sitting across from her. "Now, did you see it?"

She looked out her window to where a sliver of frost outlined the bottom ledge. "I noticed it. This isn't good," she sighed.

"When would it ever be good?" I asked.

She raised an eyebrow at me.

"Sorry," I waved my hand, "that was rhetorical. Now that I'm at my full power, I should be able to control this. How is Trip able to cause a frost in June?"

Eden put down her pen and rested her hands on the desk. "He's at his full powers, too. It's even more pertinent that you find the Amulet first to stop the inevitable."

"Is this what will happen if Trip gets it before me?"

Eden looked at me thoughtfully. "It was said that whichever sister found the Amulet first would rule the weather year-round, no exceptions. That's not to say they would rule it fairly, keeping the seasons as we know them to be. The assumption has always been Beira would keep the world in a permanent winter. It stands to reason Trip would honor that rumor."

"Like the White Witch," I surmised.

She smiled. "Yes, except there are no lions, kings, or queens to help you."

"Just you," I smiled back.

"Yes, me, Logan, Norah, and whomever else you ask for help, but it ultimately comes down to you. You have to rule to keep the seasons equal, so we can stabilize the climate and stop the utter destruction of the world as we know it."

"I definitely didn't eat enough breakfast to stomach doom and gloom so early in the morning."

"I'm not sorry for reminding you, Bridget. This is why you're here," Eden said, picking up her pen and placing it in a pencil holder. "We need to get you ready for your journey ahead."

"I know." In my brain, everything felt so far away, like when you're seven and someone asks what you want to be when you grow up. One day, you'll be that grown, but at seven, it feels light-years away from where you are. My time as that seven-year-old was quickly dwindling, and I was feeling less prepared now than I had been when I was actually seven.

"Go get ready for Logan. You're training first today and having lessons with me after lunch."

I nodded and stood. "Eden, do you honestly think I can do this?" I quietly asked.

She looked me in the eyes and said, "Yes, Bridget. You can do anything you put your mind to if you believe in yourself the way I believe in you."

"Now that you're warmed up, grab some water and meet me on the mat," Logan said as I wiped my face with a towel.

I sighed internally, already tired from my burst of energy during the warm-up. I was still on edge from my conversation with Eden, and I channeled that into this session. Logan had me practice open palm strikes after running for ten minutes straight, then had me lift weights in a circuit of triceps, biceps, and deltoids. My arms felt done for, and we'd barely started our practice. I chugged some water, wiped my mouth with the back of my hand, then trudged back over to Logan, who was standing next to a dummy. It had been way too long since I'd done any form of physical labor, and I was deeply regretting not keeping up with my regiment from Cay.

"Since it will be nearly impossible for you to avoid fighting, we need to focus on sparring. Today, we will go over the basics: kicks, throws, and knife skills."

I frowned and shook my head. "I have powers. Why do I need knife skills?"

Logan smiled. "What if you're incapacitated to a point where you can only use your muscles and a knife?"

"Wouldn't I have my powers to fall back on?" I placed my hands on my hips and bent over, stretching my back. "And where would I get a knife?"

"It's better to be prepared than not," he said, ignoring my last question. "Now, a groin strike is completely useful when your assailant's adrenaline is not pulsing at an all-time high. The rush will prevent them from feeling the pain or doing enough damage to stop them in the moment, even though they'll feel the pain later."

Logan leaned back on his left leg and swung his right leg up, kicking the mannequin in front of him. "This is called a stomp kick. The goal is to send a kick into the side of a person's knee to weaken them."

He did the kick again, going slower this time. "If someone is throwing a punch at you, this is a good kick to affect their balance since you're going to aim for their weighted leg."

Logan demonstrated this with an exaggerated movement. "Now, to get the kick to work, you must lift your knee as you kick. I know it feels counterintuitive, but if you don't, you won't have the driving force behind the kick to knock them down. You try, but go slowly," he said, tapping my left leg to show me where to stand.

I planted my feet and kicked, aiming for the knee.

"Not bad, but kick above the knee. Kicking below gives the other person a chance to move their leg and makes this kick ineffective. It also gives them a chance to defend themselves."

I tried the kick again but caught myself kicking with the ball of my foot.

"Oops. I'm supposed to kick with my heel, right?" I asked, getting back into position.

Logan nodded. "Yes, that's where the strength is coming from."

I tried again and landed my kick where I wanted it.

"Good! Do it again."

I did it again a thousand more times. My right leg was feeling numb from swinging and kicking, and my left leg was tired from holding me up.

"Take a break and grab some water," Logan said. "When we come back, we'll switch legs." I shook my right leg to get some feeling back as I headed over to chug my water.

"You're doing good," Logan said, taking a sip of his own water.

I wiped sweat off my forehead before saying, "Thank you. I'm feeling comfortable with this move. I'm ready to learn more but not today." I gave him a weak smile.

"Tired already?" he teased. I huffed out a breath.

"Come on," Logan said, slinging his arm over my sweaty shoulder, "it wasn't that bad, was it?"

"My sore spots will have aches tomorrow," I replied, leaning into him. We were both gross and sweaty, but Logan still smelled wonderful, woodsy musk mixed with his natural scent.

"After this, let's get you a hot shower."

"I hope you mean with hot water," I joked back, pulling away from him.

Logan blushed. "No comment."

I was surprised at the something in my stomach that flipped with his reply.

"Ready?" he said, placing his water bottle on the floor by the mirror. "We have kicking with the left leg now."

I groaned and promised my body lots of aspirin whenever this torture was over.

I practically fell asleep in the shower after the intense training, but I made sure to scrub my body from all the sweat combined with the scent of gym mats. Remembering my promise, I took a couple aspirin just before I brushed my teeth. As I turned off the light and climbed into bed, I imagined Cay was there to help with my growingly sore muscles.

"You know you can heal yourself now, oh, great one?" I pictured him sitting on my bed, one eyebrow raised.

Yes, I thought back.

"So, you don't need me."

I frowned as I snuggled deeper into the mattress. *Lies. I always need you.*

A sharp pain in my chest jolted me from the fantasy, and I realized how deeply I missed Cay. My cousin, my confidant, my best friend. Where was he? How was he?

"Cay," I whispered into the darkness, "please be safe."

CHAPTER 14

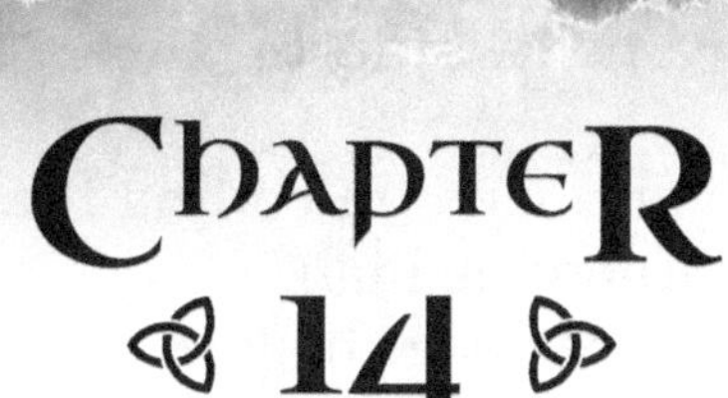

I stumbled to my training with Eden the next morning. She winced as I limped out to the field carrying the *Book of Brighde* with me.

"Rough night?" she asked, gesturing for me to sit on the large red blanket spread out next to her.

I cringed as I lowered myself onto the ground and dropped the book. "Rough Logan. I forgot what it was like to train with him."

Eden smiled. "Ah, yes. I've heard he can be particularly tough in the earlier sessions."

"Understatement of the year." I leaned back, crossing my legs in front of me as I felt my body relax.

"You're in luck, then! We're going to focus on healing today. No more relying on someone else."

The shadow of my "conversation" with Cay skimmed through my mind, and I ignored the worry that tagged along behind it.

"I already know how to heal."

"You do?" Eden asked, surprised.

"Yes. I healed—" I cut myself off before I said Trip, "myself after Rose attacked me."

"So, in the heat of battle?"

I tilted my head side to side. "More like a fight. If that."

"Then we can focus on calling it up when you aren't on an adrenaline high."

"Terrific. Where do we begin?"

Eden pulled *Brighde* toward her and flipped the pages.

"Here," she pointed and handed me the book. The chapter was on Brighde's abilities and speculations about how they were controlled. I'd reviewed it a couple of weeks ago, but so much had gone on; I hadn't remembered most of what I had read.

> The key to Brighde controlling her powers is tied into her emotions, unlike Beira, who controls her powers with her thoughts alone.

Made sense. Trip and Cay had told me the same thing when we were training.

> It has been said her powers of thunder and lightning were tied to her anger and fear while her combat fighting was deeply rooted in her need to protect.

I nodded in agreement as I saw these abilities pop up when I was feeling the same way.

In a way, her fertility and combat fighting stemmed from the need to protect and nurture, as they are often associated with parental feelings. From these comes the power of healing. This power was called upon whenever Brighde herself needed comfort or when followers left offerings in exchange for health and cures. If the offerings were accepted, Brighde would appear to the suffering individuals, lay her hands over their bodies, and absorb the injuries or illnesses as if taking on the sicknesses herself.

"I'm guessing laying my own hands on my own body wouldn't work the same way as when Cay used to hover his hands over my body?" I asked Eden.

She smiled and shook her head. "No, not like that at all. Brighde uses her emotions to wield her powers. As we know, you do, too. Which goes to say that Brighde simply urged herself to heal. I believe if you are sending healing thoughts to your aches and pains, they will simply heal themselves."

I raised my eyebrows. "Just ... think happy thoughts?"

"*Healing* thoughts. Try it."

I wrinkled my nose at her but focused on summoning up a healing thought. *Okay, legs, imagine two days ago, when you didn't whimper when I stood or protest when I bent my knees.* I kept this image in my mind and sent all my good feelings toward my legs. Nothing happened. I tried a different memory, focusing on how the hot shower felt as my muscles relaxed in the spray. Feeling the warmth of the water, I felt the tension slowly ease from my body, but I was still sore. I scrunched my face up and imagined a golden glow wrapping itself around my injured legs. This felt different from the red heat I was previously using. Like it was special, just for me. This glow hovered over my legs for a moment, then unfurled itself. Opening my eyes and looking down, I didn't see anything specific happening, no glowing or audible sounds of my body being healed. Yet, I jumped up like I hadn't done a mile of sprints last night.

I gaped at Eden. "It worked," I whispered.

She laughed. "Then why does it seem like you saw a ghost?"

"Because nothing has ever worked for me right away like this!" I jumped around, ran in place, and did twenty jumping jacks. My shoulders protested, but I sent them healing thoughts, too, and they moved without a hint of pain.

"This is incredible!" I gave Eden a hug. "Thank you!"

"For what?" she asked, hugging me back.

"For everything! For the first time, I feel like I may have a chance at surviving this war."

After spending the rest of the morning training with Eden, I skipped to lunch and grabbed a sandwich before my afternoon training with Logan. I saw Mat,

Oliver, Ginger, and Franny sitting at a table, chatting, and laughing away. I wanted to go over and tell them my good news, but Norah's warnings crept up and smacked me upside the head. No one could know who I truly was. Slightly deflated, I headed up to my room to eat alone because I couldn't trust myself not to say something. I ate my lunch on the floor as I reviewed more of *Brighde* and cleaned to get ready for my afternoon.

"Ready to rock and roll today?" I asked Logan upon walking into the gym after lunch.

"I am, but the question is, are you?"

"Absolutely! I learned how to use a new power, so I don't feel any pain!" I did a stomp kick to show him how energized and flexible I was.

"Perfect. We're starting with leg raises, squats, and burpees for your warm-up."

I groaned. Just because I could heal myself didn't mean I had to like causing myself pain.

We pushed forward with the workout, reviewing the stomp kick from yesterday as well as the palm strikes. My formerly sore arms felt fresh and able to handle the strikes with ease.

"You're doing really well," Logan said as we took our first water break.

"Thanks. It helps I have a good teacher," I said, smiling at him. He grinned back at me, and my stomach did a little flip again. When had Logan developed that great smile?

"I know this is different than you're used to with Cay," he said, putting his water down.

"Very different. He was actively trying to kill me with his drills, while you're only trying to maim me."

I put my water down by his and trotted over to the mat again.

"Kill you? That's an exaggeration," Logan scoffed.

"Not even! But at least with him, I had Neit to work out with. Now, it's just you." I made a show of sniffing him.

Oh, my God. His scent was addictive, and I had to stop myself from sniffing him again. I blushed, immediately covering my nose and mouth. Logan looked at me, smirking.

"At least Neit smelled better," I teased, dropping my hands and sticking my tongue out.

Logan burst out laughing. "It's like you want me to give you harder drills."

I grinned. "Bring it on, dog boy."

Logan grinned back at me and shook his head. "Don't say I didn't warn you!"

He hadn't been kidding. Besides the squats, leg raises, burpees, and my daily mile run, we ran through the stomp kick a million more times, and he added basic punches.

"I'm sorry for saying you smell!" I said as I swung at the punching bag. My arms were feeling the burn, which was nice because they matched the sensation in my legs. The healing powers I'd learned were hard to control when my focus was split between landing the punch and trying to stay upright.

Logan smirked at me. "You're not really sorry."

"I am! Promise!" I backed up and took my basic stance again. Swinging my hand, my punch didn't have the same oomph from before, probably because my arm was jelly.

"I need a second," I said, heading over to my water bottle. After taking a few sips, I lifted the neckline of my shirt and wiped my face with it. Today was not the day I should have forgot my towel.

"Come on," Logan called, "you still have elbow throws to learn!"

I leaned my head back and groaned. "I think you're enjoying this too much."

Dropping my water, I trudged over to the mat and took my place by the punching bag.

"Yeah, maybe a little," he admitted, grinning smugly.

"Is it your life's dream to see me sweaty and tired?" I asked as I swung again.

Logan pressed his lips together as he blushed. He turned away from me, grabbing his own water.

I blinked. Had I missed something?

"Was it something I said?" I relaxed my pose.

"You know what you... never mind."

"Never mind? What! You can't leave me hanging like that!" I threw my hands up, exasperated.

"Is that a challenge?" Logan nodded his head toward a bar. "Pull-ups. For the rest of the session."

"What happened to elbow throws?" I countered, placing my hands on my hips.

"Next time. Come on, I'll help you up," he said, spinning me around. I raised my arms and prepared to jump as Logan placed his hands firmly around my waist. I felt the heat of his hands through my shirt, and suddenly, I was breathless. I felt his fingers squeeze me ever so gently. A tingle ran through my body, and I wanted his hands touching more places than my waist.

"You ready?" Logan asked, concerned.

I lowered my arms and turned around, his hands still on my hips. I looked up into his dark-brown eyes and swallowed hard.

"I think I need another drink first."

Logan's right eyebrow twitched, and he dropped his hands as he took a step back. "Go for it. Are you okay?"

I blinked and nodded before walking carefully to my water bottle. I glanced back for another look at him, not exactly sure what had just happened. Then I caught him shaking his head and wiping his hands on his shorts. Like he was nervous.

I smiled.

After my near-fainting disaster with the basic punches and Logan last week, I admitted it was hard to focus on elbow throws this week. I kept thinking about the moment I knew we'd had. Even though Logan was careful always to maintain a six-foot distance during training, it didn't mean I couldn't think about him. Every. Waking. Moment.

I dreamed about it for the first few nights, playing out the fantasies I wished I could act on. They moved past his hands being on me to his lips pressing against mine, and my hands running along him wherever I could get them. This felt more like a need than a want. Every afternoon was tough for me, and it was hard not to feel distracted in my training sessions.

"...elbow throws. Are you even paying attention?" Logan waved his hand in front of my face.

"Huh? Oh, yeah." I shook my head. "I heard everything you said."

He crossed his arms over his chest. "Prove it."

I straightened my back and repeated his words back. "There are ten basic elbow strikes I can use: straight elbow, side elbow, up elbow, down elbow, back-up elbow, back-side elbow, back-down elbow, spinning up elbow, spinning side elbow, and spinning down elbow." I ticked them off on my fingers as I listed the throws.

Logan nodded. "Okay. What else?"

I frowned. "Um…" Sighing, I gave up and dropped my hands to my sides. "Fine, you win. I zoned out for a second."

"Bridget!" He came over and placed his hands on my shoulders.

Contact! All the alarms in my brain went off, celebrating Logan breaking his unspoken rule to keep away from me. I felt that rush from last week, and it took all my resolve not to take one step and push my body against his. "You have to get your focus back. You know how important it is for you to know these moves."

I nodded. "Yes, I do. But can we take, like … a day off once in a while, you know, for fun?"

Logan tilted his head to the side and pursed his lips. He clearly didn't know what a day off looked like.

I sighed again. "Never mind. Elbow throws. Go on. I'm totally listening now."

"You okay?" Logan still had his hands on my shoulders. I felt their weight pressing on me. It was reassuring and comforting.

"Fine. A little tired from the training, but I'll bounce back. Elbow throws?"

He looked at me like I'd told him I had spoken to aliens last night but continued with the lesson. "Elbows are good for close strikes, like if you're face-to-face with your opponent."

He demonstrated a move, pretending I was the target.

"That was the straight elbow. You try it now."

I struggled to mimic his move exactly, mostly because I kept watching his muscles flex as he did it.

I had to get out of here.

"You know what, Logan?" I cut him off. "You're right. I feel off and not in a good way. I think I need to call it quits for now."

Immediately, his body language switched from trainer to worried Protector.

"Are you sure you're okay? Are you feeling strange, like you … ingested something again?" He put the back of his hand on my forehead to check for a temperature.

"Logan," I started, as I pulled his hand from my head, "I'm just a little overworked from these sessions. I need a break."

He looked down at me holding his hand and cleared his throat. I let go of it, immediately regretting my choice, but I had to remind myself he wasn't mine to hold.

"Sure, okay." He stepped back and wiped his hands on his shorts again, the same way as last week. The movement didn't look nervous this time. Was I severely mistaken about our moment? Maybe it had been a one-sided experience. The shock of realization pierced my heart. It sank, sending a warning signal to my eyes, which were getting ready to flood with tears. It was time to book it out of there.

"I'll find you later," I said, picking up my water bottle. "After I rest."

"Sounds good. I'm going to shower and then come check on you."

I nodded, heading for the door. Even though my heart was crumpling in my chest, I knew I couldn't ever truly escape Logan. He was my Protector and bound by Norah's rule to literally watch me, even though I was a full-blooded goddess now.

I wondered if I could heal my own broken heart.

Chapter
❧ 15 ❧

I lay on my mattress, teary about how badly I had misinterpreted Logan last week. Not only was I sad, but also I was embarrassed, disappointed… I felt stupid. Of course, Logan wasn't making a move on me. He was teaching me self-defense, and I had been dumb enough to let myself believe it was more than that. I tucked my pillow over my head and groaned loudly. I just hoped he didn't notice the idiotic way I'd been acting. I groaned again and slammed the pillow on the bed. There was no use in lying here, beating myself up. I had to face him again soon. I might as well start now.

I rolled off my bed and grabbed my shower caddy. At least I could face him smelling like his own body wash instead of my gross sweat. I opened my door to Logan standing there, ready to knock.

"Hi," he said, lowering his arm.

I straightened my shoulders. "Hi."

Logan put his hands in his pockets. "Feeling better?"

"A little. I think a shower will help." I held up my caddy.

"Good. I'll… um… be here. Waiting."

"Good." I gestured, needing to walk past him, and he moved out of my way. I headed to the restroom, feeling his eyes on me the entire time. This time, I didn't let myself think it was for the reasons I'd hoped for.

I turned on the shower and let the water heat up. As I stepped in, my muscles uncoiled. It was official: showers had healing powers. I felt calmer and less down on myself, like I'd scrubbed all the negativity away and let it wash down the drain. I watched it circle around the gaping open mouth of the drain as it quickly plummeted down the pipe, through the sewers, on a journey to be cleansed and become positive for someone else.

Logan was sitting outside my door, like he said he would be, when I got back.

"Let me get changed, and I'll let you in," I said. I tightened the knot on my towel so it wouldn't fall.

Walking into my room, I dropped my shower caddy in its spot and let the towel drop to the floor. I grabbed a bra and underwear, not sure about what I wanted to put on. I wasn't feeling like wearing comfy pjs or a dress. I wanted a cross between casual and presentational. I threw on a pair of ripped jean shorts and a long-sleeved button-down shirt with blue stripes. It was light enough for the hot night we were supposed to be having and cool enough to keep me from sweating. My curly, wet hair was going to do its own thing, and I had a hair tie on my wrist in case it got too unruly. Taking one last look in the mirror, I opened my door for Logan to come in. Surprisingly, Mat and Franny were standing next to him.

"Hi," I said brightly.

"Hey," Franny said. "A bunch of us got a reprieve to take the night off, so we're going swimming. You two want to come?"

"Norah approved this?" Logan asked skeptically.

Mat nodded. "Yeah, it happens on occasion."

"I'm in. Let me grab my stuff," I said, turning back around. I grabbed a towel and a new swimsuit that was still sporting the tags, then shoved them into a tote bag. "Ready!"

Logan frowned. "Hold on, Bridget."

He stepped into my room and closed the door before whispering, "Do you think this is a good idea?"

"Yes. I can defend myself if any big bad comes."

His frown deepened.

"I need this," I added.

"I should come."

"Not this time."

His eyes widened in surprise. "Why not? You know, I'm your Protector."

I patted his arm. "Girls' night. No boys allowed."

Not looking away from me, Logan called over his shoulder to Mat and Franny. "Will Oliver be going?"

Franny responded without waiting, like she knew the question was coming. "Of course, he's going. Aren't you?"

Logan looked at me expectantly.

"I need this space. Please," I asked. He took a beat and moved aside. I gave him a thankful smile and headed out.

"Where's the pool?" I asked as the three of us joined Oliver and Ginger at the bottom of the stairs.

"Just on the other side of the village. It's a small hike to get there since we're walking the whole way," Ginger answered.

"Even better, we have until twenty-two hundred to get back," Oliver added, doing a shimmy with his hips and shoulders.

Ten o'clock. I wasn't used to military time, but it was becoming easier to convert since staying here.

Our little group walked out the front door, following some other groups all carrying towels and wearing sandals. It seemed only the older students were able to go out. I barely saw any first-years (besides me) leaving the school.

I heard a laugh up ahead and saw Rose with the rest of the Protectors (sans Logan) walking in the same direction as the rest of the group. I groaned internally. I knew we both went here, but couldn't I escape her for one night? I already felt the hackles raising on my neck.

"Mat," I said, jogging a little to catch up with her. "We haven't been able to talk recently, and I wanted to get to know more about your god."

She slowed down to my pace and hoisted her towel over her shoulder. "Goddess. Babd was the one who sounded the cry for war. Like a starting pistol at a race."

"Oh. Is that a power we need for our time?"

"Perhaps," Mat shrugged, jostling her towel. "It depends on if Brighde's and Beira's Seekers start another war."

I gulped, knowing that was definitely on the horizon based on my training. "If that happens, what would you do?"

Mat looked at me and grinned. "I can change the tide of the war, allowing the side I'm allied with to win."

My mouth dropped open. "Badass!"

If I wasn't basically a full goddess in my own right, I'd absolutely want to be a descendant of Babd.

"I love it," she replied. "If only they would start a war."

Thankfully, we made it to the pool without anyone starting a fight. Kids stripped off shirts and shorts to dive into the clear, blue water. My group snagged a bunch of chairs with a table and settled in. Franny pulled out five bottles of soda and passed them around. I looked up and was stunned into silence. We were surrounded by beautiful, snow-capped mountains, their tips lost in the clouds above them. Tall evergreen trees from my birthday dream created a barrier between nature and industry. No matter what I saw out here, it was always surreal. A light breeze danced across my face, and I breathed in deeply. Any residual bad feelings I'd had earlier dissipated into the air, and the tension I was carrying in my shoulders relaxed. The sun dipped in the sky, leaving pink and purple swirls mixed with light blues in its wake. I felt at peace for the first time in a week.

"Earth to Bridget?" Ginger asked as she tapped my arm.

"Sorry, the sites are really stunning. What's up?"

"We were going to change and then jump into the pool. Are you coming?"

Four pairs of eyes stared at me.

"Hell, yeah! Let's go." I picked up my bag and headed toward the changing rooms.

I changed into my suit and walked back to the pool in time to hear a splash.

"Cannonball!" Oliver yelled as he jumped into the deep end. Waves rippled away from his body as he landed in the water.

"Six points for the splash, but only two for the waves." Franny gestured around him. "I don't see anyone besides you wet."

I giggled as I sat on the edge with my feet in the water. The sun wasn't much lower than it had been before, but the temperature was dropping. I closed my eyes and felt warmth in my stomach, spreading to my chest, down to my feet, and finally out of my fingertips. When I was done, the air was warmer, and the pool felt more inviting.

I slipped into the water and let it rush over my head. Free falling to the bottom and shooting back up was exhilarating. All my worries and fears drifted away as I floated on my back. Suddenly, water was crashing over me, and I righted myself, coughing.

"Sorry, Bridget," Oliver said, laughing. "I was aiming for Mat, but she moved at the last second."

"Well, you know what they say about payback," I said, grinning. I cupped my hands and sent a push of magic with my wave. Oliver looked up as the wave grew above his head. The Firestarter was soaked. He popped up from the water, laughing.

"I need to learn that trick," he exclaimed, pushing his hair and water off his face.

"I thought you were a Firestarter like Oliver," Mat said, frowning. She swam a little closer to me.

"I have many talents," I replied as I swam away. I ducked under the water and kicked my feet, propelling myself toward the other side of the pool. When I came up for air, I saw I'd swam nearly half the length of the pool. The sun was peeking out from behind the mountains as a dark-blue sky trailed behind, like a blanket covering a sleeping world. I leaned back and stared at the stars for a bit. The water bumped against me as the other kids swam past. I floated in any direction the water took me, and soon enough, I was suspended in one spot. I frowned, wondering what had happened to everyone else. Lifting my head, I didn't see Ginger or Franny. A few kids were in the pool, but nearly everyone else was sitting on the side. I looked to see if Mat or Oliver were at our table, but no one was there. Our stuff was untouched. I even looked for Rose or Natalia. Rose was looking at me with an evil grin. Rolling my eyes, I swam toward my stuff and heard a scream from the pine trees just on the other side of the fence. I jumped out of the pool and ran barefoot toward the noise. Alarms were ringing in my head, warning me of danger.

I scaled the fence without a second thought and jumped over. I didn't have to run far before I met my friends facing off against someone in dark clothes.

It was summer, far too hot for that.

I did a quick check that the Amulet was still hidden in the high neck of the suit as I assessed the situation.

Oliver was standing across from the stranger, a fireball lit in his hand. Mat was lying on her side next to the bad guy. I took in a sharp breath. Was she breathing? I was too far away to tell. Ginger was hidden between two trees, looking down at her hands and mouthing something to herself. I watched as a root poked its tip out of the dirt and snaked toward the stranger. Without blinking, the stranger shot an icicle at the root, chopping it in half. The root stopped moving, as if it were dead. Ginger's nostrils flared, and she repeated the process. Oliver was shooting flames at the person but was being deflected by a thick shield of ice. I scanned the area but didn't see Franny. I stepped out from the shadows and got between Oliver and the stranger.

"Oh, here you are," the man snarled at me. He didn't seem extremely tall, but he was positioning himself into a fighting stance, lowering his body. The black T-shirt and dark jeans did very little to hide his muscles, and for a second, I doubted myself.

"I'm new to this. Are we having witty banter before I kick your ass?" I twitched my eyebrows, teasing him. Brighde's birthday energy was sending little shocks throughout my body, building up for something good. I was really hoping it was the lightning again, but I wasn't in control enough to know.

He growled and shot an arrow of ice at me. I lifted my hand, and a sunbeam poured from my palm. *A sunbeam, really?* The arrow was melted, and a puddle soaked into the dirt. I shrugged. *Whatever worked!* I felt a crackle under my skin, and I knew the lightning was up next. Not waiting for him to attack, I took a step forward and released the energy. Bolts of lightning flew from my hands and hit my target.

His body lifted off the ground as I electrocuted him, ice flying everywhere. Ducking to avoid being hit, I only stopped when he fell from the air and landed on the broken root. Everything was silent. The guy wasn't moving, and I was worried I'd killed him. Stepping carefully in his direction, I saw his chest rising and falling, and relief washed over me.

I turned to face Oliver, but his dark-brown skin was pale, and his eyes were frozen open.

"Oliver!" I breathed. "No!" Ginger got to him first and touched his arm. She jerked back and covered her mouth.

"He's ... frozen."

"Not possible!" I touched his skin, and there was nothing but solid ice. I cried, "Oliver, no. Oliver. Not you."

A wheezing cough came from behind me, and I whipped around to see the evil man who'd frozen my friend starting to stand up, smiling.

"You thought you could win against a disciple of Scotland's most powerful god?" He was now standing straight and outright laughing. "You're what we're told to be afraid of? This little girl with tears in her eyes?"

He doubled over from laughing so hard. Instantly, I saw red. Thunderclouds rolled in above us, darkening the night sky. With them roaring so loudly and deeply, I felt the vibrations in my chest. The unnamed assailant stopped laughing and looked up. I called up the wind to create a tornado. Whipping it around the man, I pulled him further up and into the cone as I had wind currents hold his hands and feet down. We heard nothing but his screams for about a minute, and then everything went silent.

The tornado gently placed his body on the ground and disappeared as quickly as it had formed.

"What did you do?" Ginger asked, frightened.

"What I had to." I focused back on Oliver, my heart breaking all over again.

"Wait, where's the other one?"

"What?"

"There were two of them. Where's Franny?" Ginger desperately started searching the perimeter of the trees, not going far from the rest of us. I encouraged the sun to shine its light brighter, knowing the reflection would bounce off the moon. It was just above us, and we needed more light since our phones were still at the pool.

"Franny!" Ginger called. "Franny!"

My stomach grew sick, and it took all my strength not to cry, to keep it together until this was over. I looked back at Oliver and gently touched his face.

"I'm sorry. I'm so sorry," I whispered. His eyes were still frozen open, his skin still blue.

"I'm going to fix this. I can fix this," I said, remembering my training with Eden. I placed my hand on his chest and willed my warmth to penetrate his body. My hands burned brightly, but it was no use. The ice was too thick to melt. I tried again and again.

"No, this has to work. Come on, work!" I cried. I was anxiously shaking my leg, helpless and powerless.

"Bridget, I can't find Franny," Ginger said, hurrying back to me. "And Mat is still knocked out from an ice blast."

"Well, I can't save Oliver," I said, the last of my resolve breaking. I knelt, sobbing at the loss of my two friends.

I failed. I couldn't save Franny, and I couldn't heal Oliver. What use would I be against Deidra and whatever she threw at me?

CHAPTER
❧ 16 ❧

"**B**ridget?" Ginger asked, pointing behind me. I spun to see an unmovable Oliver, but nothing appeared to have changed.

"His eyes," Ginger said. I looked into his eyes and noticed tears sliding down his cheek and freezing.

Hope burst in my chest, and I placed both my hands over his heart. "Come on, Oliver. Don't let go!"

The healing lit my palms, and a golden red pulsed through. I gritted my teeth and focused all the renewed energy into his body. The ice was thawing slowly, but it was better than not at all. I separated my hands and placed each of them on his face.

"I will melt you," I promised him. Finally, the ice above his eyes dripped and broke, and Oliver closed his eyelids. I moved my hands to his fingers, then his elbows, then his shoulders. With each part that thawed, Oliver was able to move it stiffly. I worked my way around his body, thawing every frozen part. When I finished with his left foot, Oliver collapsed before we could catch him, his right foot still frozen.

I hugged him fiercely, willing my body heat to keep him warm. I never wanted any of my friends to go through this again.

"Where's Mat?" Oliver asked, his voice gravelly.

"She's breathing, but unconscious," Ginger answered, rubbing Oliver's arms to help restore blood flow. Once I focused on melting his right foot, Oliver was freed. Suddenly, a gray wolf slinked out of the forest and curled against Oliver's limp body. It looked content as Ginger stroked its fur and whispered something in its ear.

"They're helping me keep him warm," she told me as another wolf trotted over to her and sat on Oliver's legs.

I nodded.

Knowing Oliver was taken care of by Ginger, I skirted past the stranger to go help Mat. She was breathing fine but still out cold. I tried to heal what I could, but I was exhausted from Oliver, so there wasn't much more I could do. I slid my arms under her armpits and dragged her to Ginger and Oliver. If she woke up, I didn't want her to be alone. Summoning any remaining energy I had, I walked over to the stranger.

He wasn't breathing, and his skin was a sickly blue. Swallowing back bile, I checked his pulse on his wrist. Nothing. I checked it on his neck.

He was dead.

I sat back hard in the dirt. This man had lost his life because of me. Something I'd done had killed him. I'd done it out of anger and revenge, not self-defense. Cold guilt mixed with dread washed over me like an ice bath, and I remembered I was barefoot and wearing nothing but a bathing suit. My stomach heaved from everything I was feeling, and I vomited bile next to me. Closing my eyes, I tried to soothe my body and calm down, but when I opened my eyes and saw the man I'd killed, I threw up again.

I had to get up and walk away. I had to move, but I couldn't. I was stuck there, numb. All I could do was stare at him.

The moon was still bright, casting its light upon us, and I noticed a marking on the guy's wrist. Wiping my hands on my bathing suit first, I took a gulp and flipped his wrist over. It was a tattoo of the Amulet. Both halves, together.

"How could you be so reckless?" Norah yelled at me and Logan while she paced behind her desk. I'd discovered the unnamed man I'd killed had a tattoo of the very Amulet we were all hoping to find. Logan, Eden, Zachary, and Norah came charging into the woods to find us when we'd missed curfew.

Both Mat and Oliver were at the hospital under the watchful eyes of Eden and Zachary while Ginger was safely tucked into bed with some lavender oil and chamomile tea to help her sleep. It was a long two hours before she was able to calm down enough to close her eyes.

No one could blame her. She had watched one friend almost die, one be kidnapped, and one murder a man.

"How was I being reckless?" I challenged. "I didn't walk around flaunting my powers! I was trying to save my friends."

"Leaving without Logan? Franny is missing, Mat and Oliver were both injured." Her voice deepened as she stopped pacing and faced us. "A man is dead. Would you like me to continue?" Norah raised a gray eyebrow, throwing a challenge of her own.

"I heard a scream and saw my friends being attacked. What was I to do? Stand there and let them all get hurt?"

"Of course, not."

"Then tell me what you would've done in the moment."

Norah pressed her lips into a firm line. I shook my head.

"You can't. You would've done the same thing." I sat back in the chair and folded my arms over my chest. I noticed Logan was being extremely quiet. Looking over at him, I saw his eyes were glued to Norah. He was sitting ramrod straight, and he never moved a muscle. I wasn't sure he was even breathing.

"Taking a life, especially out of rage, is never the answer."

I shut down. I could still hear his malicious laughter as Oliver stood frozen, mocking me and my powers. I hadn't intended to kill him, but right now, I couldn't say I was sorry he was gone.

"Logan, do you have anything to say?" Norah asked more calmly than she had been towards me.

He finally blinked and said, "This is my fault. I shouldn't have let Bridget go without me."

I stared at him. I wasn't a puppy needing house training. I didn't need a babysitter.

"What are we going to do about Franny?" I interjected.

"Based on what we know, this was very clearly an attack from Deidra. I will speak with Eden, and we will do what we can to find her."

"That's it? Deidra's been rallying troops to fight me while simultaneously hunting for the Amulet, and all we have is me, you, and Eden? Where's my army?"

Norah gave me a sharp look. "There are much bigger things at work here, Bridget. Trust me when I tell you that we will find her."

That feeling of hopelessness was creeping back in, and I was still dealing with the adrenaline crash from saving Oliver. I'd had little time to recover, but I was ready to get back out there.

"We will continue this debrief in the morning. Afterward, you will get back to your studies and your training. Both of you are dismissed for the evening."

We stood without another word and left her office.

"Why were you a zombie in there?" I hissed at Logan as Norah's office door closed.

"You shouldn't have gone by yourself." He headed toward the steps without stopping.

"Hey!" I grabbed his shirt. "I'm not six. I made the choice to leave and the choice to intervene. *This is not your fault.*"

Logan turned to face me. "I am your Protector. My job is to keep you safe until you're ready. Tonight proved that you're not."

Not saying another word, he trudged up the stairs, leaving me alone.

"Wow, you look like you had a rough night," Rose said as I was brushing my teeth in the restroom. I spit out foam and looked at her in the mirror.

"Go away. I am not in the mood." I continued brushing.

She tsked. "From what I hear, you never are."

I finished brushing my teeth, rinsed my mouth, and put my things away. Turning around, I was face-to-face with Rose. My patience was at an all-time low after Norah and Logan.

Tendrils of lightning snaked from my fingertips, and I wrapped them around Rose's arms, pinning them to her sides. I closed my fist, pulling them tight. Her eyes went wide as she struggled to get free.

"Tell your boyfriend I'm coming for him." I released her and walked out, leaving Rose's cough echoing off the restroom tiles.

At the rate my anger was growing, I was going to need to do something to expel the burning underneath my skin. My thoughts flashed back to Rose, but I wasn't worried she'd tell. If she did, she'd have to admit her involvement with Trip and Beira's side. While the Academy was home to all the gods' descendants, Norah wouldn't like Rose sticking her nose into this fight.

My electricity snaked its way down my arm, pooling in my hands as it crackled. I looked at my window, the darkness suddenly inviting. If I left now, I could try to find Franny and maybe get Norah off my back. At the very least, I could release the building pressure. Storming to my window, I threw it open and yanked out the screen. I leaned over the sill and deeply breathed in the night air. It tasted sweet and like freedom, the dark whispering for me to come outside. Feeling invigorated, I called upon the wind to collect me from my window. Swinging my legs over the sill, the wind cradled me as I floated gently to the ground. I looked up at my window, the only one lit in the sea of dark rooms, and grinned. Turning on my heel, I ran toward the whispers, the shadows created by a glowing moon. Breaking through the tree line, I followed the path that led me to Trip before. Maybe it would lead me to him again.

The only sounds I heard were my heartbeat and my feet pounding in time. Panting, I pushed myself further into the brush, jumping over fallen logs and ducking underneath hanging branches. Nothing and no one could stop me now.

Pushing up my left arm, I let the lightning inside burst out of me, directing through the tree limbs and exploding in the sky among the stars. Slowing down, I grinned and let another bolt fly through the air. Who cares if anyone sees me? They already knew where I was. I clasped my hands together and spun in a circle, watching the lightning dance to the rhythm I set. When that no longer entertained me, I called upon the rain to soak the land around me. The cloud was gray in the filtered moonlight as it floated past me and sprinkled water on the trees and plants. The gentle rain became harder, and the muffled sound of rain against dirt turned into the wet sound of water slapping against mud. When I felt everything was fully saturated and my powers seemed satiated by my outburst, I sent the rain cloud away and stood in the darkness of the forest. My ears strained to hear the sounds, but the forest was silent, barring my own breathing. The Amulet warmed against my skin, and I took that as a sign to run. I launched my body forward, back toward the school. Jumping over debris and dodging branches, I felt the Amulet burn, and I knew I was no longer alone. Calling upon the wind again, I formed it into a wide tornado, allowing it to scoop me up.

"We'll find you again," a darkly sinister voice chuckled in my ear. I whipped my body around but saw nothing but clouds. Chilled to the bone, I urged the tornado faster until we reached the tree line by the school.

"Don't leave yet," a softer, higher voice behind me called. "We want to play."

I threw a blast of lightning bolts behind me, hoping it would delay or stop whoever that was. The tornado crossed the length of the field in minutes as I zeroed in on my open window.

"Goodbye," the first voice whispered behind me. I had the tornado dump me into my room and immediately sent a web of lightning to cover the window as I rushed to get the screen back in place. Electrifying the netting, I clicked the screen into the window and slammed the glass shut. I backed away from it, then pressed my body against my door. I wasn't afraid of the dark, but that night, any sleep I got was with the lights on.

Lugh and I traveled the path to the Otherworld, though we weren't properly invited. The murky mist swirled around us, and soon, we were in bright sunshine with a colorful rainbow overhead.

"He really is one for the drama, isn't he?" Lugh said as we walked past happy souls up to the castle where our cousin resided. "I'm the Sun God, and even I think it's too bright here."

The trees lining the road were bright green, glowing like the sun had bestowed a kiss on each leaf. Birds perching on their branches chirped a cheery song. All were in harmony with one another.

"It's better than the alternative," I replied, thinking of the desolate weather we'd left behind. Arwan was waiting for us at the top of the castle steps.

"Cousins!" he excitedly exclaimed. "I was so happy to hear of your arrival. Please do come in."

He turned and walked inside, his robe twirling at his feet. Lugh and I exchanged a look, following our host inside.

"Please forgive the mess. I'm redecorating," Arwan said as he sat on a large throne. Rolls of fabric were draped everywhere, shades of sunny yellows, happy blues, and cherry reds. Wood piles were stacked in the corner, and chairs were stacked up the wall. I ignored it all.

"Cousin, you know that my Amulet has disappeared," I started.

"Must we dispense with the niceties?" he asked, hurt. "No 'How are you, Arwan?'"

"Yes, forgive us," Lugh injected. "How are you, cousin? Is my grandfather around?"

"Balor? He's around here somewhere." Arwan smiled and leaned toward Lugh. "He's deeply unsettled as he has no one here to torture. I won't allow it."

"You are truly benevolent, cousin," Lugh replied smoothly.

"Cousin," I said drawing Arwan's attention. "My Amulet?"

"Yes, yes. Beira lost her half and you yours. I heard all about it. Horrible, just dreadful." He pouted to show

how sorry he was about the loss. I resisted raising my eyebrow at his lack of true compassion.

"We are here to seek your advice," Lugh explained, "about the farmer you keep under your protection?"

"Oh, yes, yes, he is such a lovely little human. You know, he made a deal with me many, many years ago to tend my gardens and take care of my flock if I let him live a little longer to see his daughter marry. He was extremely sick, you know."

"How long ago was this deal made?" Lugh asked.

"Let's see now... about thirteen years."

"Surely, his daughter has been married by now," I said in a huff.

"Oh, yes, yes, she has been married, but he had asked if he could see his granddaughter marry. She was just a wee little one when the second deal was struck."

"What did he offer in return?" Lugh asked, taking the bait. I wanted to kick my brother to stop him from distracting Arwan, but I couldn't do it without being obvious.

"You mean, along with his undying loyalty? Why, to stay here and take care of my vineyard." Arwan gestured to a pasture outside the window, which had rows and rows of vines growing waywardly.

"It seems that his time in the Otherworld will be well spent," I said, trying to take back the conversation. "What will happen with his worldly possessions once he has crossed over?"

Arwan waved his hand. "That is not of my concern. His descendants can squabble over the remains."

The delay was grating on my nerves. "Arwan, there have been words spoken in hushed tones that your farmer has my Amulet."

"Who has spun such lies?" he snapped angrily, pounding his fist on the arm of the throne.

"Lies? Are you to tell me he doesn't have my Amulet?"

"Yes, that is exactly what I'm saying." He sat back in his chair and crossed his legs.

Anger rippled in my chest. A wasted journey. More wasted time. Beira must know where her half is now, while I'm here placating a fool.

"Cousin," Lugh cut in. "May we check in on your farmer for you? To see if his granddaughter is ready to marry?"

Arwan stroked his chin, clearly deciding if he would spill the secret of the farmer's name.

"Fine, but one of you must return here and confirm your findings. I am too busy myself with renovations to check on him."

I prayed it wouldn't be me.

"Absolutely, cousin. It would be my honor," Lugh bowed deeply, and it was all I could do to stop my eyes from rolling.

Arwan floated down from his throne, a scrap of paper in his hand. "You'll find his location here." I reached out my hand to receive the scrap, but at the last moment, he pulled his hand away.

"I want no harm to come to him," Arwan said to me.

"I think you're confusing me with my sister," I replied. He gave me a little smirk and handed over the paper. I unfolded it and read the location out loud: Alba.

I didn't want to get up that morning. Still freaked out from the night before, I tried to shake the creepy feeling that skittered down my back. I sat up and swung my legs over the bed as the dream and the whole of yesterday came rushing back to me.

While the dream was telling—it was the break I'd been hoping for in my search for the Amulet half—I wasn't looking forward to facing the day. My friends wouldn't be at breakfast. Logan was mad at me, himself, or both. I was sure Rose had told Norah about what I'd done to her, but I didn't care. Nothing was as bad as the crushing guilt sitting in my chest from losing Franny and killing that man.

I knew I'd only been protecting my friends. Without me, Oliver and Mat would have died. Ginger could have been hurt. Who knew what else could have happened? Focusing on the images of my friends being hurt gave me feelings of fiery rage again, similar to last night. The lightning pulsed under my skin. Beira's side didn't value human life as much as I did.

And yet, Franny was still missing. I sighed, the vengeance melting away as quickly as it had come on.

I had still killed someone.

The nameless man who probably had a family waiting for him to get home.

A home he would never see again with a family he would never hug again.

The guilt radiated in my eyes and poured out as tears. I threw my arm over my face and let the tears fall. I'd killed him. Crying eased some of the pain, but it didn't hide the one truth I had to admit: I'd most likely have to kill again.

I swallowed that thought down, hoping my stomach acid would break it down, digest it, and eliminate it from my body. I rubbed the Amulet half around my neck, hoping for some comfort, instead feeling nothing but cool stone.

My room was dark as the sun refused to shine through my window. *I deserved this*, I thought as I eventually dragged my butt out of bed. I put on black leggings, a dark-gray shirt, and black, slip-on sneakers.

Wind whipped outside the dining room windows, throwing leaves, branches, and whatever else was in its path. Rain splashed against the rooftop, pounding to be let in.

I nibbled on my roll and jam as I climbed back up the stairs, then heard a mild explosion from one of the science labs. The door squeaked as it swung open, and stinky black smoke filtered out. Coughing students and a teacher left the room, probably searching for fresh air.

"Ahem," a sharp voice said from behind me. I turned to face Eden, who looked exhausted after a long night of watching over Oliver and Mat.

"Morning," I said once I'd finished my bite.

"We will be training outside today."

I frowned and looked past her toward the door, shadows of last night dancing in my brain. Should I tell her and risk getting into trouble?

"Yes, I know it's miserable out there, but this is your doing, and you need to fix it." I sagged at the light chastising. I definitely couldn't tell her. It was one thing to hear it from Norah, but disappointing Eden was more than I was willing to bear.

"Get changed, and I'll meet you in the courtyard in ten minutes." She turned on her heel and headed toward her dorm.

I should have stayed in bed.

"Again," Eden called into the wind. It was so loud, like a high-speed train rushing all around us. My back was to her as I faced the rainstorm head-on. I closed my eyes and tried to focus, calling for the wind to calm and the rain to slow its descent. My dark mood only proved to be unmovable as the storm raged on. A tree was ripped from the soft earth and carried down the field, out of sight. Distressed, I hoped I didn't kill another person when that tree landed.

"Focus!" a voice came from behind me. Shaking my head to shake off my blues, I stood firmly against the funnel beginning to build.

"Bridget, control your emotions! You must, or the whole school will be destroyed!" Guilt oozed from my pores, mixing with the water droplets sinking into my shirt. The rain slowed, but the earth started to shake. That sinking feeling in my gut sank like a stone as the ground split under my feet.

"No!" I cried, desperately calling on the wind to come carry me away. A light puff pushed me aside as the gaping hole yawned, asking for someone to feed it.

Eden grabbed my arm and pulled me away from my mess.

"I know you're upset about what happened," she yelled. "But you have to let that go! I know you were only trying to protect your friends."

"I almost killed them!" I shouted back. I crossed my arms over my chest and looked away. My shameful fog started to make an appearance, and I was descending fast into a darker mood.

Eden took a step forward and wrapped her arms around me. "But you didn't. You did what you needed to do to keep them safe. You saved them."

I pushed her away. "I lost Franny. I almost lost Oliver." Rain poured over us. "I killed someone."

Eden just watched me, letting me get it out.

"How do I keep doing this? How can I face anyone after what I did?" Falling to my knees, I hung my head and sobbed. My spirit was so broken, and I didn't know how to stop the spiral of shame and misery.

With two squishy steps, Eden knelt in the mud with me, sealing me in a hug again. This time, I hugged her back and buried my face into her shoulder. The tears flowed out of me, and the harder I cried, the softer the rain became. Finally, the wind calmed until it was a gentle breeze, and a twilight sun popped up, as if it wasn't fully ready to come visit. Eden held me until I was quiet, and the turbulent weather around us was gone.

"I know you didn't mean for any of it to happen," she said softly. "This, unfortunately, is the price of war."

A sobering feeling grew from my chest and blossomed like a vine all down my body.

"I'll never be okay with killing someone," I said quietly, drying my eyes with the palms of my hands.

"Good. No one should be" was the reply.

When we headed back inside, Zachary was standing at the stairs, looking like he was waiting for us.

"I wanted to give you an update," he said to Eden, eyeing me carefully. "The students who were injured are recovering nicely from their injuries. Mat will be released tomorrow to come home."

I sighed, not realizing I was holding my breath.

"That's excellent news," Eden replied, then turned to me. "I know you have met, but have you been properly introduced to Coach Zachary?"

I shook my head.

"Allow me. Coach Zachary's in charge of the Protectors, making sure they are ready for service. He's trained some of the best Protectors the past Seekers have had."

"Nice to meet you," I lightly smiled. He looked at me, wearing dark circles under his eyes and a slight grimace. I wasn't sure if that was for last night or because I looked like a soaked raccoon who'd lost a fight with a honey badger. Honestly, it could have been either option.

"You, too." He looked back at Eden. "I've updated Norah with this information. If you'll excuse me, I have training to attend to." Without waiting for a response, he walked away, his posture reminiscent of a military man.

Yeah, I absolutely felt off about him. And something in my brain told me the feeling was mutual.

CHAPTER 17

"Spin kick, punch, elbow!" Logan yelled at me again. He had me running these sets until my body could do each move from muscle memory. After my morning the day before with Eden, I was spent. I'd had to rely on my muscles remembering these moves.

"Again!" The lighthearted Logan, who had taught me these moves, had left the building. I wasn't the only one who had changed after that night. There was still no word on Franny, and I hadn't been able to see Mat or Oliver since the pool. I blamed myself for it all, so I could only imagine how hard Logan was being on himself.

"Again!" I pushed myself to repeat the movements and fought against the fatigue crawling up my body. Logan watched me, pacing, never once breaking his stare.

"Are you getting tired?" he asked. It was the first thing he had said to me today, outside of yelling "again" and barking orders.

I put my arms down and nodded. "Yes. You know how it's been. I'm exhausted."

"Do you think they're tired? Deidra is probably planning her next attack without even thinking of stopping. What's on your mind?"

He met my eyes for the first time in what felt like forever. I frowned and took a shuddering breath in.

"I'm hoping Mat is okay, I hope Oliver forgives me, I want to go find Franny, I want to find the Amulet, and I want everyone I care about to be safe."

Logan's posture softened. "Then don't stop. Fight through the tired. You have to defeat her so no one will ever have to worry." He nodded. "Again."

I took up my stance and silently prayed to Brighde for some support.

The next morning, I went about my day, trying to avoid as many people as I could. I didn't have the energy to keep my head up, knowing people were still upset with me. I almost made it until a soft knock came from the other side of my bedroom door a few minutes before dinner was served. I opened it to find Ginger standing outside. She didn't look her best. Her blonde hair was uncombed, and she had purple smudges under her red and puffy eyes. She pulled her rumpled shirt down.

"Can I come in?" she asked wearily.

I nodded and stepped back. She walked past me as I closed the door, and I heard the bed squeak as she sat.

"I know you're not a Firestarter," she said quietly, looking at my floor.

I didn't know what to say, but I was so tired of lying to people.

Ginger looked me in the eyes. "You're the Cuardaitheoir, aren't you?"

I slowly nodded. She blinked at me and sighed. "I figured when I saw you save Oliver and call up the wind to—" she said, but her voice caught.

"I'd ask if you're okay, but ... I probably could guess," I said. The bed sank under my body weight as I sat next to her.

"I've never been so scared," she whispered.

"Me either."

Ginger laid her head on my shoulder, and I wrapped my arm around her. We stayed like that way past lights out.

I opened my blinds after a restless night and looked out. It wasn't sunny, but the air felt sharp, like just before the leaves turned and fell off the trees back home. I furrowed my brow. It was July, not autumn.

Breakfast was a quick affair. Ginger wasn't in the dining room, and I wasn't interested in discussing how I'd nearly killed my friend with anyone. I grabbed some coffee and a roll and headed to meet Eden.

"Morning," I said, sipping the sweet nectar in my cup.

"Good morning," Eden replied. "Finish your breakfast and get ready. We need to hasten your learning now that things have escalated."

I stuffed the last bit of bread into my mouth and placed my cup down.

"Ready," I mumbled through the bite.

She leveled me with a look. I swallowed and stood at attention.

Eden shook her head. "As you know, you have your second test of powers ahead of you. Normally, there is a longer period between the tests, but we just don't have that kind of time anymore."

I took a deep breath, readying myself for the battle ahead.

"You will be tested on your Brighde powers: fertility, healing, and of course, weather." She paused, as if waiting for a reaction from me. When I didn't reply, she said, "If you're ready, we'll start with healing. Come with me."

We walked out of the building and started down the pathway that led to town. I was enjoying the cooler temperatures even though it was meant to be summer. My sweatshirt wasn't thick enough, and though I had a shirt underneath, I still shivered slightly from the chill.

"Eden, I remember Norah telling me the Academy existed before the town was here. How did that happen?"

"Well," Eden began, "A descendant named Cana Cludhmor, the goddess of music, dreams, and the harp, wanted to start a music school for others. He wandered the lands until he found this unknown piece of land and built it here. Once the relatives of the other gods' descendants saw what he had started, they wanted to start schools in their god's honor."

"So, how did they all end up here?"

She gave me a knowing smile. "Of course, when they all came to study and see how his school was faring, they loved the location and landscape and convinced him to let them send their disciples here."

"Hence the name Danann Academy." As we reached the outskirts of the town center, Eden headed left. We passed houses with tulips lining their windows and gingerbread-colored buildings with white edging. I felt like I was in a snow globe scene, minus the snow.

"Yes," Eden nodded. "The Children of Danu, and their future kin, have always had a place here, even if we didn't always call it the Academy. That name has been updated to match changes in the early twentieth century."

"Are there books on this in the library? You know, in case I can read for fun again?" I joked.

"I'm sure there are a few volumes you could look at."

We stopped at an unbecoming structure. It looked like a family home more than an animal hospital, which was what the blue sign said.

"I'm guessing I'm saving sick animals?" I asked, taking in the run-down building.

Eden smiled. "Yes, animals with little chance of survival. It's time-sensitive, so we must hurry."

"I thought I was keeping my abilities a secret?" We entered the front door and walked into a waiting room full of animals, from farm-style to the typical house pet.

"Norah set this up, so the only person here is the doctor, Aarti Gupta. She is also a descendant of Dil and is very knowledgeable about animals."

"Unfortunately, even my skills are sometimes limited. Hi, I'm Dr. Gupta." A tall woman with light-mahogany skin and long, curly, onyx hair pulled into a ponytail smiled at me as she tucked her hands into the pockets of her lab coat.

"Nice to meet you," I replied, smiling. Something about Dr. Gupta made me feel at ease, which made sense, with all the patients she had.

"Norah explained that you're exhibiting healing powers and that you'd like to explore that more." She gestured with her hand to the room full of animals. "All of these animals have life-or-death injuries, but don't worry. They came in today, so there is still time to save them."

She walked over to a pig on the floor with a large gash on its side.

"This pig, Heinrich, was accidentally cut with a piece of farm equipment. His breathing is shallow, and though I stopped the bleeding, there are internal injuries that can lead to hemorrhaging."

I didn't wait for any other information. Rushing over, I dropped down and placed my hands over his body. Focusing the energy to my palms, my hands glowed that familiar healing red, and I felt the damage done internally.

"You'll be okay, Heinrich," I whispered. Slowly, the punctured lung was healing, tube by tube, until it was able to fully inflate. Fusing the blood vessels stopped the bleeding as torn muscles and ligaments under the skin reformed, like brand new. I saw the new lung fully inflate as the pig took a deep breath. I left my hands over the skin, watching as it stitched itself in a straight line and smooth out, leaving no trace of a scar.

I sat back on my heels and gave Heinrich a gentle pat on the head. He lifted his head, snorted at me, and lay back down.

"Very well done, Bridget," Dr. Gupta said. She examined the pig and gave me a thumbs-up. "He looks good. Polly, here," she pointed to another pig, "is experiencing Brachyspira hyodysenteriae."

"Which is...?"

"Swine dysentery."

"Poor Polly." I placed my healing hands over her lower abdomen and got to work. I didn't have to work as hard as I had with Heinrich; Polly was suffering from dehydration.

"Has she been eating?" Polly looked extremely underweight to me.

"No."

Polly's body responded faster to my healing than Heinrich's had. She was up on her feet in no time, snuffling around and smelling the floor.

Dr. Gupta didn't praise me this time, but she moved onto the next animal, a cat.

"This little one is suspected to have rabies."

I gulped. Rabies wasn't curable after about forty-eight hours, even if caught in time. Would I be able to stop a disease like this?

The tawny-brown cat was shaking and swiping at me as it cowered in a corner under a chair. I peeked my head down, so it could see my face.

"Hi, kitty." I didn't want to put my hands under there while claws were coming at me. How close would I need to get to heal it?

I lay on my stomach and stuck my arms under the chair, not close to the cat. Another swipe told me to keep my distance. Letting my red glow do its thing, I pushed the light toward the animal, hoping it would calm down.

The people behind me were silent as the animals groaned or cried in pain. My heart was breaking for them, and I vowed to heal all as soon as I figured out the problem in front of me. The cat hissed at me and swiped again, proving that I needed to be closer. Reminding myself I could heal, I crawled back out and took off my sweatshirt. Wrapping it around my hands, I got back underneath the chair and hoped the cat wouldn't launch itself at my head. Inching forward, I was able to reach the cat without any attacks. Though it was still shaking, it stopped swiping and sniffed me. Placing my hands on its furry body, I willed the red light to push past the cloth and into its body. I watched as the cat stopped shaking and slowly started behaving. After what felt like forever, it purred and stepped over my arms to my face, where it proceeded to lick me.

I breathed a sigh of relief and crawled out again from under the chair.

Dr. Gupta's mouth was hanging open as Eden looked full of pride.

"Who's next?" I asked.

The hot shower I took that night after my combat training with Logan was deeply needed. He was still cold toward me, but my session with Eden left me shaken. Seeing all those sick animals broke my heart. I felt gross on the inside, witnessing the broken and bloodied creatures. Maybe after I save the world, I could go around saving the animals. My stomach turned, and I leaned against the cool tile to stop my head from spinning. If all my sessions with Eden were this harrowing, I didn't know what I was going to do.

"Norah?" I knocked on her door and waited outside.

"Come in," a voice from the other side responded. I entered and closed the door behind me.

"You needed to see me?" My hair was still wet from my shower. Logan had been waiting by my door and reported that Norah needed to speak to me before I'd even had the chance to put my shower stuff down.

She sighed and sat at her desk. "I know you've been having a hard time lately," she started.

"That's an understatement," I replied.

She nodded. "Bridget, I'm sorry to say it, but there are pressing issues at hand."

I perched on the edge of the chair across from her desk.

"Eden's teaching today was a necessary, radical lesson. You are to sit for your second test by the end of the week."

"That seems fast. I thought I had another two weeks."

"Under normal situations, you'd have more than two weeks, but honestly, we need you ready more than ever now."

"Why? What's happened?"

Norah opened a drawer and pulled out a piece of folded paper. She unfolded it and handed it to me.

NO ONE BUT THE GUARDANTHEOIR
COMES TO COLLECT THE GIRL.

I didn't even pause.

"When do I leave?" I placed the note back on her desk.

"Bridget, I can't let you go," Norah said gently. "It wouldn't be the best decision right now. I need you out there, looking for the Amulet half. That's why I need you ready."

I shook my head back and forth. "No. If I'm to start implementing my trainings and actually use my powers besides heating up bowls of water or bringing out the sun, then I need to go meet who-ever this is and get Franny."

Norah pursed her lips, remaining silent.

"Do you know where she is?" I prompted. Norah stared at me until she finally sat back in her chair in defeat.

"No, but this letter was delivered this morning by way of the milkman. We'll send one back and see if we can set up a meet."

"Let me know when it's scheduled." I stood to leave.

"Bridget," Norah started, "know that I am not willing to lose her life because you aren't prepared. Until we know when the meet is taking place, you are to be training, studying, and practicing every waking moment. Too much is at risk."

The mystery man's cold, dead body flashed before my eyes. I swallowed.

"I understand."

"Bridget?" I heard Logan's voice outside my room just past curfew. I opened the door and let him in.

"What's up?"

"I ... couldn't sleep," he admitted. "Also, I'm sorry for how I've been acting."

"Yeah, me too." Giving him a soft smile, I sat up by my pillows and pulled the blanket over my legs. Logan sat at the edge of my mattress.

"Penny for your thoughts?" he inquired.

I sighed and covered my eyes with my arm. "Everything is overwhelming me. I feel like I won't be ready in time to pass my test. I won't save Franny and Oliver, and Mat will hate me for not helping them sooner, and Eden is bumming me out with her healing tests."

"Sick animals?"

I sat up quickly. "How did you know?"

He smirked. "I heard about it through the grapevine."

We fell silent as the moments passed. I didn't know what else to say, and he wasn't talking.

"Hey," I nudged his leg with my blanketed foot, "Penny for your thoughts?"

Logan gave me a small smile. "I should've been there."

"Come on. We've been over this."

"I should have been there to help you. Maybe Mat wouldn't be unconscious, and Franny wouldn't have been taken."

"That's not fair. If we head down that path, then we can play the blame game all night. What if I noticed something a little earlier? What if I knew how to throw a shield up? Oliver wouldn't have turned into a human popsicle. What if I was just three seconds sooner, would Franny still be here?"

Logan looked at me, sadness in his eyes.

"I feel stupid and guilty, too. But if we play the hypothetical game, then nothing will change. Yes, Mat and Oliver were hurt, but they are now safe and alive. I have to believe Franny isn't hurt, even if she isn't safe. If I lose hope, then I've lost my friend."

"You're right," he replied. "I wish things were different."

I scooched toward him, wrapped my arms around his arm, and rested my head on his shoulder.

"Me too."

As he leaned back against the wall, I readjusted and snuggled into him, falling asleep.

Sometime in the night, I woke up, and Logan gave me a kiss on the forehead before pulling the blanket up to my chin. Wrapping the memory around me, I fell back asleep. When I woke up the next morning, I was alone in my room.

Frustrated, I slammed my book shut. Eden had given me Tuesday morning off to brush up on *Brighde,* and I was aggravated by the whole ordeal. I was tired mentally and emotionally, stressed out beyond belief. I had no escape. Norah checked in on me whenever she could, like she didn't want me to take a break. If Logan hadn't been here, quizzing me and making me laugh when I needed to, I didn't know what I'd do. For a moment, I wished I didn't have powers and was going to college like everyone else.

I leaned back in my chair and groaned. How selfish was I? Franny's life might depend on me, and I was whining about reading a book. I rolled my shoulders. My muscles felt tight from sitting for so long. I needed a break. Glancing at *Brighde*, I grabbed my phone and dashed out my door.

The hot sunshine felt good against my face. Risking torch burns, I turned my head up and closed my eyes, soaking in the vitamin D.

"Hey, you," Logan said, trotting next to me. "Going anywhere?"

I smiled weakly. I knew my new marching orders had been passed to him, and he was playing nice before I was shipped out. "Nowhere specific. Just needed to get out."

"Care for some company?" He was also probably told not to leave my side.

I shrugged. "Sure."

We walked toward the mountains, heading away from the main town. As we walked farther away from civilization and from Norah, the stress dissipated.

"So, how are things going with Eden and Norah?" Logan asked, breaking the silence.

"Fine, I guess." I paused. "I feel ... more ready than before, but like I'm going to fail," I admitted. "I feel like everyone has pinned their hopes on me to save the world. I feel like no matter how hard I study or train, I'll never match up, even with my full powers."

I stepped over a stump.

"Bridget, you have to give it time," Logan replied. "You know you're smart and that you'll be able to handle whatever Eden and Norah can throw at you, but cut yourself some slack."

"I don't have time!" I exclaimed. "I have my second test on Friday, which I'm anxious for, and I'm a live wire waiting to hear about the meet."

"Still no news?"

I shook my head.

"You're putting too much pressure on yourself," Logan stopped. "What you need is a mental break."

"Where and when can I find one of those?" I asked teasingly. Logan paused for a second.

"Come on," Logan smiled, taking my hand. "I know the perfect place."

I followed him through the brush of the forest, scanning for any shadowy voices that could pop up. I still hadn't learned who or what they were.

"Where are we going?" I asked, snapping a twig under my feet.

"It's a surprise," he said. I heard the smile in his voice.

"What kind of surprise?"

He looked back at me. "The kind that would be ruined if I told you."

I rolled my eyes. I was in no mood for Logan's surprises. Something moved in the bushes, causing me to jump. Logan chuckled.

"Is the big bad Cuardaitheoir scared of a little bunny?"

"You have no idea what was in that bush! It could've been the bunny from Monty Python."

Logan stopped and turned to face me. "Come on, I won't let anything happen to you," he promised. He stepped closer and gently rested his hands on my hips. I flushed slightly, remembering our earlier training sessions when it felt like he was flirting. I was right.

"That's because it's your job to protect me," I said. I felt those butterflies dance in my stomach as I realized what was going to happen.

"That's not the only reason." He moved, shrinking the space between us. Logan bent his face closer to mine, his eyes closed. The heat radiated off his skin as my eyes instinctively shut.

"Wait," I said, putting my hand against his chest. When I opened my eyes, his lips were hovering over mine. I imagined how easy it would be to just move a fraction of an inch and know how he tasted.

"This isn't..." I whispered.

"No?" Logan asked. Pressing my lips together, I shook my head.

"I want to, but not now. Not with everything going on," I explained. He took a step away from me. I felt colder from the loss of his body heat.

"You're right," he said, swallowing, "But aren't you allowed a little fun?"

"I don't do fun like that. I'm not a 'fling' girl."

My whole world had turned on its axis. Logan was trying to kiss me, and I was trying not to feel guilty about enjoying myself while my friend was missing. I wanted to kiss him too, more than I wanted to admit to myself.

Thankfully, Logan had spared me the pain of going on. "I know you were really into Trip, but it's okay to not take things so seriously all the time. Relationships are meant to be fun, even when the world feels like it's ending. Or, at least, they give you a hand to hold as you watch the world burn."

I looked up at him. "That sounds more like a platonic friendship. I mean, I don't have a ton of experience, but I know the person you choose to be with should be supportive and stand with you even when it's not fun. A relationship is more than just fun."

He sighed. "Why must you fight me on everything, MacNamara?"

"I only fight you when you're in need of an education, Carter."

"Oh? You think *you* should school *me*?" he teased, pressing his hand across his chest.

"Yes." I laughed.

He tilted his head back. "You know, this is not how I expected this ... walk ... to turn out."

"Is that because you expected to get lucky?" I asked, crossing my arms.

"I plead the fifth."

I raised an eyebrow. "That doesn't work here like it does at home."

"Rats."

I laughed. "Okay. Lead the way to the special place." I gestured for him to go ahead, leaving my hand in the air. "Maybe your pride will heal by the time we get there."

Logan stuck his tongue at me, turned toward the darkness of the forest, and stepped into it, slipping his hand into mine.

CHAPTER 18

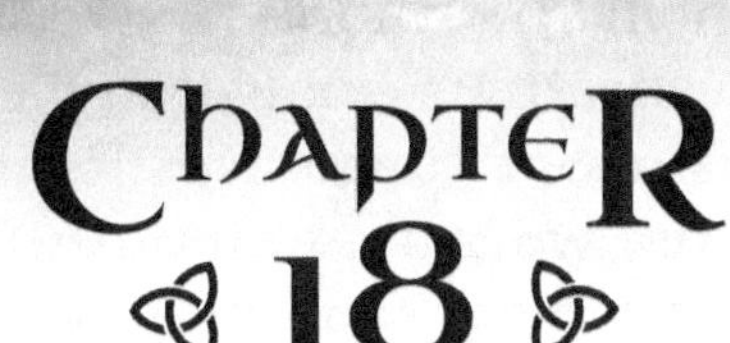

"Where are we going?" I asked, ducking my head under a low branch. The sun was starting its slow descent, so the air was cooler than before. I shivered and wished I had more than a thin, cotton T-shirt covering me.

Logan stopped. "Do you really want to know?"

"How about, 'How much longer until we get there?'" I countered. We'd been hiking for over an hour.

"Almost there," he replied and continued walking.

We climbed over hills and through streams and brush, the failing sunlight filtering through the leaves. My mouth felt sandpapery, and I wished one of us had brought a water bottle.

The sound of rushing water gave me life, and my second wind kicked in as we climbed up tiny, metal staircases. When we got to the top, Logan stopped on the wooden bridge that crossed the water.

"We're here," he announced.

"Where is here?"

"The Choleren Gorge. We can go further up, but since it's nearly dinner, I thought we could stop here before we go back."

I gazed down the ravine, the spray of water coursing underneath us, showcasing greens, blues, and even flashes of turquoise. Rock walls towered around us, worn and smooth to the touch from years of droplets sanding down their sharp edges. Breathing in deep, I smelled wet, musty rock hanging in the air, but it wasn't unpleasant. It was calming. The air was cool and refreshing on this hot day, and I wanted to dangle my legs off the bridge just to feel the breeze from the surge of the water. Standing there was an amazing experience. As I stood with Logan, the frustration and negativity seeping out of me and washing away with the river, I felt calm. Peaceful. I smiled, in spite of myself.

"Logan, this is nice." I leaned against him and let him put his arm around me as we stood, mesmerized by the water flowing under us.

We didn't leave the ravine until the sky turned pink.

As the morning sun streamed through the window, my mind replayed yesterday's events as I lay in bed. Logan liked me. I still felt the whisper of his fingers on my skin, a ghostly imprint of what could have happened. My brain was in such a haze that I could barely handle it. I was used to neat, little boxes, everything compartmentalized and organized in its place. Now some boxes were shifting out of order and morphing into triangles. It was pure chaos in my head, and my heart was suffering because of it.

I had to put it aside. Franny was my priority, as was passing my test in two days. I lay in bed another moment, allowing myself to wallow in the warmth of Logan liking me.

I got up to head to the restroom and nearly tripped on Logan sitting against my door.

"What are you doing?" I asked.

"I was told to sit here," he stood. "Norah is worried something is going to happen to you. Just doing my Protector duties." He yawned.

"Were you here all night?"

He shook his head. "Just before dawn."

I paused. "What happens if I'm attacked in the middle of the night?"

Logan's mouth opened, but no sound came out. I smiled and sauntered past him toward the restroom to get ready for my day.

I whipped my hand up, causing a swirling vortex of air toward the assailant, knocking the knife off its trajectory. A rock flew at my head, so I sent a push of wind at it, collecting it in the gust. I sent it back to Eden and nearly hit her, but she ducked just in time.

"Good!" she exclaimed. It was day three of my training, and my test was less than forty-eight hours away. Today's focus was on my weather powers, which I loved. Healing was just as good, but last week's session was still a shadow in my mind, so I was happy I wouldn't have to work on it today.

Fertility felt like a simple power, but I didn't know how I could use it in battle. It didn't matter at the moment; those were tomorrow's lessons.

Eden set fire to a patch of the woods, and I promptly called upon a quick downpour to douse the flames. Sad my training was causing so much destruction, I looked at the charred woods and scorched brush.

"Don't worry! That's part of your fertility practice," Eden commented as she walked next to me. I summoned the sun back to dry us off and lifted my hair into a bun, securing it with a hair tie.

"Can't wait. What's next?"

"Lightning. I know you've been able to manipulate bolts, so we should see how far you can take them."

I took a deep breath and nodded, focusing my energy on digging for that spark. I felt it ignite in my stomach as I mentally pulled it through my arms and out my fingertips. Lightning zapped out of me as I aimed my bolt to the sky. I didn't want to cause another fire. Trees crackled in the air above us, their branches snapping like fireworks. I closed my fist around the next bolt, crossed my arm over my chest, and whipped it away from me, the tip of the bolt nipping at the leaves of the trees. I was careful not to singe them, as these trees had seen enough today. I calmed the spark inside me, and the lightning died out.

"You're getting better with your powers."

I looked at Eden, feeling tired. "Thanks. I've been practicing."

She looked at her watch and clucked her tongue.

"You need to head to Logan for combat training. We've worked on your weather powers enough. I think you're ready for the test."

"Finally," I said, grabbing my gear. "I'll see you tomorrow."

I walked through the door, getting away from the damage I had just caused. As it shut behind me, I headed to the gym and dumped my things on the floor before starting my workout.

Logan had me review all my learned moves before letting me try out something new. Thankfully, I wasn't being tested on hand-to-hand combat on Friday. I didn't feel ready to be tested on that yet.

"How aware are you of your surroundings?" Logan asked me as I came back from my water break.

"Pretty aware?" I guessed.

"Let's test that. What in this room was moved?"

"Everything moves in this room," I pointed out.

He shook his head. "No, something moved from point A to point B. Yesterday, it was in one place, and today, it's in a new spot."

I scanned the room to see what looked different. The weights were by the mirrors, and the dummies were positioned in the opposite corner of the chest press. The treadmills were where they normally are, and the kettlebell tower was next to them. Except now, it wasn't. It had been moved to the other side of the weights.

"Kettlebells. They moved there," I pointed.

Logan nodded. "That's right. It's important to know who and what is around you at all times. It could be the answer between being attacked or stopping your attacker. Starting now, every day, something is going to be different, and you're going to have to tell me. If you're wrong, you'll have to do three rotations of your basic moves set."

"Seems fair. I'll be ready, Coach," I smiled. I couldn't help but feel lighter around him, especially after our hike yesterday. I bit my lip, thinking about the almost-kiss, and then I shook my head. Now wasn't the time to dwell on that. Franny was my focus.

Eden spent the next lesson trying to get me to understand how my powers of fertility could be used in battle. It wasn't going well, as the weight of my guilt and frustration were simmering right under my skin.

"You could encourage trees to grow and vines to wrap around enemies."

"Still feels like I'm limited, using this power."

Eden rubbed her eyes. "Bridget, work with me. You need to think creatively when it comes to using your powers in the field. You don't know what you'll encounter out there."

"Fine," I replied. "I'll think about it and keep making trees grow."

"The test is tomorrow. You don't have the time to think about it."

I chewed the inside of my lip and looked away.

"Don't think; just do," Eden instructed.

Taking a deep breath, I faced the tree line on the opposite side of the field I'd practiced in. Scanning, I saw a sapling struggling to grow in the shade of the taller surrounding trees. I focused on the little tree, willing the other trees to spread their branches as sunshine went from filtering through to fully immersing the foliage. Drenching the tree in sunlight, I pulled water from the air and circled it around the tree before pouring the liquid on the roots. I kept this pattern going, breaking a sweat from the exertion. The sapling sprouted branch after branch, growing taller until it was the size of its neighbors.

I took a breath and relaxed.

"Not bad," Eden remarked. "Do it again."

Finding another young tree, I repeated my process, this time a little faster. The same thing happened.

"Better. Again."

I did this for another hour before Eden decided I was done.

"Wait a minute, Bridget," she said as I started to leave. "I know you're tired and probably annoyed with me for pushing you so hard today."

I didn't respond, waiting to see where this conversation would go.

"Dangerous times are ahead, and it's my job to make sure you're prepared." She paused and waited for me to reply. I hesitated, unsure of how to say what I wanted to express.

"I know some crazy stuff is going to happen to me and the people I care about out there." Don't think I'm disillusioned to this. It's all anyone talks about." I sighed. "I'm so sick of being reminded every day that if I fail, people die and the world is going to blow up or evaporate, or whatever. Not everything has to be doom and gloom, twenty-four seven. Just ... try to remember, I'm only eighteen. Some lessons can be skipped, even if it's for the greater good."

Feeling unsettled, I was done with the conversation, so I left before Eden could say anything else.

"Not a bad session today," Logan noted as he picked up his water bottle and towel. He taught me a new defense—gouging eyes. If I was in close contact with an assailant, I could wrap my hands around their face just above their ears and push my thumbs into their eyes. Gross, but effective. I was happy that I was able to please one teacher, especially after my conversation with Eden. I rolled out my shoulders, loosening the tightening muscles.

"Thanks. Who would have thought gouging eyes was fun?" Grabbing my towel and bottle, we headed toward the door. The air between us was charged with our unfinished business.

"So—" he started.

"About—" I said at the same time. We both grinned at our fumbled start.

"You first." He gestured, taking a drink of his water.

"I know the other day didn't happen the way you were hoping it would," I started, "but it's important that you know…"

The butterflies were back, and my stomach flipped.

"Know…?" he prompted. I stopped and faced him, allowing the few others in the hall to disperse before I spoke again.

Go for it, I told myself. "I want it to happen, too."

"It…"

I rolled my eyes. "Come on. I know you know. I want to kiss you, too. Even though we established now isn't a good time."

He looked smug. "Oh, yeah?"

"Yes."

The smugness didn't go away.

"Can you not make me feel any more awkward about telling you than I already am?" I hated being this kind of vulnerable.

Logan just smiled and slid his strong hand into mine. "Okay, MacNamara. Let's start off slow."

Logan didn't kiss me that night, which was good because I was trying to ignore the silly smile that wouldn't leave my face as I was climbing into bed. My test was the next morning, and I needed all the sleep I could get if I was going to face whatever challenges that were thrown at me.

I strolled onto the field the next morning, where Eden and Norah were waiting for me.

"Ready?" Eden asked me. Norah said nothing but moved to the side.

"As I'll ever be," I answered.

"You may begin. Show me how you can control the weather."

I cracked my knuckles and shook out my limbs, relieving any tension. First, I summoned rain clouds and tugged on a ribbon of water. It released buckets on us, but it watered the ground as well. Green shoots of various plant life germinated under the wet dirt. I pictured the seeds sprouting tails and willed the sunlight to redirect its shine on the patch of field. While they were doing their thing, wind was up next. Feeling the breeze, I picked at the scab that was starting to heal from almost losing my friends, and I let those feelings flow. Hurt and pain rattled out of me in the form of a tornado twisting around us, climbing higher and higher until the point of the funnel lay at my feet. The cyclone blotted out the sun, spitting water, debris, and dirt at us, getting angrier as the moments went by. Not wanting my plants to suffer, I slowly reined in my feelings until the twister calmed and released the shame of my failure. Fog clung to us like static electricity, sticking to our clothes. I couldn't see my hand in front of my face. I let the fog hang there as I figured out my next step. It dispersed, and I nudged the sun to warm us back up. By now, the plants were growing. Blades of grass, flowers, tree saplings, and prickly bushes bloomed around us. With a light sprinkle of rain, the foliage flourished, completing their grand entrance.

The tree saplings were nearly matured, so I focused my water and sun routine on their roots and wished to see the trees as tall as skyscrapers. Our heads tilted back as we watched the trees shoot up in a ring around us, growing closer together and ultimately providing shaded relief. Now for the big finale. I lifted my face to the sky and called the black clouds of thunder to rest above us. The sudden shift caused the sun to be eclipsed, and nothing but darkness surrounded us. Thunder grumbled above us, the sound growing with each new peal. I felt lightning build in my blood stream, aching to get out. I let the sparks fly from my fingers. A single twitch of my forefinger released a stream of lightning straight into the sky. It cracked above us, signaling my excitement and anger. I wrapped ropes of lightning around the clouds, watching as they closed in on themselves. Grinning, I whipped them around, careful to avoid marking my new trees but narrowly missing the adults. Sobering up slightly, I was cognizant of what the next part of the test was. Pushing the clouds away, I snapped one more bolt of lightning, allowing a branch to crack and fall on my leg. The bone shattered, and I screamed. Taking huge, gulping breaths, I sent those warm, healing thoughts to my leg and waited painfully for the bones to reform under my skin. The sun was peeking around a white, fluffy cloud as the last piece pushed back into place. I bent my knee, testing its flexibility, and stood.

No one said anything for a few minutes. Norah was admiring my fertility work, sniffing the flowers as she ambled from bush to bush.

"You did well," Eden said quietly, "but that wasn't the agreed plan. We know you could heal yourself, but you were to show you could heal someone else."

"I wasn't going to hurt anyone for the sake of a test."

"Even though you're refusing the 'healing others' portion of the test, that still was a very good presentation, Bridget," Norah remarked, essentially ending the conversation. She walked over to me. "It seems your studies have paid off."

"Thank you, Norah," I replied gratefully.

"You passed this test, but there are more to come," she warned. "But that is for tomorrow. Today, you rest, as you've been through enough for now."

She waved us toward the building. "Now, let's get something to eat. I skipped breakfast for this!"

I collapsed onto my bed after lunch with Eden and Norah. If Norah hadn't been feeling chatty, the meal would have been a very silent one. I picked up my cell phone and mindlessly scrolled through my social media. Pictures of my friends' summer vacations filled my feed, and I got another pang of homesickness. It was hard lying to your best friends when all you wanted to do was talk it over with them.

My phone rang, and my mom's number popped up.

"Hi, Mom," I answered, happy to talk to her. I pushed myself up against the pillow and settled in.

"Hi, sweetheart. Did you pass your tests?" I heard her voice getting choked up. "How was it?"

"It was intense, but I'm relieved it's done. I wish I could tell you all about it, but … you know." I picked at a loose thread on the blanket.

"Oh, Bridget, one day" was all she said. I heard a metal clang in the background, and I was immediately back in her kitchen, helping her bake cakes and eating the frosting when she wasn't looking.

"I got your birthday present," I said, changing the subject. "I'll see if I can have it shipped out. I want you to be able to open it on your birthday."

"I can't wait!"

We paused, knowing the real things we wanted to talk about were too dangerous to discuss, just in case someone was listening in.

"I miss you," I said, blinking back tears.

"I miss you, too." Mom sounded as if she was doing the same.

"Tell Dad I love him."

"I will. I love you."

"I love you, too." We hung up as I let the pain of missing them wash over me.

Chapter
19

"This isn't me," I said as Logan and I stepped outside the next morning for our run. Now that my test was over, my days were crammed full of physical activity with Logan, which was no problem for me.

Normally, our workouts and trainings didn't include a dark and cold forecast of snow. I rubbed my hands up and down my arms.

"This doesn't look good," Logan commented, glancing up.

Bleak clouds floated above us, making me wish I was wearing more layers than I had on.

"If I don't find the Amulet soon, who knows how long we'll survive?"

Logan cocked an eyebrow at me. "Depressing much?"

"Did you even really think about what could happen if I don't regulate the seasons? Crops could die out, which could lead to sick animals. Famine could become an even bigger problem, people could get sick, and for all we know, the human race could be wiped out."

I felt the color draining from my face as I thought about what genuinely rested on my shoulders.

"Whoa," Logan stepped toward me and placed his hands on my shoulders. "Breathe. You're putting too much pressure on yourself to solve it all at once. Break it down: First, look for the Amulet. Second, kick Deidra's butt. Third, party because you saved the world."

Smiling, I looked up at him. His eyes were deep and solely focused on me.

"Baby steps. First, find the Amulet," I repeated. "Got it."

He looked as if he was going to kiss me but then thought better of it, which was incredibly disappointing because I wanted to kiss him, too.

The moment passed, and we jogged toward the hiking trail behind the school. My thoughts wandered as we kept pace with each other, our breathing in sync. With every step, my lungs expanded and contracted, keeping in time with my footsteps. I snuck a peek at Logan as he jogged ahead on the trail through the narrow part by the tree lines. The muscles in his shoulder tensed as he lifted them slightly when he ran. His calves flexed as he pushed off the ground, showing me how developed they were.

I flushed as I remembered the dream I'd had about him after our hike to the gorge. I kept replaying the moment in the woods where he'd tried to kiss me. His hands on my body. His warmth radiating off his skin. I wished I'd kissed him then, if only to stop torturing myself for not knowing how it would be.

"Don't check out my butt!" he called back to me. I heard the grin on his face from where I was.

"No promises!" I yelled.

I mean, he *was* right in front of me.

We were engulfed in the forest. It looked weird with the green leaves shadowed in the cloud cover. I was used to bare branches in this weather, not lush grass and rich, peaty dirt. We ran and increased our speed, me following him through the woods, dodging fallen trunks and leaping over stones. Logan made it to a small clearing that was just ahead and jogged in place, waiting for me.

I was breathing heavily by the time I reached the clearing. Cardio still hated me, even though I did it all the time.

"Jog lightly in place, so you can rest your heart for a minute," he instructed. I gave him a thumbs-up and slowed my pace.

"You okay?"

I nodded while taking deep breaths. "I ... still ... hate ... cardio."

"Okay, okay, you can pace," he said, taking my wrist in his hand to check my pulse. I frowned. He'd never done this before.

"I'm still alive," I joked. "Barely."

"I'm checking your resting heart rate. If it's too high, I may have to change up the workout."

I stopped moving. "Hard pass. I don't even like what we do now."

Logan dropped my arm. "Ouch. Tell me how you really feel."

I bit my tongue because I was not ready to tell him how I felt. I guess I'd given something away since his face lit up, and he grinned.

"So, that's how you feel," he stepped closer. Against my better judgment, I pushed him away. Again.

"Stop, I smell, and I'm offending myself."

Logan laughed. "I smell, too."

"Lies. I've smelled you before, and you don't normally smell terrible."

He took a step closer. "Should I be concerned you're walking around smelling me?"

"I don't!" Giggling, I shook my head.

"Do you limit yourself to just my skin, or are you sniffing my clothes, too?"

My mouth dropped open, and I stepped back. "I do not sniff anything of yours!"

He took another step toward me, shrinking the space between us. "My shoes? My body wash?"

"Oh, my Goddess, I hate you," I laughed, moving back again. Unfortunately, my foot landed on a loose rock that was leaning against a tree root. I stumbled back, but Logan grabbed my hand and pulled me against him before I could fall.

"My hero," I said, flushed.

This moment had *kiss* dancing all over it, and I felt myself stretching up to meet him... just as his phone rang.

To both of our chagrin, Logan swiped up to take the call as I adjusted my body, so I wasn't in danger of tripping on something.

"Yeah? Okay. On our way." He hung up.

I looked at him questioningly.

"We have to go. Norah needs us back. Now."

We took off running back to school without another word.

Norah was waiting for us at the front door.

"No time to waste," she announced as we walked inside past her. "The meeting has been set."

My heart dropped, and I whirled around. "When is it?"

"Tomorrow, sundown, at the clearing in woods on the other side of the mountain."

I nodded and moved to head upstairs.

"Bridget," Norah started, "You are not to go alone."

"But the first note said no one else but me," I replied, turning around. "I can't take the chance that something will happen to Franny because I brought along a buddy."

Logan launched into Protector mode by standing at attention, remaining silent, and allowing Norah to respond.

"Foolish girl. How do you know you won't be walking into a trap?"

I blinked. Norah had never called me a name before. I was stunned for a second before I got my wits back.

"I don't, but that's a chance I have to take."

She shook her head repeatedly. "No. Logan will go with you."

"Fine."

"And," she said, "Eden and Zachary will be on lookout close by, just in case."

She waited for me to agree to the terms before saying, "Be happy I'm not sending along more. And above all else, be smart."

Then she turned on her heel and left.

At dinner that night, I stepped into the dining room and looked to see if my friends were around. It had been too long since I'd talked to them, my embarrassment getting the better of me. I didn't even know if they wanted to talk to me. Mat walked past me, heading toward our normal table. I tried to believe she hadn't seen me but found it hard.

"Hi," I said, approaching the table. Mat, Ginger, and Oliver all looked up at me, expressions ranging from nervous, to anxious, to interested.

They exchanged looks before Oliver spoke up. "Hi."

"May I join you?" I rested my hand on the empty chair across from him. Looks were exchanged again before Oliver nodded yes. I sat, extremely uncomfortable. It helped to remind myself they probably felt worse than me.

"So... how've you been?" I asked.

No one spoke right away, everyone shifting in their seats or looking away from me. My stomach dropped, and I wanted to cry.

"I get it. I let you down." I looked Oliver in the eyes. "I never, *ever* meant to hurt you. I'm sorry. That was the worst night, and I didn't help make it better."

I shifted my gaze to Mat. "I'm sorry I didn't get there in time to stop you from getting injured. I thought we were all still in the pool until I turned around and heard someone screaming."

Ginger's eyes were wide as I looked at her. "Thank you. If you weren't there, I don't know if I could've saved Oliver alone." I gulped back the lump in my throat. Tears wouldn't help right now.

"I'm going to save Franny," I said softly to all of them. "Nothing will keep me from bringing her home."

As I stood to leave and pushed in my chair, I heard another one scrape and saw Oliver standing. He walked around the table to face me. I held my breath, waiting for the screaming to start. Instead, he hugged me tightly. I froze, shocked and afraid to move, as if I were going to scare him off. After another two seconds, I embraced him back and squeezed. Two more chairs scraped as more pairs of arms encircled us.

We stayed like that for a minute before Mat and Ginger let go. Oliver released me but kept his hands on my arms.

"I never blamed you," he said gently. My lip quivered as I tried to keep myself together.

"None of us did," Mat said, stepping into my line of sight. Ginger followed, shaking her head to echo what Mat had said.

Mat took my left hand as Ginger took my right. Oliver kept his hands on my arms before saying, "Go bring our friend home."

"I've never been happier to not be alone," I whispered to Logan in the back seat of Norah's car. Eden was driving, and Zachary was in the front seat. His long legs were tucked up to his chin, so I couldn't imagine the ride being comfortable.

Logan slung his arm around my shoulder and pulled me in.

"I wish we *were* alone and weren't driving to this meeting," he whispered into my ear.

"Focus! Tonight is not about rainbows and unicorns," I said.

He chuckled, his breath brushing against my cheek. "I really want to know what runs through your head as you fall asleep if you're dreaming about unicorns and not me."

My stomach flipped as my cheeks burned. I leaned away from him and looked out the window. We were winding down the long hill that led to a road in the peak of the valley. From there, we would cross and drive the car halfway, leaving it at a campsite, before hiking to the clearing. Eden and Coach would scope out the area around the clearing, checking for any threats. Logan was to follow me from a distance and back me up if I needed it. I was hoping I wouldn't.

We killed the car engine, and I began my trek up to the clearing. My powers were tingling under my skin, ready to be there when I called upon them. I scanned the trail the best I could in the dusk light. I didn't want a flashlight because I was afraid it would draw attention. The downside was I didn't have one, so I couldn't see clearly if someone was coming at me. My ears were straining, listening for any unnatural noises in the forest. The only thing I heard was the soft tread of my foot as I walked into the clearing.

No one was there except me. A gentle breeze dragged across my arm, and I jumped, releasing a small arrow of lightning to the forest floor.

I heard a sound from across the way. Applause.

Franny stepped out from behind the tree line, clapping her hands at me and laughing.

I looked around to see if anyone else was there.

"We're alone," she called. "Well, I am, at least. If I know you, Logan is here somewhere."

"You're not a kidnapping victim, are you?" I asked, feeling less blindsided than I should've been.

Franny barked a laugh. "Oh, you are smart. Dee said you were smart, but I didn't believe it. That's twenty francs I owe her now."

"And you're not a Protector?"

She laughed again. "Nope. That was just my cover."

"Go on," I said. "I can wait."

Franny stopped walking, keeping a good distance between us. "Wait for what?"

"This is the part where the minion reveals some big plan or makes a snappy comment about my imminent death." I took a breath. "So go ahead. I can wait. I have all the time in the world."

She grinned, her teeth sparkling. Even in the dim lighting, I saw how clean and cared for she was.

"Oh, Bridget. I'm not going to do any of that."

"No? Then why am I here?" I was biding my time as I observed her, reading her body language. I knew she was sent to kill me, or at least distract me while someone went through my stuff, looking for the Amulet half, which is always around my neck. The Amulet grew hot against my skin, but I ignored it. I didn't want to draw attention to the one thing she was looking for.

"Not to be killed, if that's what you're thinking."

I crossed my arms over my chest and rested my weight on my back foot. "Then what, pray tell, are we doing here in the middle of the woods, wasting my time?"

Franny's smile creeped up her cheeks as she looked down.

"Did I ever tell you what my real powers are?"

The ground beneath me rumbled, as if I were standing in the epicenter of an earthquake. I jumped to the right just as a massive mountain grew out of the dirt, and another one pierced the sky behind me. As I took a step to run, two more mountains pushed up from the ground, enclosing me in a giant circle. I looked up and watched as they kept growing taller.

I was not prepared for this. *Think, think!*

"Hope you're having fun in there," I heard Franny call out from behind one of the mounds.

"The best time! You should join me!" I yelled back.

"Oh, thank you for the invite, but I respectfully decline. I have a date with your Protector. Though I don't know how much longer you can call him that. Au revoir!"

The mountains moved again, resting their points together, covering my obvious exit.

Icicles ran through my veins as blood rushed to my ears. *Logan can protect himself. Stop and think.* Lightning would be useless, as would thunder. Rain would cause a mudslide, which could kill me.

Branches.

I touched the dirt. It was healthy and moist, perfect for growing. Immediately, I called upon water and the sun to help broken roots become whole again. I caught the sun before it set, and I was able to drag sunlight through a tiny crack in the top. The beam shone against the sidewall, and I did everything I could to will those roots to grow.

After a few strenuous minutes, a branch popped out above me, and I jumped to grab it. As I hauled myself up, another grew just above me. I grabbed it and followed the path of branches that led me to the top. When I reached the last one, I dangled, trying to claw my way out. *Stop. Think.*

I could pop the top of the cage off like an exploding soda bottle.

I called upon the gentle breeze and coaxed it into a strong draft. It whipped around and around until it formed a small cyclone. I pushed the cyclone up, allowing it to touch the cover that trapped me inside. The lower branches were sucked up into the twister, along with some loose dirt and rocks. I didn't bother healing whatever cut or bruised me; there would be plenty of time for that later. The dirt above me finally caved in, dropping its bulk into the cyclone. I released the tornado out of the dirt enclosure and let it disperse on the outside. I heard a dull thudding against the outer rim of the mountains from the debris being thrown about.

I let go of the branch I was clinging to with my right hand. Blood pooled in my fingers now that I wasn't holding it up. I let the lightning inside me build up, keeping it locked until I had enough stockpiled. Just when I thought I couldn't hold back anymore, I aimed my hand down and released. The lightning shot up high, and the wind I'd called caught me and placed me gently on the other side of the cage.

I didn't have time to pat myself on the back. Instead, I raced toward the cabins where we'd left the car. I didn't see Logan or Eden when I got back. Zachary was running toward me as I circled the car.

"What happened? Where are they?" I demanded. My heart was pounding as adrenaline pumped through my body.

"I don't know," he said. "Eden and I split up to cover more ground. I went right, and she went left."

I turned to run back toward the trees, desperate to find at least one of them. I made it as far as the cement stations, which were placed at the end of the paved road, before I saw Logan carrying Eden.

"Eden!" I rushed over to help him. I wrapped my arm around her and put her arm around my shoulders.

"I'm okay," she whispered. "I will be."

"Franny came out calling my name but found Eden instead," Logan explained. "By the time I was able to get there, Franny was already trying to crush her with a mountain."

We made it to the car, and Zachary took Eden from me. The two men helped get her into the back seat, and they climbed into the front. I slid next to Eden and buckled up. Her head was bleeding, and she was cut all over.

Without a word, I lifted my right hand to her head and let the red light do its thing. The bleeding slowed until it finally stopped as the skin knit itself back together. I brought my left hand up and slowly scanned her body, healing whatever injuries she had received. By the time we got back to school, the only thing Eden felt was exhaustion.

Zachary parked the car and went around to help Eden inside. I got out and watched, torn between going in or getting back out there.

"You can't do any more out there tonight," Logan said, coming up alongside me.

"I swear, I'm going to make them all pay for what they're doing."

He nodded. "You're not done for tonight."

I looked up at him, confused.

"When Franny was assaulting Eden, I heard her saying how the poison didn't hurt you, and the fire didn't slow you down, so she was going to take the people you cared about. Knowing that would cripple you."

"Franny poisoned me?" I was gutted, knowing someone I'd thought was a friend had tried to kill me.

"No. She set your room on fire," he said. "It was Rose who poisoned you."

Not even Logan could stop me from bursting into Rose and Natalia's room, picking Rose up by her pj shirt, then holding her against the wall.

"I should kill you right now," I threatened. "For everything you've done. Bullying me when I first got here, the torment you laid on me every chance you got, *poisoning* me!"

Rose swung her arms out and broke my hold. "Wolfsbane. It's a bitch, isn't it?"

"You would know." I heard Natalia climb out of bed and leave the room without a word. Surprising, given how defensive she was toward Trip about Rose. I had half anticipated her attacking me.

"How cozy, just you and me," Rose snarled. "Want me to tell you the pillow talk Trip and I shared as we lay in bed?"

"Sure. Tell me everything, so I know how I can destroy you both."

"Bridget!" Norah's voice was at the threshold of the room. "What are you doing?"

Now I knew where Natalia had gone.

"Since you're in a sharing mood, do you want to tell her?" I asked Rose. Rose smiled sweetly at me.

I glared at her. "Rose admitted to poisoning me with wolfsbane. I'm sure if we gave her another minute, she would've confirmed it was Deidra who made her do it."

There was a glint in Rose's eye as she shook her head. "Trip," she mouthed. I curled my fingers into a fist, ready to strike. Thunder boomed dangerously outside her window. As I lifted my arm, someone else's wrapped around my waist and hoisted me up.

"Logan, please make sure Ms. MacNamara makes it to my office," Norah said as we passed her. She turned to the room. "Rose, we will need to call your parents."

"Logan, you can put me down. I know how to walk."

I squirmed until he dropped me. I landed with a thump on the floor.

"Thanks," I retorted, standing.

He shook his head. "I know you're livid at Rose, but that wasn't the best plan."

"I could have died. Eden was hurt tonight, and I'm sick of being told I don't know what is going on. I'm going to get answers any way I can."

"You can always die! You're not invincible. And Eden is fine, thanks to you," Logan pointed out. "This recklessness needs to calm down."

"Is this my Protector talking or my friend?"

"Both. I don't want to lose you, and not because it's my job to make sure that doesn't happen." Logan sighed. "I don't know what I would do if something happened to you."

I swallowed thickly, my anger leaching into the air. I didn't have a chance to reply as Norah marched past him and stormed into her office, her door left open.

"I don't have all night," she said from inside. I nodded and walked into the office.

"How stupid could you have been tonight? Attacking Rose like that? I fear what would have happened if Natalia hadn't come to get me." Norah didn't even wait for me to walk completely into the room before she laid into me.

"I wouldn't have killed her, if that's what you mean."

"Don't be glib. You're in enough trouble as it is."

"Me? What about Rose? She can go around poisoning me, and she's allowed to have breakfast with us tomorrow?"

Norah let out a deep sigh and sat in her chair. She motioned for me to sit as well.

"No, Rose will be going home tomorrow, as we don't condone attempted murder on classmates. But that doesn't excuse your actions tonight." Her tone softened. "Bridget, you cannot behave the way you did. I know how frustrating and scary this is, but a full-on attack isn't the best course of action."

I crossed my arms and legs, sitting back in the chair. "So, I'm just supposed to get used to this? Attempted murder? Constant warfare?"

"Yes."

Well, that was hurtful.

"You're the Cuardaitheoir. You're going to have to expect this to happen to you. I can assure you Trip is on alert all the time."

"You speak to him?" I asked, accusingly.

"Not anymore, but he was a student here. And we taught him the same things. Be careful, be mindful, and be aware."

I seethed, feeling betrayed. How could she not have told me?

When I didn't reply, Norah continued, "It's been a long night, but there was some good to come of it."

I raised an eyebrow as an invitation for her to go on.

"We learned how you were poisoned, who poisoned you, how your room was set on fire, and have decided Franny is no longer welcome on this property."

"Because of me?"

"More because of Eden. We don't condone attacking teachers, either." She smiled a little. "Go on to bed. It's getting late, and you can brief me in the morning."

"Goodnight," I said as I left her office.

I was surprised to see Oliver sitting on the stairs when I got back.

"You didn't get her?" he asked as I sat next to him.

"No. She's not coming back."

He just nodded.

"I'm sorry," I said.

"It's okay." He hesitated. "She's evil or something, isn't she?"

I took a deep breath and sighed. "No one is completely evil, but... yeah, she isn't our friend anymore."

Oliver leaned over and kissed me on the cheek. "Thank you for trying to save her. And thank you for saving me. I know I didn't stand a chance the first time, but I got your back if you ever need me, Cuardaitheoir."

I froze, kicking myself for allowing yet another person to know the truth about me.

"It's okay," Oliver said. "I won't tell anyone."

I smiled sympathetically. "When did you know?"

"When you thawed me. No one could do that besides a full-blown Seeker."'

I wrapped my arm around his shoulder. "I'm glad we're on the same side."

He wrapped his arm around my shoulder. "Me too."

CHAPTER 20

I had a hard time falling asleep after my conversation with Oliver. While I was touched by his offer to help, I was fighting waves of anger at Rose and Franny for trying to hurt Eden and me. I turned onto my side.

Maybe Logan was right. I was being foolhardy for rushing into things. My impertinence had nearly caused me to get kicked out of training for going after Rose like I had.

No regrets, though. Not with her.

I sighed and rolled onto my back. I felt moronic about my behavior even if it did get me some results. I reached over and grabbed my phone from my nightstand.

[Bridget: Sorry about tonight. You're right. I wasn't thinking. Got those pesky unicorns on the brain.] Send.

My phone vibrated in my hand.

[Logan: No need to apologize. It's not easy to have successful missions. People lose their heads. Just remember that for next time.]

[Bridget: I'll try.]

[Bridget: What would you have done if you were me?]

The dreaded three dots appeared and disappeared before I got his reply.

[Logan: I'm not the Seeker so I don't need to worry about it. But if I was, I would have played my cards close to the chest, not showing my hand. Could have used Rose for info.]

I coughed out a laugh.

[Bridget: Unlikely. She hates me, remember? I'm Trip's ex. She sees me as competition.]

A minute passed before my phone vibrated.

[Logan: Are you her competition?]

[Bridget: Only for the Amulet. 🙂]

[Logan: Goodnight, Bridget 🙂 Sweet dreams. But don't dream of unicorns.]

I giggled.

[Bridget: No promises!]

I placed my phone back on the nightstand. I then rolled over, got comfortable, and drifted off the sleep.

I had flashes of Brighde and an unknown male running through the valley, looking for someone.

"Bres..." a voice whispered. "Husband..."

I didn't have time to process it before we ran up the mountain back to the clearing, but no one was there except us.

Not Brighde, me. Not Bres, Logan. He turned around and brushed a piece of hair off my face.

"It's always been you," he said.

Another flash, and he was gone. I was alone in the clearing, hearing laughter around me but not knowing where it was coming from.

"I will fight you!" I called out, readying myself for a battle.

"And you will lose," came the reply.

Suddenly, I was back at home, on the riverbank of the Tuckahoe River, watching myself and Trip break up. But we ended it in the library. Why was I here?

"Bridget, it's always been you," Trip said as he leaned in for a kiss.

All of a sudden, I was hovering over myself sleeping in bed, but I didn't recognize the bed or my sheets. Where was I?

Without warning, Logan was in front of me again, but this time, he was in my room and shaking me.

"Wake up! Bridget, wake up!"

I jumped to Brighde, following Bres... no, following Lugh, over hills and through trees.

"There he is!" Lugh called. I watched them come up on a man who was pushing a wagon of hay down toward the shore.

"Do you have it?" screamed Brighde. "Do you?"

"Have what?" The man replied, his Scottish accent thick.

"My necklace."

"I only have the one I'm giving to my girl, who will hopefully marry me once I propose." He stuck his hand in a pouch and pulled out the Amulet I wore around my neck.

"We found it, Lugh. We finally found it!"

I woke with a jolt and sat up, clutching the Amulet. Brighde had found the Amulet half. Where was Beira's?

The next morning, I dressed for my all-day training with Logan. After grabbing breakfast, I stopped in to see Norah and give her all the details on what had happened, not just the abridged version she'd let me get away with the night before.

"Where are we starting today?" I asked, dropping into a seat.

"Good morning to you, too," Norah replied dryly. She closed the book she was writing in and folded her hands in front of her. "We should start in the beginning."

"We stuck to the plan: Logan and I in the clearing or adjacent, Eden and Zachary on the outskirts, looking for bad guys."

"What did Franny say when you saw her?"

I shrugged and shook my head. "Nothing that's helpful. Besides how she's now hashtag Team Beira."

"Did she do anything to you?"

I could still taste dirt even after I had brushed my teeth. "Yeah, she trapped me in a giant cage of dirt."

Norah raised her eyebrows.

"You didn't know she was able to do that?" I asked, surprised.

"We did, but I didn't know she was advanced enough to create something like that."

I huffed. "Well, not only can she create cocoons out of mud; she's graduated to fake kidnapping scares and generic villainy."

Norah gave me a small smile. "Bridget, I'm sure this was hard for you, losing a friend. I'm sorry to say, she probably won't be the last."

"That's not really comforting."

Norah chuckled. "I'm not in the business of comfort. You know being a Seeker is not all it's cracked up to be. Having powers is the fun part. The rest is merely responsibility."

I looked away and pursed my lips. I knew she was right, but why did things need to be so black and white?

"I think we're done for now," she commented, looking at her planner. "I have another appointment, but we can pick this up later."

"Looking forward to it," I replied, getting up and leaving.

After leaving Norah's, I found Logan lifting weights in the gym. I stopped to appreciate the sight. He caught me in the mirror and grinned, showing off his ability to lift heavy pieces of metal. I bit my lip and wistfully sighed. Logan placed the weights on the mat, wiped his head on a towel, then walked over to me.

"Like what you see?" he cheekily asked, smiling.

Schooling my features, I gave him a little shrug. "Maybe."

His grin got bigger. I couldn't help but smile back. "What's on the agenda today?"

"What do you want to do?" he asked.

"What? *I* get to choose?" I feigned surprise, pressing my left hand to my chest. He took my right hand and started leading me back toward the station he'd just been at.

"I figured after last night, you could use some freedom to make your own choices."

I scoffed. "You're the only one, I swear."

Logan furrowed his brow. "I'm sure I'm not the only one."

I leaned away from him, and he dropped my hand.

"Am I lifting weights, too?"

"Are you okay?"

"I honestly don't know how to answer that."

"Try." Logan sat on the bench behind him and rested his elbows on his knees. His attention was solely on me.

"Can we go for a walk instead?"

He stood and ushered me out the door. "Okay. Let's go, then."

We walked out and headed toward the open fields, away from the town. As we strolled along the path, the sun shone down on us, and I basked in its warmth. Who needed coffee when a sunbeam worked just as well?

As we made it to the middle of a field blooming with wildflowers, smelling light and sweet, I slid my hand into his and squeezed. He squeezed back.

"Tell me what's on your mind," Logan said as we strolled through the flowers.

"Did Cay ever tell you about my dreams? The ones with Brighde?"

"I think so."

"I had another one last night, and it was weird. I kept seeing random snapshots of my life or some twisted version of it."

Logan didn't say anything, waiting for me to continue.

"I dreamed Brighde found the Amulet." He stopped and faced me, and his eyes lit up.

"Really? Did you see where it was?"

"No. It was too quick, but I think they found her half with Andrew."

Cocking his head to the side, he asked, "They? Beira and Brighde?"

"Brighde and Lugh. I have this bad gut feeling, and I can't shake it. I don't know what it means. I'm not a fan."

Logan hugged me, pulling me close. I closed my eyes for a minute to stay present. His skin against mine was sticky from his workout and the walk. Floral and spice mixed, creating a balance between his soap and our surroundings.

"I wish I could be your hero," he said softly.

I pulled back and peered up at him. It was the first time I'd heard anyone wanted to be there for me, not just the Seeker part of me. Something warm filled my belly, and I realized I would be able to rely on Logan in a way I couldn't rely on anyone else.

I stood a little taller and leaned in to kiss him. If this wasn't the moment, then I didn't know what would be. He bent his head and leaned down.

"Whoo!" Someone whistled as they rode a skateboard past us. I jumped back like it burned. Logan tugged me back and leaned his forehead against mine.

"I promise," I whispered. "Even if I have to use my powers for our first kiss to happen, it will happen."

He laughed and kissed my cheek. "Coffee? Light and sweet?"

I smiled. "I would love that."

I took his hand as we walked back to the Academy, smiling the whole time.

Climbing the stairs to my room, I felt lighter and happier than I had when I'd woken up this morning. Coffee turned into lunch, which turned into supper. We spent the day walking around, exploring the town, and spending time with each other as Bridget and Logan, not as Seeker and Protector. It was time I knew I needed but didn't know how to get.

As I entered my room to grab my shower stuff, I knew being with Logan would be different and much better than being with Trip had been. Logan's support made me feel protected in a way that I'd been missing. He had my back, something Trip could never do. My gut had always known Trip hadn't been there for me, but I didn't listen, and now I was embroiled in this war, constantly feeling four steps behind him.

Nothing felt like a fight with Logan. It was easy.

I headed into the restroom and turned on the water for the shower. Stepping in, I felt the water rush over me, already rinsing off the sweat of the day. I still had Logan's body wash from when my room had caught on fire, and I breathed deep. The woodsy scent relaxed me and was silky against my skin as I ran the loofah down my body.

Stepping out and drying off, I felt at peace, but I wasn't tired anymore. I needed to do something, see someone. I got dressed in my pjs and tiptoed down the stairs to Logan's room.

I decided to take a chance. I couldn't get Logan out of my head. I know he felt the same way, but I was done hesitating. I made it down the stairs without anyone else hearing, silently creeping over the squeaky floorboards.

"Hey," I whispered to Logan as I knocked softly and peeked around his door.

"Hey, yourself," he said, sounding confused and happy. "What are you doing here?"

I hope you don't mind," I said, flushing slightly and closing the door behind me. It wasn't like he could really see my face in the dark. "I ... wanted to say goodnight."

I felt so stupid. What did I think would happen? Sneaking into his room at night would lead to nothing but trouble and broken hearts.

Logan pushed off his covers and sat on the edge of his bed. Shirtless.

Oh, good heavens, I was definitely in trouble.

"Goodnight? That's all you wanted to say?" he asked, raising an eyebrow, smiling like he'd won the lottery.

"Well, no..." If I never found the Amulet, at least I could teach classes on seduction. Like the old saying, "Those who can't do, teach." I'd be broke before the first class.

Tiptoeing to avoid making any noise, I took a step closer to him.

"I've been thinking..." I said, moving toward the bed.

"About what?"

I was close enough to reach out and touch him.

"Our almost-kiss in the woods. And in the field." I stopped moving, unsure of what to do next.

Logan made no move toward me. "What about it?"

"I can't stop thinking about it." I could see his chest rising in the moonlight. He was breathing faster than before.

"Is that so?"

I nodded and then remembered he probably couldn't see me. "Yes."

"What exactly are you thinking about?" Logan reached for my hand and dragged little circles on my wrist with his thumb, making me melt.

"You. Me." I was a statue, aching to kiss him.

"Is that all?" His voice was velvet.

"No."

He towered over me, never letting go of my wrist. Moments passed, and he didn't say anything. The silence was becoming unbearable for me. Heat coursed through my veins, and it took all my strength not to lean forward and press my body into his.

"Did you want to know what it would feel like?" he whispered into my ear. I closed my eyes and tried to steady my breath. Logan's lips grazed their way down my cheek, down my neck, and back up again.

"How exciting it would feel with someone who wants to learn all of your sensitive spots," he said, caressing the small of my back. Logan slipped his hand under my shirt and left a trail of silky touches as he made his way to the front of my pajama shorts, where he stopped at the hemline under my abdomen. I shivered from his touch as my breath quickened. My lightning followed his fingerprints on my body, leaving me a little jumpy, and it took monumental effort to push it away.

"How good it would feel to have my lips on yours?"

I opened my eyes to find Logan looking back at me.

"I want to know," I whispered, "how it would feel to be with you."

Logan smiled and brought his mouth down to meet mine. My body lit up with excitement, but he paused before touching my lips.

"Are you sure?" he breathed.

I answered him by wrapping my arms around his neck and pulling him into me. We kissed tenderly for a moment, testing, tasting each other. Logan's lips were soft against mine. My body was pressed against his until I couldn't tell where I ended, and he began. He nibbled my lower lip, and I couldn't take the anticipation anymore. I moved my mouth to be fully over his and pressed hard. He slipped his tongue between my lips, drawing me in closer. Kissing Logan was different from kissing anyone else.

I skimmed my hands up his strong back, feeling the definition in his muscles. I pushed him back toward the bed, not wanting to break contact. Logan was what I wanted, and in this moment, I needed him.

"Wait," Logan said, pulling away. Why would he stop after he'd just kissed me like that?

"Yes, this is really happening."

He smiled and kissed me again, this time less rushed than before. He sat on the bed and placed me on top of him. We stayed like that, me straddling him as we kissed, for a few minutes. I hungered for the sensations of his face brushing against mine before I nudged him with my body to lie down. Logan flipped over to straddle me instead, supporting his weight with his left forearm and eliminating any space between us. My knee was pressed against his hip. Logan's other hand trailed down my body, leaving a line of fire where his fingers had been. He slipped his hand back to my shorts and up my thigh only to stop there, leaving scorched skin. I was so hot, and I was ready to burst. I pulled him closer to me, yearning to feel his bare chest against the exposed part of mine.

Logan moved his kisses from my mouth down to my collarbone, nipping my skin playfully.

"Did you use my body wash in the shower?"

"Yes. Thoughts?"

His face dipped lower after he lifted his eyes to mine, slowly making his way down over the curve of my breast, leaving hot breath in his wake. Logan spent time kissing around my belly button before he led his trail of kisses down to the top of my shorts.

I tensed.

"Are you okay?" he asked, frozen.

"Um... uh-huh."

Logan breathed deeply and sat back on his knees.

"This would be your first time, wouldn't it?"

"Having sex?" I asked, my voice high. I felt the bed shift as Logan pushed back.

"First time for anything besides kissing?"

"Yes," I whispered, suddenly feeling very juvenile and vulnerable.

"Hey," he whispered, moving gently, so I could see him. He brushed a curl off my face, his fingers trailing softly over my cheek. "I wasn't going to do anything but kiss your body. But it's cool. We don't have to do anything you aren't ready for or don't want to do." He paused. "In fact, I think we should wait."

"Really?"

"Yeah. Bridget, it's no secret we like each other, but I don't want to rush you or force you into anything that you don't want to do. I want you to lead the way. I'll be here." He smiled. "Not because it's my job either," he teased.

I shivered slightly without his body heat. "Thank you."

Logan leaned over and gave me a sweet, lingering kiss.

"Anything for you."

I fell asleep in Logan's arms that night and woke up happy the next morning. Smiling, I rolled over and looked at his sleeping form. His mouth was open, his breath heavy from a deep sleep. I pushed a lock of fallen hair from his face and lightly kissed his cheek before slipping out of bed and into the hallway. It was forbidden for the opposite gender to spend time in their counterpart's dorms, and I could be in huge trouble if Norah found out.

I tiptoed down the hall, lucky not to step on any squeaky floorboards. I almost made it to the staircase when I heard a noise behind me. Heart thundering in my chest, I saw the men's restroom door open and a boy stumble out. He collapsed onto the floor with a loud thump.

"Bridget, where the hell were you?" Cay asked, trying to lift his head up. Horrified, I rushed over to him.

"Cay! Cay?" I shifted his head into my lap. "I'm here. I didn't go anywhere."

"I couldn't find you," he said weakly, slurring his words.

"What you mean?"

"I searched for you. When I escaped."

Stricken, I asked, "From where?"

He didn't answer. He passed out.

Chapter
❦ 21 ❧

"Cay!" I immediately checked for a pulse. It was there but weak. Another guy opened his door and peeked out.

"Go get Norah!" I told him. "And hurry!" He took off running, heading toward the stairs.

"Cay? Can you hear me?" I asked him, as I noticed fresh wounds on his face and hands. One of the cuts looked like it was healing, but it was torn open and pumping fresh blood from his hand onto the floor. *What the hell?* Cay was supposed to be able to heal. *What was going on?*

"Bridget?" I heard Logan's and other doors starting to open.

"Cay!" Logan hurried over. "What happened to him?"

"I don't know! He came out of the restroom and just collapsed." By now, most of the floor was surrounding us, partially for the excitement of a stranger and partially because the stranger was passed out on the floor.

"Logan," I said, lowering my voice to a whisper, "Cay isn't healing." Logan's eyes widened as he saw the cuts and bruises forming on Cay's body. His eyes flickered to mine and confirmed the thought that formed a hard mass in my stomach: Something was not right with his powers.

"Move out of the way," Norah's voice carried over the crowd. The boys parted, making way for her and Zachary.

"Move on, and get to breakfast," he said, shooing the gawkers away. Slowly, they dispersed, allowing Norah to set her medicine bag next to Cay.

"What happened here?" she asked as she checked his pulse.

"He came out of the restroom and passed out," I answered.

"Did he say anything?" She examined his head, looking at the cuts.

"Something about escaping," I said. "Then he passed out."

I didn't want Norah to know I wasn't in my room in the morning. But the fact that I was sitting next to Cay—when my room was a floor up and not as close as Logan's was—was a dead giveaway I was somewhere I wasn't supposed to be.

Norah lifted his shirt, revealing a dark, purple stain on his abdomen.

"Zachary, call one-one-two and tell them to send an ambulance right away." She gently covered the spot and faced Logan for the first time. "I do not want to know why Bridget was here, but she needs to leave. This is not a matter that can be discussed in an open forum, but I fear Cay is more than a warning."

I paled at her announcement as Logan pulled me to my feet.

"Cay?"

Norah nodded. "He will get the medical help he needs. I will watch out for him. Now, go."

"Norah, let me help," I begged, hoping she'd get my hint. "I may be the best chance he has."

She looked up at Zachary and nodded once. He immediately hung up the phone. Turning back to us, Norah said, "Logan, bring him into your room."

With help from Zachary, Logan silently picked up an unconscious Cay and gently placed him on the bed. Norah followed us inside as Zachary left to shoo kids back to their own rooms.

Cay looked so broken and fragile. I wasted no time lifting my hands over his body, drawing on my training to work the red glow. I focused on the large bruise on his stomach. Internal bleeding was my biggest concern. His cuts and scrapes were less worrisome. I felt the laceration on his organs slowly knitting together as the blood vessels reformed, stopping the leakage. Cay was still passed out, but he looked less pale than before. Finally, the purple shape under the skin shrank, becoming no bigger than a smudge. Knowing that part would heal on its own, I moved over to his bleeding hand and then his face. Diverting my powers didn't diminish them, and soon, his face was healed, so I focused solely on his hand. With nothing else for me to heal, I stood back and waited to see if he would wake. When he didn't, Norah came over and put her hand on his chest.

"His breathing is fine now, and you can see he's getting color back. I think we should let him rest for now, and you can check on him a little later. Zachary will stay with him." She ushered both of us out of the room and waved Zachary in. He closed the door behind him.

"Now," she began, "Do you want to tell me why you were down here just in time to save Cay?"

I gulped. "Not really."

Norah leveled Logan and me with a look as I braced myself for another lecture. "Be safe."

I blinked. "That's all?"

Logan elbowed me in the ribs, but I ignored him.

"Do you want to be in trouble?" She gave me a patented "Don't tempt me" look. "Don't get caught. Again."

With that, she left us alone, standing in our pjs in the hallway with a sleeping Cay only six feet away.

I left Logan for my own floor. Quickly, I got dressed and brushed my teeth. I grabbed a hair tie and pulled my hair into a tight bun. A few curls fell out, but I didn't care. I was in a rush to get back to Cay and watch over him. I knew how unsafe this place could be.

I hurried back down the stairs that had once carried me to a heated night but now took me to the same room with a much different temperature. Zachary was gone, but Logan was lounging in a chair, his arms crossed over his chest.

"I'm back," I whispered as I entered the room. Cay looked more relaxed than he had when I'd last seen him. Logan, on the other hand, was still in his pjs, hair disheveled. When he looked up at me, his eyes were stormy and full of pain.

I walked over to him and wrapped my arms around his shoulders as he leaned against me.

"He'll be okay."

"How do you know?" His voice was husky.

I smiled a little. "Because *I* healed him."

He sniffed and pulled away. "I should go shower, but I don't want to leave him."

"I'm here."

Logan stood, gave me a tight hug, and left to shower.

I looked at Cay and sighed. "What happened to you? Why couldn't you heal?"

Sitting in the spot Logan had just vacated, I felt that my nerves were tight. I wanted to run out and go after whoever did this. The urge was so strong; I jumped up and started doing push-ups, then sit-ups. I needed to expel this energy. Feeling I was getting too loud, I switched to yoga poses, starting with morning salutations before moving into downward dog. My muscles felt the pull, which helped the built-up excitement. As I turned my body into the next pose, Cay stirred. Immediately, I dropped the pose and popped my head up. He didn't wake up; he only adjusted his body. The scars I'd healed were superficial compared to what mental trauma he would more than likely face. I wished I could heal that, but it was out of my reach.

Logan came back, smelling of mint.

"Anything?"

I shook my head. Logan sat on the floor, his back against the wall across from the bed.

"Penny for your thoughts?" I asked, sliding to sit down next to him.

"I'm mad that I wasn't there for him. I'm disappointed I couldn't save him. I'm murderous against whoever did this."

His comment hurt, like my saving Cay hadn't counted for much.

Remember, this isn't about you, I reminded myself.

Logan took my hand and held it in his lap, our fingers entwined. He gently ran his thumb over the back of my hand, and I realized he was calming himself down with the motion.

"You should get some breakfast," I suggested.

Logan licked his lips and looked at Cay. "I can't leave him again."

"Logan, look at me." He dragged his eyes over to me.

"You did not fail. Cay was not your responsibility. I know you're more than just friends; you're brothers. But you were where you needed to be."

His eyes shone as a single tear slipped down his cheek. I squeezed his hand that still held mine.

"Cay is my responsibility to avenge," I reminded him. "But I would love the help."

Logan swallowed, leaned over, and kissed me. This was nothing like the restrained passion he'd kissed me with last night. This was a promise and a thank-you wrapped in one.

"When did you two get together?" a sleepy Cay asked us from the bed.

We both launched ourselves off the floor and rushed to the bed. I enclosed him in a hug and tried not to crush his lungs. He put one arm around me as the other one had to support himself sitting up.

"Missed me?" he joked. It only resulted in my hugging him harder. When I finally let go, Cay barely took a breath before Logan hugged him. Speaking from experience, Logan gave strong hugs.

"Are you okay? Are you hungry or thirsty?" I asked hurriedly.

"Some water would be nice," Cay replied, patting Logan, who was still hugging him, on the back.

"Logan?"

He let Cay go and took a step back.

"Can you get him some water?" I asked, wanting to give Cay a minute to fully wake up.

"I'll be right back," Logan answered as he left.

"You're a sight for sore eyes," Cay said, looking at me. "Trust me."

He went to smile but ended up grimacing. "I'm okay, just a small stab of pain."

Logan returned with the water and handed it to Cay. He drank half of it in one go.

"Thanks." He placed the bottle on the nightstand and settled back into the pillows. "So, tell me how you two happened. I totally called it, by the way."

"Our relationship is the conversation you really want to have?" I asked him as I folded my arms over my chest.

Cay looked down, allowing some of his hair to fall in front of his face. "Yes. I can't talk about what happened just yet."

Biting my lips, I looked at Logan. He looked at me while rubbing his hand on his forehead. I turned back to Cay and nodded. "Okay. Logan pursued me for the past couple of months. During this time, I almost died, twice."

"Once," protested Logan.

"Twice. Poison, fire," I argued, holding up two fingers.

"The fire doesn't count. You weren't in the building."

"Still, it was an attempt on my life."

Cay sighed and smiled. "I missed you two."

Now that Cay was showing signs of healing, I convinced Logan we needed to tell Norah and go get something to eat. When she arrived in the room, I pushed Logan out the door and closed it behind us.

"This has been an interesting fifteen or so hours," I started as we headed downstairs.

Logan let out a laugh. "Yeah, I'd say so. From kissing to Cay. Not how I saw this morning going."

We made it to the dining room, picking up some fruit and grabbing whatever breakfast remained. My stomach growled as I poured myself a cup of coffee and added milk and sugar.

"How did you see this morning going?" I asked, as I grabbed a chair to sit. I took a sip of the sweet, hot drink and readied myself to dig in.

Logan gave a wolfish smile. "Let's just say, I didn't plan on having to witness emergency healing in my own bed."

"Kisses are definitely preferred. But still," I sighed, "Cay is here."

"Yeah, he most definitely is."

Logan was moved to another room for a few nights as Cay was still too weak to move. It cut into our kissing time as Logan had a roommate and didn't want to be more than a few doors away from Cay, rendering my room out.

Thankfully, after day five, Cay was up and about, looking and feeling closer to one hundred percent than before.

"I'm good. I promise," he said as I ran my red hands over him one last time.

"Doesn't hurt to be extra sure."

Cay held my wrist. "It just might if you keep doing it."

"Oh, how I missed you," I said sardonically, freeing my wrist. "Let's get you something to eat, and if you're feeling up to it, we can ... talk."

"About you and Logan?" Cay asked hopefully.

"No."

Cay ran a shaky hand through his hair. "You know I'm not ready," he said softly.

"I know, Cay, and I hate that you have to go through this, but," I paused, taking his hand in mine, "we need to know what we're up against."

He slid his hand out and looked at me with shiny eyes. "Please don't make me do it."

Tears slipped down my cheeks. "I'm sorry. I'm so sorry," I sniffled, turning away from him. "I don't know what I can do. I can try to talk to Norah and tell her you need more time."

Cay sniffled too. "Okay."

"I'll go now," I said, jumping up and wiping my tears. I raced out of the room and thundered down the stairs to Norah's office.

"Norah?" I called, knocking on her door.

"Come in," she answered.

I opened the door and closed it behind me. "I need to talk to you about Cay."

Norah looked up from her desk and saw the state my face was in.

"Is he worse? I thought you were healing him," she asked, offering me a tissue. I took it and wiped my nose.

"I am, and he's okay, physically. It's just... he's not ready to talk about, you know, what happened." I collapsed into a chair, feeling another bout of tears coming on. I dabbed my eyes with my tissue and then threw it out.

Norah came around to the other side of the desk and leaned against it, handing me the tissue box.

"I understand what a harrowing experience Cay must have had. But it's of the upmost importance we know what he experienced so we can be better prepared for it."

Frowning, I looked up at her. She held up her hands, palms faced at me.

"I'm not wholly uncaring to this young man. Don't think that, please," she said, taking a breath. "Unfortunately, because of the timing and the urgency of our matter, I can't be patient any longer. He must tell us what happened."

"What if he refuses?" I asked.

"Don't let him," she said plainly.

I gaped at her and shook my head. "I'm not forcing him to do something he doesn't want to do."

"You won't have to if he refuses. Now, please tell your cousin that he has an appointment with me that I expect him to keep."

I left her office, dreading telling Cay what happened. When I reached his room, Logan was sitting in a chair with him, and they were laughing about something.

"Bridget!" Cay brightened. "Logan was telling me about your training sessions with him."

I frowned and sat on the bed next to Cay. "Don't believe everything you hear."

"Cay," I began, "I talked to Norah."

He sobered up immediately. "What did she say?"

"I tried. I really did!"

Cay nodded, looking down at his hands in his lap.

"My hands are tied on this. She wants to hear your account right away. I'm sorry." I hung my head in my hands, feeling like the biggest disappointment. I failed yet again to protect someone I love.

Cay sighed. "You did what you could."

I looked up at him. "What are you going to do?"

"I'll see if I can get the words out when she asks me what happened."

I nodded, numb to it all. "Do you want something to eat beforehand?"

Cay shrugged. "Sure, why not?"

"I'll walk you both down," Logan offered, standing up. We got up and left the room without a sound, besides the soft clicking of the door lock.

"It's nice to see you up and about, Mr. McKay," Norah greeted us as we hit the bottom step. Logan abandoned us and headed toward the restroom.

"Thanks. It's good to be up and about."

"We're grabbing some breakfast, and then we'll meet you in your office," I said as we walked past.

I showed Cay where the dishware was as we headed inside to make our selection. We both grabbed plates with some fruit and rösti, a delicious mixture of potatoes and eggs shaped like a pancake. Today's version had Swiss cheese and spinach. Collecting our utensils and drinks, we made our way to a table. Cay ate carefully, as if he was worried he'd get sick with each bite.

"Do you not like it?" I asked, cutting a piece of my rösti.

He put down his utensils and swallowed before replying.

"I do, but I'm still not able to eat a full meal since..." He trailed off.

I choked down my own feelings, and said, "It's okay. Eat what you can or want. No pressure."

He gave me a smile, picked up his fork, and continued to eat. We finished our meal in silence, him focusing on his meal, me fighting my desperation to ask what had happened. I'd find out soon enough, and he deserved peace while he still could have it.

After we bussed our plates, we walked to Norah's office. I clutched his hand and stopped. Cay looked down at our clasped hands and frowned.

"We will find our answers, even if you don't share your story."

Cay faced the door and sighed. "It's now or never." He turned the knob and walked in, still holding onto me.

"Please, sit," Norah motioned for Cay to sit in one of the chairs. I sat next to him, not wanting him to face anything else alone. Eden, Zachary, and Logan were in the room. Logan stood on the other side of Cay, facing him. He had his arms crossed over his chest, intimidating. The others were behind Norah as she sat at her desk.

"Before we get into anything, Cay, how are you doing?" Norah asked, leaning forward on her desk.

Clearing this throat, Cay squirmed. "Better than I was."

"Have you been able to rest?"

He nodded. "Yeah, I can sleep." He stopped and then continued. "I don't want to talk about what happened, but I know it's important you hear about it." He chuckled nervously. "Anything for the cause, right?"

I placed my left hand on his shoulder and gave it an encouraging squeeze.

"Um, here goes... I was held prisoner by Beira's family. Deidra, Tomas, Roden..." He looked over at me, "Even Trip."

I took in a sharp breath but didn't say anything. My mind was blank, unable to process this.

"I was heading toward Zurich to scout out the descendant, but I never made it past Leeds. I was jumped and beaten by a couple of their family members. That's what they call anyone loyal to Beira, family." He stopped, seemingly lost in the memory of what had happened. Cay swung his hand out and grabbed mine before continuing.

"I was thrown into a car trunk, and we drove, but I don't know where. I passed out for some time. I only woke up when I got dragged out of the car and dumped in a barn. Then, I was tied up and left there for about two days, I think. I know it was dark when I left."

Eden placed her fingers over her mouth and wrapped her other arm around her stomach. Norah didn't move, and Zachary stood the same way as Logan: legs spread, arms crossed, and frowning. If the flared nostrils and widened eyes on my Protector's face were any indication, Trip and his family would have a bigger problem than just me.

"When they came back, I was given bread and water, and they left again. That's what I ate for my time there."

"Did they ask you anything?" Norah gently asked.

"Um, yeah. They did." He ran his free hand through his hair and rubbed the back of his neck. "They wanted to know where Bridget was and where she kept the Amulet half."

I felt a prickly icicle poking under my skin, up and down my arms, and I shifted to hide my uncomfortableness.

Cay looked Norah straight in the eye. "I never gave in. Not once."

"Cay, how did you escape?" I asked him, trying to redirect the focus. I couldn't stomach much more of this, but I wasn't going to reveal that.

"I didn't. They let me go after—" he said, then stopped.

"After what?" I prompted.

"After they strung me up, dropped the key on the floor, and left." I stopped asking questions because I didn't want to know how he got out. My emotions were fluctuating between rage and sick sadness.

Cay took a deep, steadying breath. Reliving his past month was taking a toll on him.

"One more question, then we can stop," Norah spoke up. "Where did you go after you got free?"

"I've been trying to get here without them following me. Staying underground."

Norah nodded. "That's enough for now. I'm sorry for the ordeal you went through. You can go rest now."

Cay, Logan, and I shuffled out of her office. We barely made it to the stairs before I grabbed Cay and hugged him so hard.

"I love you, cousin," I told him. He hugged me back as hard, buried his head in my shoulder, and cried silently. I rested my head against his and looked at Logan, heart breaking. He swallowed forcefully and walked away.

As I watched Logan leave, Cay sniffled and pulled away, his eyes red and bloodshot.

"I don't want to ask, but I want to understand," I began, "How come you couldn't heal yourself?"

"I don't know, really. I guess I was tired and starved. It was horrible, trying to get here. I know I made my injuries worse." He wiped his eyes on his sleeve. "I think I'm going to get some rest."

"See you later." I watched as Cay trudged up the stairs, his shoulders hunched over with the weight of whatever else is buried in his soul.

As Cay headed to Logan's room, I went to find the room's former lodger. I found him in the gym, punching a bag so hard; I expected it to burst.

Unsure if I should disturb him, I stood at the entrance for longer than was socially acceptable. He took a second to adjust his stance, and I cleared my throat.

"Hi," I said.

"Hey." Logan went back to punching the bag.

I was torn. I wanted to comfort him, give him a hug, but his body language screamed to stay away.

He huffed and dropped his arms. "Do you want to say something?"

"Nothing in particular. You?"

"I don't want to talk." Logan punched the bag again with less force than before.

"I can see that, but," I said and took a step inside the room, "we don't have to talk."

Logan raised an eyebrow and looked me up and down.

"No." I rolled my eyes. "I meant, I could work out with you, unless you want to be alone."

He threw a punch at the bag one more time, making a *thump*. "I don't want a partner right now. And I don't want to talk, but I've heard doing so could help, so okay."

Walking over to him, I took off my jacket and dropped it on the floor. If I was going to work out, I didn't want layers. I went to brace the bag for him, but Logan waved me off.

"In case I miss," he said. I moved away from the mat and stood off to the side.

"Talk to me."

"I don't know where to start." *Thump*.

"How do you feel?"

"Angry." *Thump*.

"Why?"

"Because I wasn't there. I should've been there." *Thump*.

"That's it?"

"No." *Thump*.

"Care to share?"

Thump, thump. "He is my best friend, and I failed him." He hit the bag again, making the *thump* resonate in the empty gym. With the last punch, Logan leaned against the bag.

"I failed him, and now he won't look at me," he answered softly. I moved slowly toward him and put my hand on his back.

"Do you think he thinks you failed?"

"I don't know what he thinks. He won't talk to me about it."

"Logan, he's barely talking to anyone. He didn't even want to tell Norah about what happened, but he knew it was important for her to know."

He pushed off the bag suddenly. "But I'm his best friend! What could he tell her that he couldn't tell me?"

I shrugged. "Maybe you should ask him."

"How are you not raging right now?" Logan regarded me carefully.

"I'm too sad this happened to feel the anger yet, but I know Cay doesn't need anger right now."

"What does he need?"

"To feel safe and supported."

Logan let out a deep sigh. "I think I need to go for a run. Can I find you later?"

I nodded. I wasn't sure how it would be received, but I hugged Logan. I needed it more than he did at that moment. Thankfully, he reciprocated, hugging me tightly.

I was able to close the door to my room before I doubled over and sobbed.

Chapter
22

The next morning, I heard a knock on my door as I was getting dressed. I opened it to find Logan standing with his hands in his pockets. I stepped back to let him in.

"I'm sorry," he said. "Obviously, yesterday was a bad day, and I didn't do well with it."

I smiled sympathetically and tucked a piece of my hair behind my ear. "You didn't do anything you need to apologize for. You felt what you felt, and that's ... good."

He stepped forward, closing the minor gap, and pressed his lips against mine. Strong arms pulled me closer as he deepened the kiss. I wrapped my arms around his neck and pushed up on my toes, matching his intensity. It was so nice how we just fit—our bodies, our minds, our thoughts. We were like two puzzles pieces joining together.

"I should have done that yesterday instead of sending you away," he whispered when we broke apart.

"Yesterday was not good for kisses," I whispered back, giving him another kiss. He ended the kiss and rested his forehead against mine as we stood there enjoying the moment.

My stomach protested the delay of breakfast, interrupting us. Logan lightly laughed.

"Can I take you to breakfast in town?" he asked.

"Only if we invite Cay."

Logan kissed me again. "Deal."

The three of us headed to town, Cay sandwiched between Logan and me. The sun shone brightly.

"Did you sleep well?" I asked Cay. "I know that mattress can be lumpy."

Cay eyed me up and down. "Why, my dear cousin, do you know how *Logan's* mattress feels?"

My cheeks were on fire from how badly I blushed. "Shut up, you. I've sat on it."

Logan and I exchanged a look behind Cay's head. He didn't know I'd spent at least one night there.

"Sure."

"So, did you sleep okay?" I repeated, ignoring him.

"Yeah, it's fine. I've slept in worse places." We continued in silence for a few more minutes. I felt the palpable tension Logan had mentioned in the air. Pulling out my phone, I sent a quick text to him.

[Bridget: Are you going to tell him about what we talked about yesterday?]

My phone vibrated in my hands with his reply.

[Logan: Now?]

[Bridget: No better time. I'll hang back if you want me to, to give you privacy.]

[Logan: May be a good idea.]

I turned off my screen and tucked the phone into my pocket. I walked slower so as not to make it obvious I was leaving them alone.

"What are you doing, Bridget?" Cay stopped and asked.

I exchanged another look with Logan.

"Stop. Just tell me what's going on," he demanded. I raised my eyebrows at Logan and shrugged.

Logan sighed. "It's me, Cay. I'm sorry I didn't have your back."

Cay whipped around on Logan, surprised. "You're sorry? It's not your fault; it's mine."

"How?"

"I shouldn't have gone alone. I should have had some kind of backup, but I was so sure I could do it by myself, so I told you to go to Bridget."

The conversation made me feel like I was eavesdropping, so I backed up to stick with the original plan.

"Bridget, stop moving," Cay threatened, facing me. "Are you mad at me, too?"

"What! No, Cay, no one is mad at you for anything. If anything, we're mad at ourselves because we let you go through that alone."

"I was always meant to be alone. Logan was always supposed to be here with you. I'm just ... collateral damage."

Furious, I stalked back to him. "Listen up, Cailean McKay. You are *not* collateral damage. Without you, we wouldn't have made it this far. I wouldn't be here."

"Yeah, man, you're important to the team," Logan added.

I looked between the boys. "I know this is easier said than done, but we need to let go of any guilt or anger we have. Logan, you are where you're supposed to be. Cay, you are the heart of this team, and I wouldn't have made it through the past year without you. Can we all promise to try to let those feelings go?"

Logan and Cay looked at each other.

"I can," Cay said.

"Me too," Logan agreed.

"Good. Let's go because, if I don't eat soon, I can't be held responsible for what I do." I linked my arms through each of theirs, and we walked into town like Scarecrow, Dorothy, and Tin Man on the yellow brick road.

After our healing session this morning, we traipsed back to the school to regroup.

"I'm not sure if I can get back out there yet," Cay said, lounging back on Logan's bed. I was sitting cross-legged next to him, and Logan sat in his desk chair.

"We get it. But I have to go," I replied.

"Not alone," Logan said, furrowing his brow.

"I don't want to, but if I have to, I will." Though his expression didn't change, Logan didn't say anything else.

Out of nowhere, something pricked at my memory: a bad feeling about where we needed to look next for the Amulet. It was my turn to furrow my brow as I shifted on the bed.

"Everything okay?" Logan inquired. "I know you want to do this alone."

"That's not it. Just... Brighde. That dream I told you about? How she and Lugh found the Amulet? That bad feeling is back, and I feel like I know why, but I..." I sighed. "I don't know. I can't put my finger on it."

Cay adjusted his position. "What happened with the dream?"

"In my dream, Brighde found a half of the Amulet from a fisherman."

"Way to bury the lede," Cay remarked.

"I used to not put stock in my dreams, but ever since I got my powers, all my dreams have been about the Amulet. This one definitely felt like a message. I just couldn't figure it out, and it's not like I can ask her." I huffed. It was frustrating, to say the least.

"Too bad. Any more telling dreams?"

I shook my head. I was thoroughly sick of sorting through all this mess. Eden was still healing from her attack, Norah was running the school, and saving the world was left to three teenagers who had no idea what else to do besides walk into danger without a formulated plan. For once, could *something* be easy?

"Bridge?"

I was startled by Logan's voice and his hand on my knee. "What?"

"Where'd you go?"

"Just thinking how unfair this whole thing is. Again."

Cay slid his leg out on the bed and touched my thigh with his toes.

I looked down and grinned evilly. "I hope those socks are clean."

Cay pretended to be upset. "My socks are cleaner than his hands." He gestured to Logan, who was touching my knee still.

"I washed my hands!"

By now, I was laughing and feeling better. I missed the camaraderie of my friends. Picking up my phone, I sent another text to Logan.

[Bridget: I like your hands on me xoxo.]

His phone buzzed with my text. He read it and smiled.

"If you're going to sext, get out of my room," Cay said, throwing a pillow at me.

Laughing, I threw it back. "It's not your room. You leave!"

"No! I sleep here now. Go to your room. You clearly need your own time, and I am going to soak up all the rest I can before you drag me out again."

Logan waggled his brows at me, and I smiled, standing.

"Okay, you win. We're out." I grabbed his hand and pulled him out of the room; I was laughing the whole time.

Logan ended up going to the training room, and I went to talk to Norah. There was something I needed to share that I'd held onto for too long. Her door was open, and she was sitting at her desk, rubbing her eyes with her hand.

"Norah?" I called softly as I knocked and looked in. She dropped her hand immediately.

"Yes, come in," she said. I closed the door behind me and took my normal chair.

"I need to tell you something. Before I do, I know I should have told you sooner, but I was holding out hope that he wasn't evil until Cay told me."

"What? Who? Bridget, please speak plainly."

I inhaled a deep breath and released it. "I've seen Trip here before. When I first got here and I had kitchen duty with Rose, he would meet up with her. He told her..." I couldn't tell her what he'd said about me. That still felt too personal. "He told her where she could find the Amulet, told her to search my rooms."

"Bridget! Why didn't you—"

I held my hand up. "Please let me get this out. The last time I saw Trip, he was in the woods behind the fields. I accidentally knocked him out, and when he woke up, he wanted me to work with him to find the Amulet. A truce. He suggested we share the Amulet together." I cringed at the memory.

"What did you say?"

"No, obviously. But I wonder if my turning him down had something to do with Cay being taken."

Norah didn't say anything, presumably waiting for me to continue.

"That's all," I confirmed.

"Bridget, let me say this one time: Nothing you did caused Cay to be kidnapped. That is completely on Beira's family. Understood?"

I nodded.

"Now, for the rest of it, why didn't you tell me sooner?"

I shrugged. "I don't know. I guess I felt if I told you he was in cahoots with Rose, you wouldn't have believed me. Because when I tried to tell you she did maggot magic on my food, you didn't listen. I thought I could handle it."

Norah pursed her lips. "I'm sorry that's how I made you feel. You can tell me anything, always."

"I know that now. But since Cay said Trip had a hand in what happened, I felt like you should know."

"Better late than never, I suppose, though this would've been useful earlier." She sighed. "Anything else to share?"

Suddenly, I wanted to unburden myself with the night I first attacked Rose.

"One more thing," I started, sitting on the edge of the chair. "The time I found out Rose poisoned me wasn't the only time I attacked her."

Norah sighed and pursed her lips. "I see."

"I almost forgot about what happened, but I think it's important you know." I took a deep breath. "I snuck out that night."

"What?" She picked up her hands and dropped them on the desk.

I held up my hands. "What I'm going to tell you isn't me trying to relieve guilt. I think I was chased when I was outside."

"What do you mean?" she asked, frowning.

"Yes, I snuck out and ran outside. I had my full powers and a lot of pent-up energy. I ended up in the forest, and I let off a few lightning bolts and some rain. Nothing damaging!"

She didn't say anything, so I continued.

"All of a sudden, I got a creepy feeling like someone was with me, but I didn't see anyone. I heard two voices whispering in my ear, saying I should stay there because they wanted to play." I shivered, remembering how scared I was. "I called up a tornado to drop me off in my room, and then I electrified my window."

"Have you seen them since?"

I shook my head. "No, thank goodness. I've been scared, but that was a whole new level of freaked out for me."

"And you never saw them?"

"No."

"Leave this with me, and I'll find out who those voices were," she said. "And Bridget? No more leaving the Academy without my knowledge or permission. This isn't the time for a Cuardaitheoir rebellion."

"I won't. And thank you."

"Anything else I should know?" Norah folded her hands in front of her.

"No. That's it." I stood to leave. "Thank you for all you've done for me."

Norah smiled graciously. "Anytime."

Climbing the stairs, I headed back to my room. I wanted to dig into my dream and figure out why I was feeling like something horrible was going to happen. As if what had happened to Cay wasn't enough. We'd agreed to let our guilt go, but like I'd said, easier said than done. At least Norah was looking into the scary voices I heard. With everything that's been going on, I had forgotten to look into it, though it doesn't feel like something that should be ignored.

Sitting on my bed, I opened the *Book of Brighde*, hoping for some insight. I skimmed page after page, chapter after chapter, but nothing was clear about the Amulet.

> It was known the sisters did not get
> along, but things were made worse
> when the Amulet halves were lost.
> The sisters fought immensely, and
> the Amulet was never found.

That was completely wrong. I slammed the book shut and groaned, flopping back on my pillow. What would happen if I didn't find the other half? Was there another Brighde Seeker who would pick up where I left off?

I gasped.

What would happen if I *didn't* make it?

I sat up so quickly, the book fell on the floor. I was eighteen. I should have been having the time of my life, enjoying a carefree summer with my friends before I left for college. I didn't even apply because I'd known that this would derail any plans I had.

Trapped. I felt trapped in a future I didn't ask for and got stuck with. I knew there were swarms of people who would love to be in my shoes, but I wasn't them. I loved reading fantasy, but I didn't need my life to imitate art.

I needed to get out of here. I needed air.

I ran out the front door, my legs carrying me away from everything. Faster and faster, I nearly knocked people over. I weaved in and out of town and headed down the mountain toward the main road that splits the valley. The necklace was pulsating on my chest, urging me to ditch training and get on the hunt. I did my best to ignore it most days, but lately, it had been pushing harder. I felt trapped by the school, by the Amulet, by my destiny. My mind—and my powers— couldn't take it anymore.

As I flew down the hill toward the road that splits the mountains in half, some of my anger washed away, like flower petals caught in a current. I slowed down as I got closer to the road, but no one was coming, so I jumped over it and up the trail across the street. Large trees loomed over me, creating a cocoon of safety. I could hide here, and no one would find me.

I was tired of feeling like I wasn't good enough or strong enough to fight whatever comes my way. It was like I was battling with two enemies: Beira's kin and myself.

I pushed myself up the hill harder, jogging past a cluster of buildings, following the dirt path into the woods. Storming my way between two trees, nothing stopped me as I shoved forward through the brush. I wanted to scream until my voice was raw and sore.

Coming to a little break in the trees, I stopped and panted. I felt my powers twitch under my skin, signaling their desire to break loose. I spun in a circle and saw no houses, no people, and no animals around me. I was completely alone. I picked up a small boulder and launched it at a tree. Grunting, I picked up another rock and hurled it in the same direction. The physical action made me feel better. *This is for you, Trip! For all the bullshit you lured me into.* I ran at the tree and jump kicked it, but its trunk withstood my weight. *That's for Eden and Norah, keeping me in the dark when I should have been clued in.* I grunted and breathed out heavily. *I didn't forget about you, Brighde. Giving me all your knowledge and powers to save the world. Who said I wanted that power?* I punched the trunk, feeling my knuckles shatter from the impact. Cradling my hand, I quickly drove my healing to my right hand, and the fragments fused back together under the skin. I remained standing, bent over with my hand to my chest. My breath was coming out slower and more evenly as my pounding heart resumed its normal rhythm. Tears pricked my eyes as my anger gave away.

I was an amalgamation of all the things people told me I was: daughter, friend, Seeker, goddess. Who did I think I was?

I stayed like that until the sun set. I wasn't ready to go back, so I threw my powers up and held the sun in the sky a little longer. These woods held nothing for me. They were a safe space when I needed to get away. I wasn't going to stand here feeling sorry. I was a daughter. My parents loved me and sent me here to protect me. I was a friend. My New Jersey friends always kept me grounded and offered support when I needed it the most. My friends here were funny and charming, and they made me miss home a little less. With Cay and Logan, it was like I'd brought a piece of home with me.

I was a Seeker. One of only two currently looking for the Amulet and the only one who had a piece of the prize. The Amulet warmed a little against my skin, as if giving me a gentle hug. I was a goddess. Brighde's power flowed through me and gave me strength when I had none. I stood and released the sun from my grip.

No one else in this world could do that. Realization settled on my shoulders as I headed back toward town.

I understood why my family had been fighting for hundreds of years to find the Amulet. It was in my soul, coursing through my veins and seeping into every thought. It was my destiny to defend my birthright and control the weather. I was Brighde's heir. I was her last hope. I was the Cuardaitheoir.

CHAPTER 23

When I woke up the next day, Cay was waiting at my door with his fist raised.

"What possessed you to stand outside my door and wait like that?" I asked as I brushed past him to use the bathroom. He trailed behind me.

"I'm hungry, and Logan didn't answer. I think he's still sleeping. I was about to knock when you opened the door."

I turned and held my hand up to his chest. "Wait here."

Finishing in the bathroom, I swung the door open and saw Cay leaning against the wall across from me.

"Breakfast?" he asked hopefully.

"You know," I said, heading to my room for my clothes, "you can go and get food yourself."

He followed me like a puppy. "I know, but I kind of feel weird going by myself, given everything."

My resolve softened a little, and I sighed. "Okay, give me a minute. I'll get dressed. But I can't hang out for long. I have to go through the *Book of Brighde* to find out where the other half is."

"Let's eat in your room, and I'll help you."

I smiled. "Deal."

We headed downstairs and grabbed some granola, fruit, coffee, and muffins before heading back to my room, where Logan was waiting at my door.

"I heard you were sleeping," I said, giving him a quick kiss.

"Nah, I went for a run. I was seeing if you wanted to get breakfast, but..." he said and gestured to my plate.

"Yeah, Cay beat you. Why don't you grab something and come up? We're about to go through the book to see if it can tell me more about the Amulet."

"Okay. I'll be right back," he said, giving me a kiss on the cheek. Logan left us as I opened the door to my room.

"You two are too cute," Cay cooed.

I blushed. "Shut up."

He sighed dramatically as he walked into the room. "Really. I mean it. You two are perfectly matched."

The blushing didn't stop. "Well, thank you."

I set my stuff down on my dresser and made sure I took a sip of my coffee, buying me time to cool my cheeks off.

"Minus the feeling of being at school again, I could totally get used to this life," Cay said, settling onto my bed and tossing a raspberry into his mouth.

"Yeah" I agreed. I picked up the book and dragged my chair over to my breakfast. Opening it up, I started from the beginning, wanting to make sure I didn't miss one clue. Neither of us spoke for a few minutes as we ate our breakfast, and I read a few pages.

"If you stare any harder, cousin, you'll go blind," Cay joked. I slid my eyes over to him.

"Something in here has to give me an inkling about where to start looking. Alba? That's not a current country name, and I haven't found any references on what it could be now." I flipped the page and took another a sip of coffee.

"Maybe that's something we Google?"

I shrugged. "Probably would be faster than looking through this. Though it kind of feels like cheating."

My door opened, and Logan came in carrying his breakfast. It was similar to ours, but instead of a muffin, he had an omelet. Not saying anything, he placed his food on the floor and sat next to it.

"Any luck yet?" he asked me, picking up a fork and his plate. I shook my head no.

"We're planning on using the Internet if the book doesn't help," Cay filled him in. They continued holding a conversation, but I only partially paid attention as I scoured the pages for mentions of Alba or the Amulet. I played with the frayed edges of the ribbon bookmark tucked in between the pages I had read. Turning page after page, I wasn't any closer to finding out where the Amulet was, and my eyes were getting a little tired.

"I'm done for now," I said, closing the book. "Someone else can have a go."

"I'm guessing no luck so far?" Logan asked sympathetically. He had finished his breakfast and left the empty plate on the floor.

I took a bite of my muffin and chewed. "No. I'm at a loss."

"Google?" Cay suggested.

I waved my hand at him, taking another bite. "Have at it."

Cay picked up my phone from where I left it on my bed last night and held it up to my face. It unlocked, and he went to work.

"Where's your phone?" I asked him.

"Lost it" was the curt reply. I didn't press him for any more information and let him use mine.

"You okay?" Logan asked me.

I sighed. "Yeah, just tired of feeling ... lost. I don't know where to look, and I feel this pressing urgency to find the Amulet, like, yesterday."

"I'm sorry." He offered his hand up to me. I took it, and he rubbed little circles on my skin.

"It's not your fault," I said with a weary smile, resting my arm on the dresser. I absent-mindedly ran my hand over the bookmark, pulling at the threads that were already unraveled. The book itself was a bit tattered, probably from being a thousand years old. The pages were yellowed and smelled musty, which I found extremely satisfying. The corners of the cover were bent or crumpled from being tossed or stuffed in places over the years. Even the binding had seen better days. There was a gaping space when the book was opened that didn't quite seal when the book was closed. Pieces of paper were hanging out of it, and I pulled on those instead. I tugged them off and tossed the fragments onto my abandoned plate. One piece didn't want to come off, no matter how hard I pulled. It was starting to bug me, so I let go of Logan and used both hands to tear the piece off.

"I think I found it," Cay said, sitting up a little in my bed. "It says Alba is the former name of Scotland." He looked up at me. "Well, that was easy."

"Scotland. That makes sense. Now we know where to start," I said, still working on the paper. The more I pulled, the more came out of the book, and I was beginning to think I was ruining it. But the paper didn't feel like it had been bound with glue; it didn't feel worn like the pages inside did. No, this was much older and felt more delicate, so I was trying to be careful when I tugged.

"What are you doing?" Logan asked.

"This piece of paper is stuck," I said, getting more out. "But it looks like more than just a piece of the book."

"What do you mean?" Cay replied.

The paper slid out, and I looked at it in my hand. Opening it, I saw faint handwriting on it in a language I wasn't familiar with.

"It's a note," I told them, brow furrowed. "And it's so old; it's in a language I don't recognize."

"Can I see it?" Cay asked, jumping up. I gave him the note and stacked our plates. I didn't want to invite bugs into my room if I could avoid it.

"Want me to take these down for you?" Logan offered. I smiled.

"Thank you. I would really appreciate it."

"Done." He picked up the stack I had created and left the room, leaving Cay and me.

"I've seen this before," Cay said. "But I don't remember where."

"Google?" I joked.

"Maybe..." he drifted off. "There is a library here, right?"

I nodded.

"Would you mind if I did a little research to see what this says?"

The Amulet flashed hot on my skin. I didn't ignore its signs.

"Actually," I held out my hand. "I think I want to try to solve something this time. You figured out Alba, after all."

He handed the note over and fake pouted. "Fine, have all the fun."

I stood up and patted him on the cheek, like my grandpa had always done to me. "I will."

I headed to the library and left Cay to find Logan. The Amulet warmed under my touch, telling me I was doing the right thing.

There was class in the library when I walked in. They were studying something about the biology of plant life in the area as I walked past them to the history section. I figured if I could look back far enough, something would tell me what this was. Maybe there'd be a sample of it or a way for me to translate it.

I pulled three books down, all centering around Scotland and their gods. Given the fact that Brighde and Lugh were headed to Scotland in my dream, I felt like that was the best place to start. Sitting at one of the tables away from the biology class, I opened the first book and looked at the index for any references to old Scotland and languages.

I did see a chapter on the Jacobite Rising of 1745, but it didn't give me a language sample of what they spoke. I left the book open to that chapter to use it to cross-reference, but I opened the second book in the meantime. This book had a section on the Kingdom of Alba, which was the era I was looking for. The chapter mentioned how the kingdom came to be, who ruled it, and what daily life was like. After skimming page after page, a paragraph jumped out at me, saying the language that was spoken was Goidelic, currently known as Gaelic. The Amulet warmed under my shirt, and I knew this was the right answer. Taking my books and moving to a computer, I took the folded note out from my pocket and placed it on the table. I looked up the alphabet for Gaelic and found a ton of sites that could help. I printed out what I thought to be the most complete alphabet after comparing different sites to the note. Snagging the sheets from the printer, I dropped the books off on the reshelve cart and booked it to my room for some privacy. I didn't know what this said, but I didn't want to take any chances.

When I got to my room, I closed the door, then hopped onto my bed. Grabbing the pencil I'd been using for my dream journal, I looked up each letter to see if it matched a modern English one. I was mostly in luck—some letters matched but not all.

Sorting it all out took me longer than I would have liked to admit. Some of the writing was faded enough that I couldn't figure out which letters they were. By the time I was done, I was able to decipher about half. I filled in the blanks the best I could and read it to myself.

Cuardaitheoir,

The Amulet is not truly lost.

I had to guess on "lost," given I could only translate the "o" and the "t."

> HALF HAS BEEN FOUND IN ALBA, BUT NOT THE
> HALF I NEED.

Based on the dream I had, I was guessing the person speaking was Brighde.

> MY HALF IS MISSING AND IS NOT WIT ARWAN
> FISHERMAN.

Wait, the fisherman from my dream? There was a line underneath this one that was too faded for me to read.

> IT MUST B FOUND BFOR THE MAGYCK RUN OUT.
> I CAN FEEL IT WEAKNING.

This definitely feels like Brighde, even if the writing is stilted.

> IT NOW IS YOUR RESPONSIBILITY TO FIND IT.
> TO OWN IT. TO (MISSING WORD) IT. DON'T LET
> HER FIND IT FIRST.

That was it, short and sweet. I reread it and tried to fill out more letters, but overall, the message didn't change. I had to find the Amulet because the pieces were losing their powers. My last dream told me the Amulet was in Alba, and I knew she got the half because it was on my neck. It began to burn a bit hotter than normal.

"Ow, okay!" I gently moved the necklace off my body to stop the pain.

What am I missing, Amulet?

I read the letter again, slowly, waiting after every line for the Amulet to respond. It sat like a lump on my chest, not giving any more hints. I was confused and sat back in the chair. What did Brighde mean when she said the Amulet wasn't lost? I still needed to find Beira's half, which *was* lost.

The Amulet half heated up again as I completed my last thought. I flinched. *There is still a half to find,* I mentally told it. It warmed against me, and I wondered if I could get direct answers from it as I recognized its pattern. When I was right, it was warm, and if I was wrong or something was urgent, it burned. I sat up a little straighter, smiling. This could work.

Amulet, is Brighde's half still missing? I thought it would be an easy way to lay the groundwork for our conversation, but instead, the Amulet grew hot and then died down.

I frowned. That didn't make sense. I had Brighde's half already, didn't I? I was her Seeker, after all. I tried again, rephrasing the question.

Amulet, has Brighde's half been found? Again, it burned and then cooled down.

Amulet, are you Brighde's half? I needed clearer answers if I was going to get to the bottom of this.

The Amulet burned against me so hotly, but it didn't matter. I think I understood what it wanted me to ask.

Amulet, are you Beira's half?

It gave me the comforting warmth I've grown to rely on, and I fell over onto my pillow, excitement and fear surging through my body.

Holy shit. I didn't have Brighde's Amulet half.

I had Beira's.

Chapter
24

Two days later, Logan, Cay, and I had nothing but backpacks full of clothes and essentials as we climbed out of Norah's car at the Zurich train station. Eden drove us now that she felt better.

I was keeping my discovery to myself for now, paranoid that if the knowledge that I had Beira's half was revealed, I'd be an even bigger target than before.

"Thank you for everything," I said to Eden. "I'm sorry for all the times I was ungrateful and a pain."

She smiled and hugged me closely. "Never. Everything we went through was worth it to get you here."

"You'll take good care of *Brighde*?" I left the book with Eden, not wanting to risk anyone else getting their hands on it.

She let me go and smiled. "Always."

"You two take care," she said, facing Logan and Cay. "Don't do anything stupid, and keep each other safe."

She hugged the boys and turned back to me.

"Norah asked me to give you this," she said, handing me a piece of paper. "She said you'd know what it's about."

"Thank you." I was eager to read the note, but I slipped it into my pocket to read when I was alone

Eden said goodbye once more and then left. It was in our best interest to keep under the radar as much as possible, so we paid for our tickets in cash and mostly kept our phones off.

We were finally leaving Switzerland to find Andrew's family and whoever had the Amulet. Since Cay had figured out Alba was modern-day Scotland, we had mapped out our travel plans, packed, and were ready to get going.

Our train was leaving in an hour, so we had time to kill. It was still early in the morning, and many people on the train looked tired. I felt alive. My nerves were one thick cable wire, intertwining my excitement and anxiety together. The Amulet burned hot against my neck, mirroring my feelings. Things were finally happening.

A whistle pierced the air, signaling the train's arrival. The three of us stood by the tracks, leaving room for people to disembark from the car. When everyone departing was off, we climbed on, slid into a cabin, and got settled. Our first stop was Paris, and we had about five hours until we reached it. I sat next to the window and peered out, watching as the train pulled out of the station. My nerves calmed as the wheels glided over the tracks, creating a reassuring clacking noise. Exhaustion pulled at me as I listened to the white noise of the rails and watched the blur of the trees outside. Leaning against Logan, I snuggled up and drifted off to sleep.

I woke up later, groggy, but more rested than I had been.

"How long was I out?" I said softly as Cay was sleeping. While he had been resting, I didn't think he had been sleeping over the last days, so I wasn't surprised to see him sound asleep now.

"About two hours," Logan replied. I sat up and stretched my back. Logan put his hand on my neck and massaged the muscles. I hadn't had a massage since I'd left the US, so I tensed up and then relaxed once I realized how good it felt. He worked out the knots by my shoulders, and I melted.

"If you keep this up, I'll fall asleep again," I joked. "Did you get any rest?"

Logan shook his head. "Someone needed to keep guard."

"I'll stay up if you want to nap." *And as an added bonus, I can read my note from Norah in private.*

"It's okay. I don't feel very sleepy." He leaned over and gave me a kiss. I had a feeling these were going to be fewer and further between, given our mission ahead, so I eagerly kissed him back. Not wanting to take the moment for granted, I leaned in, applying more pressure. Logan adjusted in his seat, closing the space we had between us. His mouth was cool and tasted minty, like he'd just brushed his teeth. I traced his bottom lip with my tongue, and he groaned.

Pushing me back gently, he said, "Bridget, if you keep that up, we are going to have a big problem on hand."

I cheekily smiled. "Big, huh?"

He grinned and kissed me again.

As we pulled into the station, Cay woke up and rubbed his eyes.

"I slept for the full five hours?"

I nodded. "Out cold. But come on, we have some time to grab lunch before we head to our hostel."

The plan was for us to spend at least a night in each place to check if we were being tailed. As much as I was ready to be in Scotland, I loved that I could check out some of the sights across Europe.

"Hostel or sights?" Cay eyed me, smiling as we hustled out of the cabin.

I blushed. "Sights first, if we can. I would like to see the Eiffel Tower and the Arc de Triomphe."

"First time out of the US?" Cay asked as we stepped onto the platform.

"Yes," I frowned. "Are you going to mock me for wanting to see them?"

"Not at all. I thought you'd be interested in the Catacombs."

"If we have time, we should see everything."

"First thing we should do is get something to eat," Logan chimed in. "I could use some lunch."

"I second that," Cay said. We headed to the closest metro station to grab a train to the Eiffel Tower. It took us roughly half an hour to get there, and I was ready to eat. We found a little café, which had sandwiches, coffee, salads, and more. I ordered a sandwich with tomato, cheese, and pesto of some kind. The boys had ham sandwiches, and we all got coffee to keep us awake. We grabbed a table on the patio and sat, taking sips of our drinks.

As we waited for the food, I looked up. The top of the Eiffel Tower peered over us, and I felt like a tiny speck. It was stunning, and I was ready to see Paris from a whole new vantage point.

"You happy?" Logan asked. Cay went back in to get a second cup of caffeine.

"Loaded question," I replied, turning back to face him. "But yeah. I've always wanted to see Paris and travel more, so as much as our mission is business, I'm going to get some joy out of it. You?"

"I'm getting there," he answered. "But you're helping."

I blushed. "Me? How?"

"I see your face when you look at stops on the map. Elation makes you glow, and I'm happy to see it."

I flushed but still had a wide, dreamy smile as I rested my head in my hands. "I can't wait! All those sites to visit and history to hear, who wouldn't be happy?"

"No one, if they're with you." He leaned over and kissed me gently. "Remember, Paris is the city of love."

"So, expect a lot more kisses?" I raised an eyebrow. "I can live with that."

"Live with what?" Cay asked, sitting back down and placing his mug on the table.

"Kisses." I said, sitting up.

"Oh, yeah. I miss those," Cay wistfully replied.

"Maybe we can find you a lovely Parisian girl," I offered.

"In the twelve hours we have left?"

"You were the popular boy at OCHS. You're handsome and charming. I'm sure you'll find someone in no time."

Our food appeared before anyone else could chime in. Without another word, we dug in, enjoying our first meal in France.

"Physical activity right after a meal was a bad idea. Why are we doing this?" Cay complained, panting as Logan, he, and I were climbing the second flight of stairs up to the top of the tower.

"Because we wanted to get the full Parisian experience?" Logan suggested.

"Because the line was too long for the elevator," I shouted to Logan.

To Cay, I apologized. "Sorry! I didn't think we'd rush to get here."

"Says the girl who kept jiggling her foot and checking her phone as we were eating?" Logan teased.

"No kisses for you!" I called behind me.

"I'm cramping, I'm cramping!" Cay doubled over.

We stopped walking and moved to the side the best we could.

"Cay," I said, "I'm sure you can handle this with ... you know."

"I'm still a little on the fritz," he replied in a strained voice. Sighing, I climbed two stairs up and turned around. Shielding my hand with my body, the healing red light lit up, and I waved it over Cay's stomach. Immediately, he breathed out in relief and stood.

"You're the best," he said. We kept walking up the stairs until we hit the first level, which had a restaurant, a cinema, an exhibition, and transparent floors.

We stopped to take a break. I peered out the windows and looked below me, soaking up every view I could. With a rush of adrenaline and excitement, I looked toward the next set of stairs to make it to the second floor. I was determined to get to the top.

Cay came over and stared out the window with me.

"It's really crowded and loud here," he commented.

"Of course. This is a busy floor." I gestured to the features. "Plenty of things to do and look at."

"Ready to head up?" Logan asked, walking up to us. I nodded as Cay looked up at the steps and winced.

"I got you," I said, looping my arm through his. Even though we were all tired from the first set of stairs, with a little help from some healing powers, we made it to the second level and took the lift to the top floor. As I walked onto the platform, I gasped at the site of Paris laid out before me. Buildings, both new and old, cars, and people stretched out far enough until they hit the horizon and disappeared. Being this high up made me feel powerful in a way my own powers didn't. I was intoxicated, rushing from one side to the next, drinking in every piece of landscape around me. Finally, stopping to look at the Grand Palais, I clutched the chain guardrail in my fingers and breathed deeply.

For the first time in months, I felt truly at peace. Nothing but the rushing wind to drown out even the loudest of sounds behind me. The sun shone a little stronger than earlier, reflecting my mood.

"Happy?" Cay asked, resting his back against the wall.

"So very happy," I breathed. Logan flanked my other side as the three of us reveled in the moment.

We stayed for the rest of the afternoon until I actually smelled myself and wanted to find our hostel.

We climbed back down the steps in search of our temporary residence. Not only did I need a shower, but also I wanted to rest for a bit and read my note. There was a growing concern that whatever illness that left Cay without his powers could affect me somehow. It was important I didn't tax myself too much. After a quick metro ride, we found our hostel close to the Louvre.

"Do you think I could find a cute French girl?" Cay whispered as Logan walked up to the front desk.

"It is an international hostel. You could get lucky." I adjusted my backpack straps as I started to feel its weight. The lobby was clean, minus a few pamphlets on the counter. One wall was a dark red, making me feel trapped. Behind the counter was a wall full of open, numbered cubbies. Some of the cubbies held keys while others were empty. We signed waivers and handed over our cash as the concierge handed Logan our key.

"Our room is through these red doors, and we're on the second floor," Logan said. "Communal restrooms and showers are on every floor, and we only have one key between us." Cay and I followed Logan as he climbed the stairs. At that point, we were all thoroughly tired of climbing stairs, and we sighed in relief when we opened our door. There was a single bed on the left side of the room and a set of bunks across from it. The frames were a bright blue that popped in contrast to the crisp, white linen on the bed. Toiletries for us were left in a basket on a little table at the foot of the single bed.

I dropped my bag by the single and sat. The excitement of the day was wearing off, and I needed another coffee to keep me going. Tomorrow, we were leaving for Brussels, and I wanted to get back out there to see more of Paris. I stifled a yawn as I kicked off my shoes and leaned back on the bed.

"Napping now?" Cay asked.

"I'm tired enough to want to sleep, so yeah." I heard the squeak of the bunk beds. Peeking over, Logan had claimed the bottom bunk and was sitting up on it.

"Before we go out again, I'm going to grab a shower," Cay said, poking through the basket of stuff. He selected a towel and washcloth, placed them on top of bag, then left. The door made a soft *click* as it closed.

"You good?" I asked Logan, rolling over to face him. He mirrored my pose on his bed, arm tucked up under the pillow and his head resting on top.

"Yeah. You?"

I smiled. "Yeah. Just so you know, I want to kiss you, but my need to nap outweighs my need to move."

He chuckled. "Right back at you, babe."

I closed my eyes and listened to the sounds of Paris as I drifted to sleep.

I woke up an hour later with Cay on his bunk and Logan missing, his bed mussed. He must have slept a bit, too.

"Logan is taking a shower," Cay said, flipping through a pamphlet.

"Where did you get that?" I asked, sitting up. Feeling groggy, I rubbed my eyes and yawned.

"Downstairs. After my shower, I grabbed a couple to learn about the sights."

"Are you able to read it?"

"Of course."

"Because you speak French?"

"Because they have English versions."

I stood and grabbed my backpack. "It's my turn to take a shower." Picking up the remaining towel, I headed out the door just as Logan was coming back.

"Oh! Sorry," he said, backing up. His wet hair was combed down, and he smelled woodsy, like pine. It was the same body wash I'd been using for the past few weeks.

"No worries. I was about to take a shower myself."

Logan didn't move out of the way.

"Uh... open sesame?" I titled my head and raised my eyebrows.

"I..." he cleared his throat, "I think you shouldn't go anywhere alone."

"What if I need the bathroom in the middle of the night?" I crossed my arms over my chest and leaned back. "Am I to hold it or go in a corner like a puppy?"

Cay hopped down from his bed. "Stop complaining. It's for your safety."

He wrapped his arm around my shoulders, and I shrugged him off.

"What about yours?"

"Please, Bridget," Logan begged. "I can't protect you if I can't be with you."

I shook my head. "No. Boundaries, boys." I pushed past Logan and headed to the stairs. "Don't follow me."

Showering was the greatest thing after a sweaty afternoon, and thankfully, I was able to shower alone, minus a few strangers who were also using the restroom for one reason or another. I dressed right outside the shower stall, behind the curtain, and squeezed out my ringlets as much as possible. Leaving them damp and down, I stuffed my dirty clothes into my backpack and pulled out the note Eden had handed me.

Bridget,

Please know this information was not easy to come by. Our library, while extensive, did not have the facts I needed to identify your harassers. Before I reveal their name, it's of utmost urgency that you remain vigilant in your search and keep yourself and your purpose a secret. I fear the person who chased you that night has truly returned, and if I'm correct, then you're up against much darker forces than the Findlay family.

I swallowed a lump in my throat as tears sprang to my eyes. Who could be worse than them?

<u>Balor is back,</u> and if he's back, it must mean he's thrown his lot into Beira's clan.

Balor? That name was a whisper in my memory, but I couldn't remember where I had heard it before. Groaning, I deeply wished I hadn't told Eden to keep the *Book of Brighde*. More research on this being would be needed if I was to know who I'd be facing. Though, if he was the creepy voice I'd heard in the woods, I almost didn't want to know anymore.

Again, I caution you to be safe, smart, and vigilant on your journey. Keeping your powers sharp and your wits about you is more important now than it ever was before.

As always, you have our support.

Norah

I returned the note to my pocket and headed back to the room, my mind spinning. As I reached our door, I made a conscious decision not to say anything until I knew more about Balor.

"I'm back!" I announced as I walked in. "As you can see, I made it out alive and unscathed but smelling *very* good."

I spun in a circle.

"You are not amusing," Cay said.

"You have no sense of humor," I replied, hanging my wet towel over the rung of the bed frame to dry. I picked up my phone and noticed it was getting close to Swiss dinner time. Unfortunately, France didn't do dinner early, based on my Wikipedia search.

"Do you want to stroll and see what's around before grabbing dinner and coming back?"

"Better than sitting around here," Cay commented, shrugging. Logan said nothing. I looked at him and held my palms up.

"Do you want to go for a walk?"

"No, but I will, since you two are going," he replied, getting up. As we put on our shoes, grabbed our bags, and headed outside, I sent a text to Cay.

[Bridget: Are you mad at me too?]

[Cay: No, but it IS his job to watch your back.]

[Bridget: He is not watching or listening to me pee. I don't care.]

[Cay: Then talk to him about it. But listen to him. He cares deeply about you, and he is extremely loyal.]

[Bridget: You just described a dog.]

[Cay: Bridget...]

[Bridget: Cay...]

[Cay: Talk to him.]

"I'm going to get a bottle of water. Anyone want anything? No? Okay," Cay said, rushing off.

I watched as his backpack bounced against his lower back, and I shook my head.

[Bridget: Real subtle.] Sent.

I sighed and looked around. While we hadn't gone very far, I saw a lush landscape ahead with trees and a few people. The sun was getting lower in the sky, and the park looked inviting.

"I know you're mad at me," I said to Logan.

"I'm not mad." He faced me but kept his focus on Cay.

"You aren't happy."

Logan sighed and looked at me. "You know I was trained my entire life to keep you safe, right?"

I pursed my lips and tucked my hands into my pockets. "Yes."

"You understand I take that very seriously?"

"Yes, but you don't have to follow me to the bathroom."

"I did it all the time in Switzerland."

"The door locked there." I stared at him, brows raised, waiting for his reply.

Logan came over and rested his hands on my shoulders. "Please, please know I don't want to listen to you in the bathroom, but when I remember how you fainted because of the poison, or the look on your face when you heard your room was on fire, or when Eden was hurt, or when Oliver almost died, my fear of losing you outweighs how weird it is for me to keep you close."

A sinking familiarity came back, and I had to ask, though I really didn't want to know the answer. "Is that why you're dating me?"

"What?" He blinked and removed his hands.

"Are you so afraid of something happening to me that you're dating me to prevent it?"

"Is that what you really think?" he asked me sadly. "That I'm like him? Only dating you because of your abilities?"

Tears stung behind my eyes. Did I really feel that way?

I wanted to answer but never got the chance because Cay came back with three water bottles. He gave Logan his and held mine out to me. I grabbed it and moved away from them, heading toward the expansive garden in front of me. I needed space for a minute to sort my head out.

I crossed into the park, barely registering the sound of footsteps behind me. Was he dating me because I was the Seeker? I stopped for a second. No. Logan had never treated me like being the Seeker was first and being Bridget was an afterthought. Yet it was a fear that lived in the back of my mind. Did I treat him like that?

I circumvented the large stone fountain, its rushing water reminding me of the river at home, how it whooshed past the house after a strong rainstorm. I shook my head. I needed to stop trying to break my own heart and take down Logan's with it. If I didn't, I'd break down here in the city of love, in a beautiful garden, where there were people to see me cry.

"Bridget, wait!" I heard Cay's voice from behind me. I didn't stop or turn around because I didn't want to talk to him, either. Right now, I wanted to be left alone.

"Yes, Bridget, stop. Don't cry," a familiar voice mocked. I looked up, and my stomach dropped. Deidra was standing in front of me.

CHAPTER
❧ 25 ❧

I gulped. Why did the bad guys *always* show up at the worst time?

"Can we skip the chitchat and just get to it?" I asked.

Deidra shrugged, and her blonde braid slid behind her. "Care to relive some memories?"

"Yes. Especially the one where I kicked your ass." The anger I had for Cay's kidnapping bubbled up and was directed at Deidra as my hands crackled with lightning. I shot a bolt at her, and she ducked, letting it hit a tree that was probably older than the two of us combined.

"Not that one. The one where Trip broke your heart."

Without missing a beat, Trip appeared, wearing that same red sweatshirt from before. My heart didn't flip, didn't beat harder in any way. My body didn't react. He was dead to me, especially after what had happened to Cay.

"What can you do?" I asked. "It's summer."

"I'm sure I can make adjustments," he snarked, walking closer to me.

"Stay away from her!" Cay yelled out from behind me. I smiled. If Cay was here, then Logan couldn't be too far behind.

"Cay still following you around?" Trip asked, peering around me.

"You say following; I say he has my back. It's still a better high school memory than any of the ones that included you."

Trip faked feeling hurt. "Ouch."

His body language changed, and he grew serious. "I'm over you, Bridget. Nothing you say can hurt me."

"Say? Probably not. Do? Oh, yes." I called up fog, enclosing us in its wispy embrace. "You forgot I had a birthday."

"Still working with fog?" he asked, amused. I smiled.

"Among other things." Roots from nearby trees snaked under his feet, wrapping themselves around his ankles. Trip looked down in surprise and shot ice daggers from his hands, slicing the roots. He stepped back from the carnage.

"Interesting. I guess you did learn something new." He shot another dagger at me, and I melted it in midair with a sunbeam.

"Lame." The ground below me started to rise as Trip shrank back. I was lifted higher than my fog and could see the rest of the park from my vantage point. Then the ground disappeared from under me, and I plummeted down. A gust of wind came and wrapped around me, carrying me safely to the ground.

"Hi, Franny," I said as she rested against a tree. Team Beira had Trip, Deidra, and Franny so far in their ranks. I didn't see Tomas around, but I was sure he was here somewhere. I wondered if Rose would make an appearance, making this an OCHS/Danann Academy reunion.

"Bringing out the big guns for little old me?" I asked Trip. "I feel so honored." Sucking his teeth, he said, "Nothing but the best for second place."

I rolled my eyes. I encouraged the tree roots to push from underneath Franny's feet and wrap themselves around her torso, pinning her arms to her sides. They kept circling her until she was nearly the size of a rubber-band ball.

"This is between you and me, Trip. Tell your minions to stand down." He looked impressed.

"You first," he nodded behind me. Logan had finally arrived and was fighting Tomas, the two of them an equal match. Cay was going hand-to-hand with Deidra, but he was holding back, probably because of his most recent experience.

I turned around and faced Trip. "You won't tell yours to stand down; I won't tell mine." The sun barely peeked over the horizon, and the darkness was only pierced by the lights from the park. Thunderclouds rolled in, answering my silent call.

Trip looked up as the first raindrop fell on his nose.

"I can work with this," he shrugged. He created hail from my rain. We both were shooting each other with precipitation. The fountain provided good coverage from any ice balls coming at my face, and I stuck my hand in the water, sending electric currents up and over the stone rim to electrify Trip. He was stunned for a minute before his body fell to the ground. This gave me time to check back on Cay, who was still fighting Deidra. It was an uneven match, as Deidra was able to create hail like Trip and pitch them at Cay. Thankfully, his healing powers were back to full strength, and he was relying on the martial arts his brother had taught him.

Incensed, I clapped my hands, creating thunder so loud it shook the ground. Deidra whirled around and saw me. She raised a hand to send ice at me, but Cay came behind her and put her in a choke hold. Figuring he had this handled, I focused back on Trip, who had recovered from being electrocuted.

"That's all you got?" Trip yelled over the din.

"I think you'd know the answer by now!" I called back, frowning.

I heard a mangled noise behind me, then a thud. Whirling around, I saw Logan standing over the body of Tomas, who looked like he wasn't breathing. Everyone ran over, abandoning all our individual fights. Only Franny remained as roots slowly grew around her, keeping her in place.

"Logan, what happened?" I asked as I knelt by Tomas. I peered up at him, and he looked like he'd faint. He needed help, but Cay got to him first, leaving me next to Tomas.

Trip collapsed across from me and held his friend's hand.

"Bridget, please help him," Trip begged, looking up at me. Desperation was etched on his face. "I know what I said, but please!"

The memory of the first man I'd killed flooded back, and I swallowed down bile. I couldn't handle watching someone else die like this, someone I knew. As much as I hated Trip now, I needed to help.

Before I could say anything, Deidra cut in, "If this was your Protector, you'd want us to save him."

I glared at her. "What about my cousin? Did you think that when you tortured him?"

She paled and shrank back away from Tomas.

"I'm not doing this for any of you, but for him," I told Trip, as I nodded toward Logan.

I let my hands glow and moved them over his body, starting at the heart. There was the faintest whisper of a beat, so I focused my power there. For about five minutes, the red hovered over his chest, and I willed his heart to beat stronger.

Tomas's heartbeat faded until I couldn't feel it anymore. I checked the brain activity. None.

I pulled my hands back from Tomas and rested them in my lap.

"No, do something. Bridget, please. Help him!" Trip screamed.

I shook my head sadly. "I can't. I'm sorry."

Deidra cried and pushed me out of the way, throwing her body over Tomas's.

I looked up at Logan as Cay slipped his hands under my arms and helped me up.

"What happened?" I asked Logan again quietly. He stared at me with big eyes full of shock and panic. It took me a minute to realize Logan had never killed a man before.

"We should go," Cay whispered, tugging on our arms.

"No!" Trip demanded, standing. "We finish this now."

"Go," I urged Cay and Logan. "I'll handle this."

They didn't move.

"Go! Please!"

Logan remained still, so I looked at Cay, word-lessly. He nodded and grabbed Logan's shirt, drag-ging him toward the park's entrance.

Facing Trip, I gently said, "This is between you and me."

He looked at me, nose red, tears running down his face. The ice had stopped before, but now it pelted us all, friends and foes of Beira. I had to tuck any sympathy away, or we would all die.

"Call a truce right now, Trip," I warned. "It's not the time to fight."

He licked his lips as he shook his head. "He deserves to pay. You all do."

Without another word, he reached up to the sky and hail swirled over his head, creating a whirlpool of ice. Feeling like I was about to die, I ran for cover, standing behind a tree to my left. It may not have offered too much protection, but it would take the brunt of the damage.

"Then send everyone else away, and we'll settle this!" I called from my spot.

"She's mine!" Trip yelled to everyone else. Only Deidra was left, crying over Tomas's body. Franny was wrapped in roots up to the middle of her torso.

The lightning in my bones flickered back to life, and I built a bolt large enough to destroy whatever he would throw at me.

Trip turned underneath his whirlpool; he was looking for me. I needed another minute. Taking the chance to close my eyes, I tapped into the fear and worry from this summer, the pain and anger. How scared and frustrated I'd been for Cay. I thought of all the times Rose had tried to hurt me, and I drew upon these feelings, feeding the lightning.

When I felt I was powerful enough, I stepped out from the tree, keeping my distance from him.

"He was my best friend! My brother!" Trip walked carefully toward me, keeping the mass of ice above his head. In the time I'd been building up energy, Trip had shaped the hail pellets into one massive formation. It was a cone of ice over his head with the point facing down.

As much as I wanted to say something to avoid what was coming, I knew nothing would work for someone who was grieving. He had to deal with it the best he could at the moment. The shock of Tomas was fresh, but that didn't mean I had let him take it out on me.

I allowed Trip to advance toward me, waiting until he was close enough to get the full brunt of my power.

Slowly, he dragged the funnel of ice in front of him, forcing the sides together until it made a spiked battering ram. With a quick flip of his wrist, the spike flew at me, aiming for my chest. I channeled my lightning into one braided mass and shot it at the tip of the spike. The two met midway as the lightning punctured it, traveled through the body of the ice, and burst through the other side. The spike splintered, ice shattering everywhere as Trip and I were knocked down from the sound waves.

The last thing I remembered was landing on cement as everything went dark.

Chapter 26

"Oh, child, it's time to wake up," a familiar voice said to me.

Dazed, I sat up and looked into the green eyes of Brighde as she knelt in front of me.

"Am I dead?" I asked her, pressing a hand to my forehead, expecting pain. I was surprised there wasn't any.

She chuckled, her curly red hair, which looked just like mine, bouncing on her shoulders. "No, you're alive but unconscious. I'm here in your dreams."

"But how? You don't have that power."

Brighde smiled. "From the goddess Caer Ibormeith, but that is not your concern right now. We have other pressing matters to attend to."

"Like what?"

"My time is growing shorter, and I have many things to tell you." She paused. "Forgive me for rushing, but you need to understand the Amulet you wear around your neck is not mine, Bridget." My fingers wrapped *around my necklace, which was warm and comforting against my touch.*

"I know it's Beira's."

She looked proudly at me. "I knew you could untangle the message."

"I had help from the Amulet." I blushed. "What I don't understand is how I ended up with Beira's half and not yours."

She nodded, leaning forward, resting her hands on her thighs. "Do you remember the memory I sent to you about finding the Amulet?"

"Wait, those dreams were your memories?"

She smiled.

"Yes. I have been sending you my memories to help you find the other half of the Amulet and rule over all seasons. You see, the Amulet responds to you, which means it's your birthright, like it was mine, to control both the warmer months and the cold. It knows you are bringing it to its mate, my half."

"So that's why the weather has been more insane, and Trip can call upon his powers during my seasons?"

I got a raised eyebrow from the goddess, but she answered. "Yes. The Amulet is losing its powers without its other half. The pieces have spent too long apart and are weakening. Once you reunite them, the weather will start to right itself."

Using my powers during the winter gives me an equal advantage against Trip and his family, plus Balor, if he was as horrible as Norah described him to be.

Brighde clapped her hands in front of my face, and I suddenly remembered her impatience from the dreams.

"Bridget! I'm trying to make sure you learn all I can give you before my time is over."

"Sorry," I shrank back, hanging my head.

Sitting back on her feet, she continued. "The memory of meeting the fisherman with Beira's half was a happy accident. We thought he was the farmer Arwan was enslaving, but we were wrong. Lugh and I tried to get the Amulet half from the fisherman, but he refused to hand it over. Arwan appeared and protected the fisherman, citing he was related to the farmer and therefore under his protection."

She rubbed her eyes in a surprisingly human way. I stared at her incredulously.

"We were sent off, but I kept tabs on the Amulet half, and I followed the trail to you."

"How did you know it wasn't your half?"

She motioned me to come forward, her one sleeve sliding down her arm. When I did, Brighde picked up the Amulet half, and it sung a lovely melody like a bird.

"It's never done that for me," I remarked.

"Not yet, it won't. See the orange-red color in the center?"

I nodded. "For summer and fall."

"My half will have white. Mother thought it would be best if the center colors that represented our seasons—orange for me, white for my sister—would go to the opposite sister. She believed it would help us understand each other and end our quarrels."

"And your half is still at large."

She frowned and cocked her head. "At large?"

"Missing," I explained.

Her face relaxed as she replied. "Yes, which is why it's more urgent than ever that you find it."

"I know, I know. We have to save the planet."

Brighde shook her head, her brow furrowed. "No, child. You don't understand. While I am coming to you in a dream, my sister is in the land of the living in a place called Scotland and is hunting for my half of the Amulet."

"Wait, what do you mean, land of the living? Like she's immortal? On Earth?"

Brighde nodded.

"Beira is alive."

Pronunciation

Cuardaitheoir (koor-DA-hoir)	Seeker
Brighde (Breed)	A Scottish goddess who, with the help of an Amulet, was able to control the Summer seasons (Spring and Summer)
Beira (Beer-a):	A Scottish goddess who, with the help of an Amulet, was able to control the Winter seasons (Fall and Winter)
Tuatha Dé Danann (TOO 'ha dA Dah n'n)	people of the goddess Danu
Neit (Neat)	Scottish God of War; the name of Cailean's dog

Cailean (Kay-lin)

Lugh (Loog) — Brighde and Beira's brother, God of Sun, Mastery, and Harvest. He helps Brighde hunt for the Amulet

Balor (Bah-loor) — An evil Scottish god who enjoyed torturing others

Bres (Brr-eh-s) — Brighde's husband; father of Ruadán

Babd (Bahb-d) — Warrior Goddess; turns into a crow and causes fear and confusion to soldiers

Arwan (Air-wan) — King of the Otherworld

Artio (Ahr-tee-o) — Goddess of the Bears; appears in Bridget's dream as a messenger of Brighde

Trottinett (twuh-tah-net) — Scooter

Cana Cludhmor (Cane-ah Clood-more) — Goddess of the Harp, Music, and Dreams

Ruadán (Roo-ah-don) Brighde's and Bres' son
who died in battle

Caer Ibormeith Goddess of Dreams
(Kai-er Ee-ber-meth) and Prophecy

About the Authors

B oth Leslie and Janice Sommers were raised in New Jersey, but have a little New York sass to them (courtesy of Janice's hometown of Bay Ridge, Brooklyn). This duo is known in their respective friend circles as the "funny one" and often are sought out to make other's laugh. Reading and writing YA Fantasy have always come naturally to Leslie, getting this from her mother, so it was a no-brainer for them to co-write a series. If reading is their hobby, then writing is their passion. Teaching herself to read and create stories at 3 years old, Leslie knew this was what she wanted to do. Though the Amulet series is their first, they have already been working on a second series, steeped in fantasy and romance. You can follow them on Twitter, Tiktok, and Instagram at lj_sommers and Leslie can be found on Facebook as Leslie Sommers. If you're lucky, you can catch them in the wild stacks of their local library, working through the new YA fantasies (and some contemporary romances) that were just released or assembling non-official book clubs with new friends.

With the secret of Beira's life now revealed, how will Bridget fulfill her destiny of reuniting the two Amulet halves? Don't miss the exciting conclusion of the Amulet series with *Brighde Restored*.

Book Club Questions

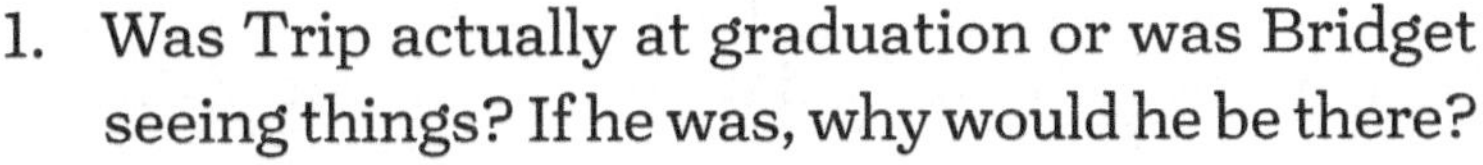

1. Was Trip actually at graduation or was Bridget seeing things? If he was, why would he be there?

2. Bridget is alone in a new country for the first time. How would you feel if you were in her position?

3. Should Bridget have saved Trip after knowing he was behind the attacks on her?

4. Is Bridget and Logan's romantic relationship a conflict of interest?

5. If you were Natalia, would you support Rose in everything she does?

6. Why do you think Bridget waited so long to tell Norah about Rose and Trip?

7. Angry that her friends were hurt, Bridget killed someone. Could she have handled it differently? How would you feel if you were Bridget?

8. Why do you think Norah was so upset after Bridget returned from the fight at the pool?

9. Why do you think Cay was unable to heal himself after he was kidnapped?

10. Why can Trip use his winter powers in the dead of summer when he is meant to be weak?

11. Do you think Bridget should keep her friends (old and new) in the dark about her true identity?

MORE BOOKS FROM 4 HORSEMEN PUBLICATIONS

YOUNG ADULT

A.R. FARINA
Welcome To Mansfield
Fire, Ice, Acid, & Heart
A Fae is Done

BLAISE RAMSAY
Through The Black Mirror
The City of Nightmares
The Astral Tower

LESLIE & JANICE SOMMERS
Brighde Reborn
Brighde Redefined

C.R. RICE
Denial
Anger
Bargaining
Depression
Acceptance
Broken Beginnings: Story of Thane
Shattered Start: Story of Sera
Sins of The Father: Story of Silas
Honorable Darkness: Story of Hex and Snip
A Love Lost: Story of Radnar

M.E. BATT
The Syphon's Daughter
The Princess of the Poison-Wastes

MEGAN MACKIE
The Vilification of Aqua Marine

PAIGE LAVOIE
Dear Galaxy

PEGGY GOODWIN
Manure

DANIELLE ORSINO
Locked Out of Heaven
Thine Eyes of Mercy
From the Ashes
Kingdom Come

VALERIE WILLIS
Rebirth
Judgment
Death

Fantasy

D. Lambert
To Walk into the Sands
Rydan
Celebrant
Northlander
Esparan
King
Traitor
His Last Name

Danielle Orsino
Locked Out of Heaven
Thine Eyes of Mercy
From the Ashes
Kingdom Come
Fire, Ice, Acid, & Heart
A Fae is Done

J.M. Paquette
Klauden's Ring
Solyn's Body
The Inbetween
Hannah's Heart

Lou Kemp
The Violins Played Before Junstan
Music Shall Untune the Sky

R.J. Young
Challenges of Tawa

Sydney Wilder
Daughter of Serpents

Valerie Willis
Cedric: The Demonic Knight
Romasanta: Father of Werewolves
The Oracle: Keeper of the
Gaea's Gate
Artemis: Eye of Gaea
King Incubus: A New Reign

Kyle Sorrell
Munderworld
Potarium

Discover more at
4HorsemenPublications.com